# THE BULL RIDING WITCH

## BY: JAMIE MARCHANT

BEWITCHING FABLES PRESS

ISBN: 978-0-9978624-5-4 print
978-0-9978624-4-7 ebook
PUBLISHED BY BEWITCHING FABLES PRESS
Printed in the United States of America

TO TINA TATUM,

A FAN OF THE BULL RIDING WITCH

AND PATRON OF THE ARTS.

THE WORLD NEEDS MORE LIKE HER

# ACKNOWLEDGEMENTS

As always, the author wishes to express her extreme gratitude to the Robrek Steele Conspiracy Writers' Group: Peg Daniels and Jim Elston. (I wrote the names in alphabetical order, so don't go quibbling about order of importance.) Peg and Jim supported me through every stage of the novel and never let up on me until I got it right.

I also owe a massive thank you to Wiley Petersen, world champion bull rider. Wiley provided me behind the scenes information about the bull riding life and graciously answered all of my questions, even the ones he clearly thought were weird. His personal assistance as well as the many training videos on his website, bullridercoach.com, helped me to get the details right. I appreciate him taking the time for a stranger in need.

Cheree Castellanos provided excellent editorial assistance. The cover was designed by Lou Harper.

# CONTENTS

# CHAPTER 1

I woke with my head pounding and my tongue coated with the fur balls of ten thousand cats. I nearly gagged at the stench that filled the air, a scent that combined the reek of the inside of a knight's armor after jousting with the odor of rotting flesh.

Confused, I examined my surroundings. Hanging on the wall facing me was a portrait of a huge bull with its head down and its heels kicked high into the air. Incredibly, a man, holding onto a rope with only one hand, sat on the bull's back. Why would anyone ride a bull? Bulls were dangerous and impossible to control.

Piled high on the bedside table were plates covered with the remains of several meals, bowls with a few dregs of sour milk, and empty bottles. The sheet I laid on was stained with various substances I didn't want to identify. Where was I? This was certainly no place worthy of me, the crown princess. Maybe I had somehow ended in the servants' quarters, although I couldn't imagine how.

I tried to sit up, and my head felt as if it were going to split in two. I groaned, and the sound was deep and masculine. What the . . .? I looked down at my arms. They were muscular and covered with hair. I grabbed my naked chest. My breasts were entirely flat, and my chest was covered with thick, coarse hair. When I rubbed my hand across my face, I felt thick stubble. I looked down at the short clothes, which were the only thing I was wearing; there was a bulge that just shouldn't have been there. I lifted the waistband and peeked. Dear gods, how had I gotten one of those? I poked it with my finger, and it twitched. I snapped the waistband closed and jumped away, but I couldn't get away from the body I was wearing.

My breath came in dizzying gasps, and my pulse raced. This was just a dream, I told myself. It couldn't be real.

From the bed, I saw a small, closet-like room with a mirror on the wall. With my skull threatening to split apart, I stumbled out of bed and tripped over piles of dirty clothes that covered the floor. I pushed through them to the other room. In a mirror stained with water spots, a man stared back at me. Medium-height, broad shoulders, shoulder-length brown hair with brown eyes to match. A scar near the right eyebrow enhanced rather than detracted from the rugged good looks. It was a face that would have drawn a second glance, even from a princess, and one that would have sent my father calling for the guards.

But it wasn't mine. I grabbed the filthy porcelain basin underneath the mirror. How had this happened? Had I gone mad? "Think, Daulphina," I told myself. "There has to be a logical explanation."

The sound of knocking startled me, and a woman's voice called out, "Joshua, I know you're in there."

Thinking the woman might know something, I stumbled through the piles of clothes to the door and unlocked it. With her brown eyes and brown hair, the woman looked like a female version of the face I'd seen in the mirror. She was about my age, early twenties. What was more, she was wearing pants like a man and a tunic of an odd fashion. How was this possible? When I had complained about the ridiculous dresses a princess had to wear, my father had assured me that the gods would be displeased, that the sun and the moon would go out, indeed that the very universe would come to an end, if women adopted men's style of dress. Yet here was a woman dressed like a man who didn't seem to suffer as much as a hangnail.

The woman wrinkled her nose. "Whoo-ee, you smell like a distillery. Just what were you drinking last night?"

I put my head in my hands, certain it was going to fall off if I didn't. "How, how did this happen?"

The woman pushed past me and entered the room. "Good Lord, it stinks in here." She picked up an empty bottle. "Whiskey? You've been drinking Jack? I thought you only drank beer. Josh, you're not becoming an alcoholic, are you?"

I shook my head. This was a mistake because it made the pounding worse. "Please. Something's wrong. You've got to help me."

"Help you? What do you think I am? Your nanny?" she asked.

I remembered who she was. Her name was Jocelyn, and she was Joshua's cousin. Oh gods, how could I know that? I didn't know a Joshua!

"You haven't been answering your phone, and Meemaw sent me over here to find out why you didn't show up last night to your birthday party. All the family was there except the guest of honor."

None of this made sense, and the world whirled around me. I clutched the door frame to keep from fainting.

"You don't look so good," she said.

"I don't feel so good." I dropped to my knees and vomited down the wooden front steps. It felt like hot lava scouring the inside of my throat. I vomited and vomited until there was nothing left inside my stomach. I collapsed onto the floor, trembling.

Jocelyn rolled her eyes and squatted down beside me. "I don't care how hung over you are. Meemaw told me to come get you, and I'm getting you. Clean up first."

"No, this isn't real. None of this is real."

"Geez, Joshua, you stay away from the whiskey."

"I never drink whiskey," I said. "It's a man's drink." A princess only drank wine, nothing stronger. At least, that's what my father always said. It occurred to me, not for the first time, that if a person were to follow all my father's rules about what a princess should or shouldn't do, she'd be so restricted that she might as well be handcuffed, shackled, hog-tied, caged, paralyzed, thrown in the dungeon, buried alive, have her tongue ripped out, her hands cut off, and turned into a brainwashed vegetable. Yet, somehow my younger sister Jenna followed most of these rules.

Jocelyn looked at me strangely. "And what are you? A little boy? Into the shower with you." She helped me to my feet. I was too frightened to resist. She took me to the adjoining room, shoved me into a small, filthy stall—short clothes and all. She turned a knob. Warm water splashed down on me from overhead. I stared. How was that possible? Was magic heating the water? If so, who was working it? And who would expend magic for something so trivial?

"Don't you have any clean clothes?" Jocelyn shouted from the other room.

Trembling under the warm water, I didn't answer. How had I gotten here? How was it I was wearing a body that wasn't mine? How was it I remembered Joshua indeed had no clean clothes? "Here's a t-shirt and a pair of jeans that aren't too bad. I'll lay them on your bed. You've got ten minutes to get showered and out here, or I'm coming in after you. Don't make me see you naked again. Despite what people think about us Alabamians, I have no interest in marrying my cousin. I'll go hose off your trailer steps. At least you had the sense to throw up outside this time."

I collapsed in the corner of the small stall. I put my arms around myself, but seeing their huge hairiness only made me shake more. I wanted to cry, but I remembered a face, red with anger, standing over me, telling me in no uncertain terms that princesses didn't cry. I pounded my head against the stall wall, but that did nothing but make my head hurt worse. Had I gone stark raving mad and now imagined I was a man? I looked down at the body. If it was my imagination, I had an awfully good one.

I tried to think back to how this could have happened. I'd been going to the Temple of Cailleach to meet my lover. Clenyeth had told me he had important information and I should come alone. Clenyeth and I had had to be careful. If my father found out about us, Clenyeth could hang.

I'd seen Clenyeth near the entrance to the cave that housed Cailleach's temple. As I hurried toward him, someone had grabbed me from behind and put a cloth that smelled sickly sweet over my mouth and nose, and then . . . And then . . .

And then, I woke up as a man.

I stared at the warm water falling over me. It had to be magic. Somebody magicked me into a man's body. Dear gods, did that mean this hairy man was in my body? Was body-switching possible? Granny had never mentioned any such thing when she taught me everything she knew about magic, not that I'd ever been anything but a disappointment to her. I never had the raw power she expected of her successor. Or was my body empty? Or dead?

I was still staring at the falling water when Jocelyn yanked the stall door open. "Joshua, I told you you had ten minutes. Damn it, what's wrong with you? You still have your boxer shorts on. Have you even washed yourself?" She turned the knob, and the water went away.

I stared up at her. "Miss, you have to believe me. I'm not Joshua."

She put her hands on her hips. "Who are you, then? The queen of England?"

"No, I'm not a queen. I'm the crown princess of Asteria. I've never heard of England."

She put her hand to her forehead. "Joshua, just how drunk are you?"

"I'm not drunk. This isn't my body. Somebody magicked me into it."

Jocelyn stared at me for a second. "I don't know what you're playing at, but it isn't going to get you out of going to Meemaw's."

I rose abruptly. "I'm not going anywhere until someone explains what's going on! Just how did I become a man?"

Jocelyn backed away. "Good God, Joshua. You've completely lost it. I'm calling Uncle Braeden and getting you locked up in detox."

For reasons I didn't understand, I felt a shiver of fear when she mentioned Uncle Braeden.

She got a small black box out of her pocket. What magic could she work with it that would summon this Uncle Braeden? I'd never seen anything like it. Dear gods, was I not even in Asteria anymore? When I'd been a child, witches at my father's court had talked of parallel realms; a few even claimed to have travelled to them. My father had thrown them out of court. Surely, parallel realms didn't exist. I'd just been taken to another country, that was all. Neuk, perhaps. That was far enough away from Asteria that things would certainly seem strange, and maybe they even had different types of magic. But it was cold in Neuk, wasn't it? It wasn't cold here.

Jocelyn started bringing the box to her ear. I didn't know how such a small box could work a summoning, especially without a lot of blood, but I knew I didn't want Uncle Braeden appearing in this room. Somehow, I knew things would be much worse for me if she involved him. I grabbed her arm. "No, I'm fine," I said. "I'll go with you to Meemaw's."

A man's voice squawked out of the box. "Hello."

I jumped back. The accent alone was enough to make me gag. This Braeden couldn't be coming through it, could he? I went into a defensive crouch.

Staring at me, Jocelyn brought the box to her ear. "Sorry, Uncle Braeden," she said. "I must have butt dialed you."

The man heaved an exasperated sigh. "Don't do it again. I'm a rather busy man." The box went silent.

Jocelyn lowered the box. "You're sure you're okay?"

"Or course, I'm sure." I straightened and tried not to sound as terrified as I felt.

She handed me a worn brown towel, and I began drying off. "Get dressed. I'll wait outside." She headed out and shut the door behind her.

Shaking, I drew down the soggy—what had Jocelyn called them?—boxer shorts, and that thing was still there. Good gods! I remembered how much Clenyeth used to obsess over his. All men seemed to be like that, viewing their thing as a possessor of mystical power, a connection to the very gods themselves. Feeling in need of divine guidance, I touched the thing again, but I felt no flash of brilliant insight that would entitle the possessors of such things to rule the world.

What was I going to do?

I told myself to handle this like the princess I was, and for the moment that meant convincing Jocelyn I was sane. I hurriedly dressed in the strange clothing Jocelyn had laid out for me—a pair of pants and an almost clean tunic of the same unusual style Jocelyn was wearing. A t-shirt she'd called it.

Jocelyn came back in. I stared at her, and she put her hands on her hips. "Well?" She pointed to a pair of socks draped over black boots tooled with more images of men riding bulls.

Obediently, I pulled the socks and boots on. Although the socks stank, the boots, unlike everything else in the trailer, were clean, shiny, and polished. I reached for the hat on the bedside table. I stared at the hat in my hand. It was the same type of hat the man in the bull portrait wore. A peasant's hat, surely. Why had I reached for it? How did I know Joshua always wore it?

"Let's go. You know how Meemaw hates waiting." She walked out. I put on the hat and followed her outside.

I stopped dead, pointing to the three carriages sitting out front. "Those, those carriages go without horses!" I'd seen paintings of such things, but I'd never thought they were any more real than the paintings of winged fairies that hung in my old nursery or the dragons carved into my bedposts. As a child, I used to pretend I was driving a horseless carriage or flying on the back of a dragon, but pretending was another thing on the huge list of things princesses did not do. I collapsed in the dirt between the trailer and the carriages.

Jocelyn let out an exasperated breath. "*Now*, what's wrong with you?"

I stared around. In addition to the small trailer I'd woken up in, there was a red barn and a farmhouse. Fields with horses and cows and hay tied into strange round shapes stretched out behind them. I dropped my head into my hands. Please, don't let this be real! Cernunnos, god of life, let this not be true!

Jocelyn grabbed my shoulder. "Joshua, c'mon! Let's get going!" For a moment, I just stared at her. "That's it! I'm calling Uncle Braeden." She got out her black box again.

"No!" I cried and stumbled to my feet. "I'm fine. I'm coming."

She paused with the black box halfway to her ear. "Are you sure? You aren't going to do anything else weird?"

"I'm sure," I said, trying to control my trembling.

"We'll take my car. I'm not letting you drive in this condition." I followed her to a blue, dirt-splattered carriage. A sign on the back of the carriage read, "Alabama." I remembered that Jocelyn had referred to herself as an Alabamian. Where by all the gods was Alabama? She got in one side of the carriage, and I climbed into the other.

I wondered what strange magic Jocelyn would have to do to make it work. Would she cut herself, or was a larger sacrifice necessary? Most magic required the use of blood. The more powerful the magic, the more blood required, and such a carriage seemed like powerful magic. But all Jocelyn did was put a key into the slot by the wheel and turn it. She didn't even act like it hurt, and magic always hurt. The only thing that hurt worse for a witch than doing magic was not doing magic. Unused, built-up power could kill you.

The carriage roared to life. I screamed and clutched the seat.

"Jesus!" Jocelyn put her hand over heart. "What is wrong with you? You're always a little off around your birthday, but today, I swear you're not yourself."

I looked away from her, trying to hide my fear. "I'm fine."

"If you say so," Jocelyn muttered, seemingly to herself. The carriage started moving. How could such powerful magic be worked so simply? Besides, I hadn't felt any magic. To mask her magic from me, this woman must be an extremely powerful witch. That fact that I could feel no magic at all terrified me almost as much waking up and finding myself a man. The carriage rolled onto the road and picked up speed. Even racing at top speeds, Ghost Rider couldn't approach this, and she was a fast horse. I would have screamed again, but I didn't dare while sitting beside such a powerful witch. We flew past fields full of horses and cows that didn't look that different from those in Asteria. It couldn't be a parallel realm if there were cows and horses, could it? But what other explanation made sense? I tried to breathe slowly so I didn't hyperventilate, especially when a carriage zoomed past in the other direction. How could there be so many of them? Just how common were witches in this realm? They were pretty rare in mine.

Fortunately, we didn't go far before Jocelyn stopped in front of a white . . . house, I supposed it was. It was too big for a peasant's shack, but not big enough for a nobleman's dwelling. The house had a wide front porch with an overhang supported by white columns, a green roof, and green shutters by the huge windows. It needed a new coat of paint.

We got out of the carriage. Dear gods, Jocelyn acted like such wondrous magic hadn't even caused as much pain as a pin prick. Jocelyn opened the front door of the house without knocking, and I followed her down a hallway to the back of the house. We passed a parlor on the right that was stuffed with floral couches covered in doilies. Everything was coated with a light covering of dust, as if the room were little used. The kitchen, where we ended up, was, by contrast, clean and bright. Huge sunflowers gleamed from the walls. The kitchen cabinets were in a contrasting orange and spotted with smaller sunflowers. I was okay with the sunflowers, but the kitchen was full of strange objects I had no names for and couldn't even begin to describe. A short woman with iron-gray hair in tight curls all over her head was puttering around, wiping down the already gleaming counters. Meemaw.

How could I know this was Joshua's grandmother?

When she saw us, she leaned against the counter and crossed her arms. "Look what the cat drug in."

I looked around for a dead mouse or bird, but I didn't see one. An orange and white tabby jumped from the top of the refrigerator onto the counter, but it wasn't dragging anything.

"Have a seat." Meemaw pointed at the table. She opened what must have been the ice box and got out a wide variety of containers made of some strange material. She started dishing food onto sunflower plates. The cat jumped down from the counter and rubbed against my leg. I reached down and scratched its head, causing it to purr.

"None for me, Meemaw. I'm not hungry," Jocelyn said.

With her back to us, Meemaw ignored Jocelyn and continued ladling out food onto both plates. Jocelyn and I sat at a plain wooden table on wooden chairs with sunflowers carved into the woodwork. They weren't ornate enough for a palace, but too fancy for a peasant's shack. As soon as I sat down, the cat jumped into my lap and started kneading me and purring loudly. I petted it.

Meemaw muttered, "I should just let you starve, but you're nothing but skin and bones. Living off cold cereal and beer." She turned, holding two plates. She gasped. "Good Lord, what's got into Oscar? He usually won't come within ten feet of you."

I froze. Could it be bad that the cat liked me? Could I use it as proof I wasn't the Joshua they thought I was? The cat butted its head against my hand to encourage me to continue petting it. I complied. I glanced over at Jocelyn, and that decided me. The powerful witch wouldn't believe me, and she'd get this Uncle Braeden involved.

Meemaw shrugged. "You never can account for cats." She put a big plateful of cold ham and other food, strange food, in front of me—far more food than I could possibly eat in two days. She put a smaller one in front of Jocelyn. She sliced a big piece of cake and put it on a smaller plate in front of me. She poured three mugs of some brownish-black liquid. She added cream and sugar to one of them, which she gave to me. The ones for her and Jocelyn didn't get cream and sugar. She sat down at the table and peered over her glasses at me. "Now, son, why weren't you here last night? Hard to have a birthday party without the birthday boy."

The scent of the food reminded me I'd thrown up everything I'd eaten, and despite my fear, I was ravenously hungry. With a valiant effort, I controlled the shaking of my hand, picked up a fork, and took a big bite of some yellowish stuff. It was one of the most delicious things I'd ever tasted. "This, this is good," I said.

"You always did like my potato salad, but don't avoid my question." Meemaw's eyes bored into me.

I flinched, causing the cat to jump off my lap. I had no idea why Joshua hadn't come, so I stalled for time by picking up the mug and taking a drink. The liquid had a strange, but pleasant flavor.

Jocelyn sighed impatiently. "You know full well why he didn't come, Meemaw. He hasn't been to one of his birthday parties since Aunt Renee was killed in that car crash on his 18th."

Meemaw reached across the table and patted my arm. "Josh, darling, do you think you're the only one who misses your momma? She was my daughter, after all. But it's been five years. You know what Oprah says about grief. It's important to let yourself feel it, but at some point, you've got to move on. Your momma loved you, called you 'her little prince.' She wouldn't have wanted you to spend all the rest of your birthdays stuck in a bottle, and don't tell me you weren't. I can smell it on you."

Not knowing what to say, I shoveled down more food. It dawned on me I was eating like a backwoods peasant, not a princess. I took a dainty bite.

Meemaw sighed. "Stubborn as a mule. Always were. Ought to tan your backside." I raised my eyes in alarm. That didn't sound good, and she had a powerful witch like Jocelyn doing her bidding. "I'm going to give you one chance to redeem yourself. Jayleen is graduating on Sunday, and you'd better be there with the rest of us Killenyens." I didn't know when Sunday was or what a graduation was, but to pacify Meemaw, I promised I'd come and hoped I got this situation remedied before then.

I took another sip from the mug. The cream and sugar made it especially good. Why was I the only who'd gotten them? Sugar was undoubtedly expensive. Was this some kind of sexist ritual that only the man was felt worthy of the extra expense? That made me angry. All my life I'd fought against being seen as less than men. I offered my mug to Jocelyn, who was picking at the food on her plate.

She looked at me like I'd lost my mind. "Why would I want yours after Meemaw put all that junk in it? I like my coffee black, thank you very much." She picked up her mug and took a drink.

So, I guess it wasn't sexist. Or were these women pretending not to like the sugar like I'd heard of peasant women who pretended they weren't hungry when there wasn't enough food to go around? I shook the thought off; there was far too much weirdness going on to worry about coffee rituals.

After I polished off the food, cake, and coffee—good gods, how had I eaten so much?—Jocelyn took me in the carriage back to Joshua's trailer. I clung to the seat the whole way. Jocelyn must have noticed because she rolled her eyes. "I'm not driving that fast, Josh. You'd drive twice as fast if it weren't for the sheriff."

I wasn't sure what she was talking about, so I just smiled through clenched teeth until Jocelyn stopped in front of the trailer.

A man hurried out of the barn. He was about Meemaw's age and had white hair and a long, bushy white beard. He was wearing blue overalls of the same material as my pants and a red plaid shirt. Jocelyn saw him and turned to me. "Go on, get out." She made a shooing motion with her hand. "I want to leave before Uncle Gilly starts talking about Zenon and alien abductions. I don't know how you stand to live around such a crazy loon."

Not knowing what she was talking about, but grateful for the excuse to get out of Jocelyn's presence, I hurriedly got out of the carriage. Jocelyn whizzed out of there, kicking up a cloud of dust.

# CHAPTER 2

Uncle Gilly ran up to me. "Whisper Willow gots colic. Go and walk her. I'll call the vet."

Surely Jocelyn could have better handled the problem than I. My training was incomplete. Still, Jocelyn was gone, and I could cure a colicky horse. I didn't have any herbs or a place to make a potion, so I'd have to use a poppet even though that hurt a hell of a lot more. Uncle Gilly headed for the farmhouse, and I headed to the barn.

Unlike the stench of Joshua's trailer, the barn had a fresh, clean, and familiar scent of straw. There were stalls for about a dozen horses and a similar number of cows. Tied to a post in the grooming area was a bay mare. The horse was rolling her eyes, snorting and groaning. I looked around, but I couldn't see materials for making poppets. I thought of my sock. I quickly took off one boot and removed the sock. Dear gods, it stank! I carefully approached the suffering mare; a colicky horse doesn't pay much attention to its surroundings and can step on you without even realizing you're there. I plucked two hairs out of her mane, stood back, and used the hairs to tie the sock up into the semblance of a horse.

I looked around for something to cut myself with. In the tack room, I found a very long knife, almost a sword, hanging on the wall. I grabbed it, brought into the main barn, and carefully made a cut a on my left thumb. At least, I meant to do it carefully, but the knife was so gods-cursed big that I slipped and cut a nearly half inch gash.

I dripped, or rather gushed, blood onto the sock. One drop should have been enough, but I was bleeding everywhere.

I sucked on my bleeding thumb for a second and then ignored it and breathed on the sock horse. I held the image in my mind of it being the living horse. A sting shot through my hand as the magic gathered. I ignore the pain, breathed again, and focused my will. It felt like a bright light was exploding inside me, and my head exploded with it. I breathed a third time, and a hard lump coalesced in the sock horse's abdomen, right where the horse's intestines must have been blocked. I just avoided screaming at the pain in my own abdomen. Good gods, I hated poppets. I used the large knife and cut a hole in the poppet where the horse's anus should be. With one bleeding and one nonbleeding hand, I gently massaged the lump toward the hole. The pain dulled to several levels below excruciating.

The mare reared and whinnied, and I had to jump back or risk getting crushed. Soaking the poppet in blood, I continued massaging the lump further toward the hole, and the horse fidgeted and snorted. I gritted my teeth against the pain and squeezed and squeezed, the lump getting slowly closer to the hole. It would only move a miniscule distance with each squeeze because that was as fast as the blockage could move in the mare's intestines.

Uncle Gilly came back and stooped over me. "What in God's name are you playing with a bloody sock for?"

I thought it would have been obvious. "It's a poppet." When he looked at me blankly, I add, "For magic."

"Magic," he snorted and pointed at the sock. "There's no such thing as magic."

I gaped at him, stunned that anyone could deny the obvious. "There most certainly is."

Uncle Gilly laughed. "That's what the aliens want you to think."

I didn't know what he was talking about, but at the moment I needed to concentrate on the spell. I ignored him and continued squeezing the lump farther toward the hole.

Uncle Gilly picked up the large knife. "What's all this blood on my machete?"

I guessed that was what the knife was called. "Be quiet. This hurts, you know."

He gave a loud humph, but didn't say anything else until I finally squeezed a lump of who-knows-what out of the sock, and the mare let out an immense fart and pooped out a huge pile of . . . you know. I sat down hard on the wooden barn floor, as the pain drained out of me and near euphoria took its place. Magic might hurt, but the aftereffects were almost always worth it.

Uncle Gilly stared at me open-mouthed. "What kind of alien technology is this?" He took the sock from my hand and picked up the lump that I squeezed out of it and sniffed it. "Where'd someone like you get this? You haven't been abducted lately, have you?"

I wasn't sure what all this talk of aliens was about, but evidently he'd never seen magic like this before. Considering how badly telling the truth had gone with Jocelyn, I hesitated. But I didn't know what else to say. "I'm not Joshua."

Uncle Gilly squatted down near me. "Then who are you?"

"I'm Daulphina, the crown princess of Asteria."

Uncle Gilly rubbed his chin. "Asteria? Is that in the Andromeda Galaxy or farther out in the Sunflower?"

Confused and still bleeding, I shook my head. "Galaxy?"

"Yeah, you know, what planet are you from? Is Asteria anywhere near Zenon?"

"I'm not from a different planet. Asteria is a parallel realm, at least I think it is."

"Parallel realm?" he scoffed. "And people think I'm crazy when I tell them about the aliens from Zenon who abducted me." He picked up the machete and pointed it at me. "You just don't want to admit that aliens have replaced Joshua with you."

"They did?" I wondered if Uncle Gilly knew something I didn't.

"How else could it happen?" He squinted his eyes at me. "Although I don't know why they'd bother with a loser like Joshua. It's usually important people they mess with, like world leaders and talk show hosts."

"It is?"

He nodded knowingly. "Of course. Our last two presidents have been aliens." He leaned closer and whispered as if he didn't want these aliens to hear. "I'm pretty sure Oprah Winfrey is, too."

I was sure I'd heard the name before, but I wasn't sure where. Then, I remembered. "Meemaw was talking about Oprah."

Uncle Gilly nodded. "She always does. Oprah creates mind slaves of people if they watch her too often. Her slaves even read the books she tells them to, if you can imagine that." He drew back and raised the machete. "But you already know all about that, don't you?"

"I don't know anything." I looked away. I could feel tears forming in the corners of my eyes, and I didn't want him to see them because, of course, princesses don't cry.

Uncle Gilly hesitated, then patted me on the shoulder and sounded more sympathetic. "It wasn't your choice to come here, was it?"

I shook my head. "Somebody did this to me."

"And they didn't give you any instructions?"

"None. I don't understand this place."

"What you going to do about it?" he asked.

Furiously, I wiped at my eyes with my left hand. "I have no idea. I don't even know where to begin looking for an answer."

Uncle Gilly scratched his head; then he smiled. "The library, of course. Aliens have been trying to control information by making everything digital, but the library in town is holding out."

I didn't know what he meant about making things digital, but could a library really hold the answers I needed? "Where is this library?"

"In downtown Hamilton, of course."

"Would they allow me to use it?" I looked down at myself. Who would allow a peasant as I seemed to be to touch his precious books?

Uncle Gilly laughed. "It's a free public library. Anybody can use it."

I gaped at him. "Anyone?" Somehow a free library seemed more bizarre than a horseless carriage. Books were expensive. The librarian in my father's palace got possessive when I even wanted to look at a book, and he had to be threatened with dismissal before he would allow me to take one out of the library. In fact, my father was the only one the librarian didn't give a hard time.

"Sure, anyone." Uncle Gilly straightened as if that settled matters and walked out.

"Wait," I said. I needed Uncle Gilly to tell me more. Maybe he didn't believe in magic and parallel realms, but he at least seemed to know something. Still, he was gone. I leaned back against the barn wall, damning whoever had done this to me. I wanted to blame my bastard brother or my stepmother, but my bastard brother was even more poorly trained than I was, and my stepmother didn't have any magic at all. Could they have paid a witch to do this to me?

I sat there for a long time, and slowly, my thumb stopped bleeding. We witches heal faster than normal people. I didn't want to leave the barn. Here, things seemed almost ordinary. I knew as soon as I stepped outside, I'd have to deal with more of the bizarre.

My stomach started growling, and I was hungry again. Working magic did that to me. I reached beside me for the bell, but, of course, there was no bell. No servant was going to bring me food.

I got up and went to Uncle Gilly's house. I knocked on the door, and he answered. "What you want?" he asked.

"I require food," I told him.

"Go and get it then. I don't feed aliens." He shut the door.

Shocked, I stared at the closed door. No one but my father would ever close the door on me. How could he expect a princess to get her own food? I'd only been in the palace kitchens once in my life.

I thought about bursting in and demanding to be fed, but I had no way to compel him to serve me.

Joshua must have food in his trailer, I thought. When I returned to Joshua's trailer and opened the door, I was hit again by the stench. I closed my eyes. "Cernunnos, god of life, get me out of here. Take me back home." But Cernunnos must not have been listening because when I opened my eyes I was still standing in Joshua's doorway. I tried Cailleach, mistress of death, and a few others. But at the moment none of the gods seemed to be on my side.

I entered and went looking for food. In a little alcove off the bedroom, Joshua had what appeared to be a kitchen. It had an icebox like Meemaw's, a counter, a few cupboards, and some strange things I didn't know the name or use of. As I stared at the strange objects, I wondered how it was that I had known Jocelyn's and Meemaw's name, but I knew nothing about the objects in front of me.

The kitchen had a basin full of dirty dishes, and every surface was covered with the same, some of them with mold growing in them. I wished Sylvia or the chamber maid were here to clean up. I opened the icebox. There wasn't any ice in it, but somehow it was still cold. More magic? Or did the cold have something to do with the aliens Uncle Gilly spoke of? I inspected the contents. Other than a large number of bottles labeled "beer" and a container that looked like it contained milk, there was nothing in it.

I started opening the cupboards. Most of them were empty, but in the last one, I found three large boxes of something called "Frosted Flakes." I liked frosting, so I opened the box. I didn't know what to make of the contents, but I was hungry, and Joshua didn't seem to have any other food. I cautiously took out one of the flakes and ate it. It was sweet, delicious, and crunchy.

As I stared at the box, I realized the words were written in Asterian. Not only that, but everyone here spoke Asterian, without an accent even. How was that possible if I wasn't still in Asteria? I tried to remember what the witches at my father's court had said about parallel realms. I recalled them saying that because the realms were parallel, or shadows of each other, they all spoke the same language.

I grabbed a handful of the Frosted Flakes and shoved it into my mouth. I thought it would be more proper to eat it out of a dish than the box, but there didn't seem to be any clean dishes. I opened the icebox and grabbed a beer. I stared at it wondering what I was doing. Princesses didn't drink beer. Why had I grabbed it? How had I known Joshua would have one with every meal? I was curious what it tasted like. I glanced around, but, of course, neither my father nor any of his spies were near. I examined the top. It said, "Twist to open," so I twisted, and the top came off. I took a cautious sip, and I sputtered it back out. Dear gods, it was terrible. The lower classes must drink it only because they had nothing better.

But at the moment, I didn't seem to either, and as my father told me, a princess is always brave. I took another sip. It still tasted bad, but I managed to swallow it. After a few more sips, the flavor started to grow on me. There was nothing resembling a table, so I took the beer and the box of Frosted Flakes to the bedroom and sat on the bed. Before I knew it, the entire box of Frosted Flakes and the bottle of beer were gone. By Cailleach, I ate a lot.

I stared out the window at the gathering darkness and tried to think of some way to get back into my own body, to my own world. I kept returning to Uncle Gilly's suggestion of the library. Would I find some explanation of how parallel realms worked there? I had to hope I could. But surely such a magnificent thing as a free library wouldn't be open at night. I resolved to wait until morning unless this was truly a dream and I woke up in my own bed. I took off the boots, but left the clothes on. I curled up on Joshua's bed. It had been the longest and strangest day of my life.

\* \* \*

I dreamed I saw myself cowering in the corner of my bedroom, dressed only in my shift. Well, it looked like me with my long curly blonde hair and slight built, but somehow, I wasn't inside the dream figure. I was watching as if it were a play. My eyes were wide and looking wildly around the room. The door opened, and my maid Sylvia came in. "Your Highness, what's wrong?" she asked.

"I have boobs, that's what's wrong!"

By Cernuous, was I watching Joshua inhabiting my body?

Sylvia sighed. "Your Highness, I know things would have been easier for you if you had been born a man, but isn't it time you dressed?" She held up one of my favorite green dresses. It had leaves and purple flowers embroidered around the edges.

Joshua put up his hands. "I ain't wearing no dress! Oh, God, how did I get here? And where the hell is here? This sure as hell ain't my trailer!" He looked around at the large canopy bed, its woodwork carved into a pattern of dragons; the two huge wardrobes with matching dragons on the doors; the ornate chairs covered in embroidered silk; and the marble fireplace. "Looks like some Louis XIV's palace or something."

Sylvia's face creased with concern. "Your Highness, are you all right?"

He wrapped his arms around himself. "Hell no! Haven't you heard what I've been saying? Somebody turned me into a woman!"

Sylvia set down the dress and felt his forehead. "You don't feel like you have a fever, but . . . should I fetch a physician?"

"No, fetch whoever turned me into a goddamned woman and make him turn me back!"

Sylvia backed away. "I'll get a physician." She nearly ran from the room.

Joshua muttered, "Maybe this is some kind of delusion brought on by the alcohol. I never should have drunk so much whiskey." His hands flew to his crotch. "It's gone! I don't have no goddamn dick!"

Sylvia returned with Uistean. I didn't have much faith in Uistean and did my own healing. There were stronger witches in the city, but my father hated witchcraft and barely tolerated me in the palace, let alone someone more powerful. "What seems to be the trouble, Your Highness?" Uistean asked.

Joshua got shakily to his feet and grabbed his breasts. "Look at me! I have boobs! And where's my dick?"

"You see what I mean?" Sylvia asked.

"My, yes!" Uistean nodded. "It's clear she has an imbalance in the humors and needs to be bled."

"What the hell?" Joshua put his hands on his hips. "Who in the twenty-first century bleeds people? Oh, God, have I time travelled or something?" He turned to Sylvia. "Can't you understand I'm not the princess? I'm in the wrong damned body!"

Uistean's eyes narrowed. "I know Your Highness doesn't believe in bleeding, but I assure it is an effective cure for when the humors are as imbalanced as yours are."

Joshua stabbed a finger at Uistean. "What I need is someone who knows how to change me back!"

Uistean opened his case and got out a lancet and bowl. "Give me your arm, Your Highness. I'm afraid your case is rather serious."

"Try it, and I'll knock your head off!" His hands formed fists.

The physician put the instruments back in his case, snapped it closed, and turned to Sylvia. "Try to keep Her Highness quiet. I will discuss her treatment with the king."

* * *

I woke up in the middle of the night, shaking and grabbed at my breasts. They still weren't there. Joshua had them. Oh gods! How had this happened?

# CHAPTER 3

When I woke up in the morning, I kept my eyes closed. It was all a dream, just a horrible dream. But I reached between my legs and felt something hard. "No, it's still there!" I cried in a deep masculine voice. I opened my eyes and stared around the room. It hadn't changed. The picture of the bucking bull was still on the wall, and the room still stank.

While I was damning whoever had done this to me, Uncle Gilly walked in without knocking. He was holding the sock I'd used to make the poppet with. "I've been up all night trying to figure out this technology you used to cure Whisper Willow, and I can't make hide nor hair of it. Mind telling me how it works."

I sat up. "It's not technology. It's magic. It's about creating a sympathetic connection between the poppet and the real object, and then what you do on the smaller scale occurs on the larger. I never did have a very good grasp on magical theory. I can't explain it better than that."

Uncle Gilly snorted. "I may be an old man, but I'm not as dumb as you think. We both know there's no such thing as magic."

"No such thing as magic?" Uncle Gilly had said something similar the day before, but I couldn't wrap my head around the idea of a world without magic.

He looked disgusted. "Course not. After all, you abducted me to your space ships when I was little older than you are and did all your experiments on me, anal probe and all. Now are you going to explain this or not." He held out the sock.

I shook my head. "I've done the best I can."

Uncle Gilly snorted again. "You aliens, always want to keep the secrets to yourself. It amuses you to watch us struggle on like ants? Have it your way." He headed for the door.

I grabbed his arm before he reached the trailer door. "Please, Uncle Gilly. I need your help. Can I use one of your horses to get to this library you told me about?"

Uncle Gilly looked down at my hand. "Anyone ever tell you your trailer stinks, and so do you? Why don't you clean up at bit and put on some clean clothes?"

I abruptly let go of him and sniffed my underarms. I did stink. A princess couldn't stink. It just wasn't done. "I don't know what to do. Joshua doesn't have any clean clothes."

He rolled his eyes. "Typical. Why don't you take them over to Meemaw's and get them washed?" he said, like I was the stupidest person he'd ever had the misfortune to meet. "If you go now, she'll probably make you breakfast, too. She's always feeding Joshua. Then you can head over to the library, but if you think you're taking one of my horses after last time, you don't have the sense God gave hamsters."

I was too shocked to speak for a moment. "If I can't use a horse, how I am supposed to get to Meemaw's and this library?"

"You drive Joshua's truck, of course." He headed out of the trailer without waiting for me to dismiss him.

My mouth dropped open. Abandoning royal dignity, I ran after him. "I can't work the magic of those horseless carriages!"

He heaved a great sigh. "Enough of this magic nonsense, but our vehicles are probably too primitive for the likes of you. Since you're too high and mighty to explain your tech to me, I should just leave you to your own devices, but I happen to need Joshua to do some chores. Come on, I'll show you how to work the truck." He led me over to one of the carriages—a beat-up, brown one. "This is Joshua's truck," he said, and opened it. The floorboard was littered with trash and empty beer bottles. "You put the key in there and turn it." He pointed to the slot beside the wheel. "Use the gear shift to put it in gear." He pointed to a stick with a knob attached. "D for drive. R for reverse. P for Park. Push the pedal on the right to go. The one on the left to stop. Turn the wheel to change directions. That's all there is to it. Have fun." As my head spun with the instructions, he turned toward the barn.

"Wait a minute. Where's the key? And how do I get to Meemaw's and this free library?"

Uncle Gilly shrugged. "Key should be in the trailer somewhere. You'll have to search for it." He pulled a notepad and pencil out of his front pocket of his overalls. "I'll draw you a map. Meemaw's is on the way to the library. It ain't far." He drew a map and explained how to get there. He abruptly walked away, still seeming angry about the sock.

I turned back to the truck. Could I do it? Uncle Gilly said it wasn't magic, but surely that was impossible. Remembering a princess is always brave, I went back into the trailer to find the key, not an easy feat considering the mess. Thinking it might make it easier to find the key, I decided to gather the laundry first.

I found a large bag. Wanting to touch Joshua's dirty clothes as little as possible, I found a pair of work gloves and gathered the clothes up from between the various messes. They smelled like he let something die and crawl in among them. I picked up one pair of pants that had been on top of a plate covered with food remains. Nasty, huge, black cockroaches scurried in all directions. I jumped back and let out a muffled scream. Dear Cailleach, get me out of this place. I stood still for several moments, but nothing else happened. I shook myself and continued stuffing the clothes into the bag. I found a set of three keys on the bedside table under a dirty pair of boxer shorts.

Picking up the boxer shorts, I uncovered a picture of some sort. It depicted Joshua, a few years younger than he was now, with an older woman. Momma, I thought, and tears came to my eyes. Good gods, Joshua missed his mother as much as I missed mine. But how was it that I felt his emotions? I felt like collapsing on the bed in sobs, but of course, as a princess, I couldn't do that.

I rigorously repressed the emotions that weren't mine. I looked at the picture more closely and noticed something odd. It didn't appear to be painted. How had it come to be?

Shaking my head, I set the picture down and lugged the laundry bag out to the back of Joshua's truck, which had some kind of shell over it. I put the bag in back and opened the front door warily. Moving carriages without horses seemed far too advanced of magic to handle with a simple key. But if Joshua had, surely I, crown princess of Asteria, could.

I sat in front of the wheel. I prayed to Cernuous, god of life, that I could work the carriage and get to Meemaw's house without killing myself or anyone else. I focused my will, braced myself for the pain, and tried to put one of the keys in the slot. It wouldn't fit. I tried the second key. It went in, but no matter how hard I concentrated it wouldn't turn, so I tried the third key. As soon as I turned it, before I'd even focused my will, the truck roared to life. I screamed, but not because it hurt. In fact, there wasn't even the smallest amount of pain. Could Uncle Gilly be right? Was I in a world without magic?

I stared at the carriage's controls and tried to remember everything Uncle Gilly had said. I grabbed hold of the gear shift and moved it to D for drive. I pressed my foot on the go pedal, and the truck jumped forward. I panicked and slammed my foot on the stop pedal. The key had allowed me to work the magic, but could I control it? All my life I had heard stories of apprentices trying spells too advanced for them. The results were always disastrous and usually ended up with the death of the apprentice.

But what choice did I have? Shaking, I tried pushing the go pedal more gently. The truck crept forward. Slowly, the truck moved onto the road that led to Meemaw's house. I hadn't gone far when another carriage zoomed up behind me and sounded a truly awful horn. I shrieked, veered off the road and into a fence post before I thought to slam on the stop pedal. The operator of the other carriage, leaned out his window, shouted something I couldn't understand, and put up the middle finger of his hand. Before I thought about it, I returned the gesture. It felt familiar, like one I'd made thousands of times before. Good gods, was Joshua in here with me? No, he was in my body. If he was here, surely, things would make more sense.

I sat there for a while trying to control my heartbeat and breathing, and more carriages zoomed past on the road behind me. By Cailleach, how could you control something moving so fast? I wanted to get out of Joshua's truck and never touch it again, but if I did that, how would I find my way back to Asteria? It seemed absurd to be struggling on my own. In my world, I was almost never alone. I had a host of servants, advisors, and hanger-ons buzzing around me. I had but to snap my fingers, and Duke Tearlach would be waiting on me hand and foot, and he wasn't the only one. But here, who could I rely on besides myself? It was situations like this my father must have had in mind when he told me a princess was always brave.

I could do it. I would make it to Meemaw's. I waited until there were no carriages on the road behind me, then I tried R and the go pedal again. The carriage eased backwards. When I got on the road, I moved the gear shift to D and pressed a little harder on the go pedal. The carriage leapt forward, zooming at impossible speed. Still, carriages continued to close rapidly on me and sound their horns. But I managed to keep control of the truck and continue down the road.

Before I reached Meemaw's, I stopped shaking. Something about operating the carriage felt familiar, like I'd done it before, although that was absurd. Still, I kept the speed as slow as I dared. I stopped the truck in front of Meemaw's and moved the gear stick to P. Good gods, it hadn't hurt in the slightest. What was this technology Uncle Gilly spoke of? It seemed much better than magic. I lugged the bag out of the truck, approached Meemaw's front door, and knocked.

Through the window, I saw Meemaw tottering toward me using a cane. She opened the door and looked me up and down like she'd never seen me before. "What in tarnation are you knocking for? I don't get around like I used to."

I remembered Jocelyn had just walked in. Meemaw obviously expected Joshua to do the same. She stared at me like she expected an answer. "It was locked," I tried.

"Lock's been busted for close to five years. You keep saying you'll come around and fix it, but you haven't yet. Not that I ever locked the door anyway."

"Er . . . I thought it was locked."

"Turn the knob next time. You know I've got Oprah on this time of day." She turned and tottered back to the kitchen.

I followed her, lugging the bag. Over the kitchen counter was a moving, talking picture of a dark skinned woman. I gaped at it. How did Meemaw make the picture move? I remembered what Uncle Gilly had said about Oprah.

"Isn't she an alien?" I pointed at the moving picture.

Meemaw looked at me like I'd lost my mind. "Don't you go listening to Uncle Gilly. Oprah Winfrey happens to be the most important person to have lived in the last hundred years, maybe the last thousand."

I pointed a shaking finger at the woman in the moving picture. "But how does she make the picture move and talk?"

Meemaw put her hands on her hips. "What is wrong with you? You act like you're scared of the TV." Meemaw reached up and touched the moving picture, and it went black. "Josh, darling, are you all right?"

I realized this moving picture must be more technology like the horseless carriage. I tried to tell myself to act normal. "Nothing. I just had a strange nightmare about her, that's all."

Meemaw narrowed her eyes. "What kind of nightmare could Oprah possibly cause?"

I scrambled around for something to say, but nothing came to mind.

Meemaw narrowed her eyes. "I bet she was lecturing you on responsibility. I've never been happy with the way you treat women. Have you ever had a relationship that lasted more than a month?"

I started, thinking of Clenyeth, who'd been my friend such childhood and later my lover. What had happened to him when I was taken? Had he been killed trying to protect me? Surely he wouldn't have allowed me to be taken without a fight. I squeezed my eyes tight. No, he hadn't been killed. He couldn't have been. I forced myself to believe Clenyeth was safe.

Meemaw was still waiting for an answer, and I tried to think what a man might say. "My relationships are my business, Meemaw."

"Humph! That's probably what your father thought when he ran out on your mother before you were even born. I won't have you doing any nonsense like that." She shook a finger at me. "If you aren't ready to take the responsibility for a baby, you use a condom. You hear me?"

I had no idea what she was talking about, but promised her I would.

"See that you do." Thankfully, that seemed to end this uncomfortable conversation, and she starting getting eggs and bacon out of the ice box. "I see you brought your laundry."

I nodded. "Uncle Gilly told me you could wash it for me."

Meemaw looked at me sideways. "Why would Uncle Gilly need to tell you when I've been doing it since your Momma died? Lug the smelly things out by the washer, and I'll whip you up some breakfast." She waved in the direction of the back door.

I carried it out onto the back porch. I sat the bag down, came back into the kitchen, sat at the table, and looked around at all the sunflowers. Oscar jumped on my lap again, and I scratched his head. I continued petting him while Meemaw cooked.

Meemaw shook her head. "Strangest thing. I can't imagine what's got into that cat." When the food was ready, Meemaw placed a large plate of bacon and eggs in front of me. She poured me a cup of coffee, adding cream and sugar. "What you got planned for the day?"

I shooed Oscar off my lap so I could eat. "I thought I'd go to the library."

Meemaw's jaw dropped. "Why in tarnation would *you* go to the library?"

I would have thought that would have been obvious. "I want to look at books."

"Books?" she repeated like it was some foreign concept. "I haven't known you to pick up a book since you graduated high school. What are you up to now?"

Before I could figure out what to say, a smile spread across Meemaw's face. "I heard yesterday at the beauty parlor that Mary Olsen's daughter, Linda, just started working at the library. She went to high school with you, didn't she?" Meemaw nodded knowingly. "Go along when you've finished your breakfast, and check out your books." Meemaw winked at me. "But remember those condoms now!"

Grateful she'd thought of an explanation, I told her I would.

When I finished eating, I headed out to Joshua's truck. I'd made it this far; certainly I could make it the rest of the way to the library. I got in and gingerly put the key in the slot. Bracing myself, I turned it, and the truck roared to life. I felt proud of myself that I managed not to scream.

Gripping the wheel tightly, I moved the gear shift to D and eased the carriage slowly onto the road. I looked at Uncle Gilly's map. As I followed it, I became more and more comfortable behind the wheel. It was as if my body knew how to operate the carriage. The farmland gave way to odd buildings, some with large crosses on them. Other carriages became more and more frequent on the road. Everyone seemed to have one. The street narrowed, and I entered a couple of blocks of shops with impossibly large front windows: Valley Title Company; Vickie's Jewelry and Gifts; Ann's Boutique and Tanning; Old School Barbershop; a couple of empty shops; Braeden Massinger, Attorney at Law. The last one caused a shiver of apprehension. It had to be the Uncle Braeden Jocelyn had threatened me with.

I turned onto Bexar Avenue and pulled up in front of a small red-brown brick building with a white portico. White letters spelled out Clyde Nix Public Library.

I got out of the truck, opened the library door, and stared at the books—rows and rows of them, nearly as many as in my father's library. Surely such a grand library couldn't be used by just anyone. A librarian noticed me and came up. She was about my age with her brown hair pulled back into a ponytail. I was certain she was going to tell me to leave. Instead, she smiled brightly. "Joshua! Good to see you."

I guessed she must be Mary Olsen's daughter, Linda. "Linda, how's it been?" I asked, praying I was right.

"Fine, fine, and you?"

I wanted to say I'd never been worse in my life. "Mighty good," I said, and as soon as I said it, a tremor of fear passed through me. I'd never used that phrase. Why would I now?

She leaned close to me and ran a finger down my arm. "Heard you're still bull riding?"

At first, I had no idea what she was talking about. Then, I remembered the picture in Joshua's trailer and on his boots. Had he done that? "Mm, yeah, yeah, I am."

She leaned even closer. "What's it like?"

I took a step back. "It's . . . it's exciting all right. Nothing like it."

She smiled, closing the distance again. "Some people think it's stupid, but I think you're real brave. I heard the rodeo's in Pontotoc, Mississippi, this weekend. That's only about an hour away. I just might come down and watch."

Good gods! She was flirting with me. "You . . . you do that," I said, certain I wouldn't be in Pontotoc myself. I wanted to escape the situation, but I hadn't gotten what I'd come for. I tried to change the subject. "I'd like to look at some books."

"You do?" She seemed as surprised by this as Meemaw had been.

"Yes, do you have anything about aliens?"

"Aliens?" Linda laughed. "You must be getting books for Uncle Gilly. I'm afraid we don't have any new ones he hasn't read a hundred times. Alice told me she always lets him know when we get a new one in."

I licked my lips. I wasn't sure aliens was what I actually wanted to read about any way. "What about parallel realms?" I asked tentatively.

Linda took a step back. "Has Uncle Gilly broadened his obsession to those now?"

I nodded.

She sighed. "I guess there is no end to the man's craziness. Come over here to our catalog and let's see what we have." She led me over to what Meemaw had called a TV. This one had a board with buttons with letters on them below. Linda pushed some of the letters. I braced for the moving, talking pictures to appear, but this time only words emerged. "It appears that we have only one," she said. "*The Hidden Reality: Parallel Universes and the Deep Laws of the Cosmos.*" She read the description of it, "*The Hidden Reality* reveals how major developments in different branches of fundamental theoretical physics -- relativistic, quantum, cosmological, unified, computational -- have all led us to consider one or another variety of parallel universes." She looked at me. "Those theoretical physics should be right up Uncle Gilly's alley."

I nodded again, worried that I wouldn't be able to understand the book since I didn't know what physics were. "Can I take a look at it?" I said.

"Sure." She led me over to one of the shelves and picked up a thick volume.

There was a table with chairs nearby, so I asked her if I could sit and read.

"You want to read it yourself?"

I tried to think of something to say. "I've got to let Uncle Gilly know if it's any good before he comes in himself. He's an old man, you know?"

Linda looked at me like this was the strangest thing she'd ever heard, but she shrugged. "Suit yourself." She leaned close, touched my shoulder, and walked off to help another peasant who'd wandered in.

I sat at the table and opened *Hidden Reality*. The book started off with a description of a child playing with mirrors and got increasingly complex. I had to read very slowly, and still I only partially understood it. Every now and then, Linda wandered by, touched my shoulder, and asked me if I was still reading. "You sure you don't want something else?" she asked on her third visit. "We have quite a few novels by Louis L'Amour."

"This is fine," I said. I wished she'd leave me in peace. It was endlessly distracting.

Finally, Linda came to me to tell me the library was closing. "You've been reading that book all day." She sounded stunned. "Did you want to take it home to Uncle Gilly?"

"You'd let me?"

"Why wouldn't I?" She picked up the book and took it to the front desk. I jumped as she made a red light flash and beep. If there was no magic in this world, what could she possibly be doing? Fortunately, she didn't seem to notice my reaction and handed me the book. "Remind Uncle Gilly it's due back in two weeks."

I almost choked. They'd let me keep a book for two whole weeks? Even at the palace, I couldn't get the librarian to let me keep a volume in my rooms for more than a couple of days.

"Tell Uncle Gilly he could probably find more at the Barnes & Noble in Tupelo. We really are a small library."

"Small?" I blurted, wondering in what world such a magnificent library could be called small.

She leaned close and touched me again. "See you Friday, and maybe we can go out to get a drink or something afterwards."

"Mmm . . . yeah, sure," I said, and hurried out the door.

When I reached Meemaw's house, it was dark. A piece of paper was taped on the door with Joshua's name written on it. I pulled off the note and read it.

"Where you been all day? Had to get to bingo. Laundry's on the back porch.

Meemaw"

I didn't know what this bingo was, but I fetched Joshua's laundry and headed back to my trailer. Had I just thought of the trailer as mine? No, I was not Joshua Killenyen. I was Daulphina, the crown princess of Asteria.

* * *

The first thing I did when I got back to the trailer was get another box of Frosted Flakes out of the cupboard. I was standing in the kitchen eating and drinking a beer—I guessed it didn't taste that bad—when Uncle Gilly came over. "Find out anything at the library?"

I shook my head. "Nothing useful." I held out *Hidden Reality*. "This is the only book they had on parallel realms."

"Parallel realms?" Uncle Gilly scoffed. I guessed Uncle Gilly had no further insight to offer because he abruptly left.

Damn it all! I hit the trailer wall. I wanted to go home. I wanted my own body back. I took the box of Frosted Flakes to the bed and picked up the book. It was hard reading, and it didn't contain a blasted thing about how to cross between parallel realms or body switching. Before I knew it, the entire box of Frosted Flakes was gone. Good gods, I ate a lot!

I continued reading until I couldn't keep my eyes open any longer.

* * *

I dreamed of my father. He was alone in his bed and looked terrible. His face and bald head were a pasty white, and he'd lost so much weight the skin hung in loose folds. He had a cancer that was beyond my power to cure, and he wouldn't allow any of the more powerful witches from the city near him.

The door opened, and my bastard brother entered. Fitzrigh was two years older than me, and we'd never gotten along. He resented me for being the proper, legitimate child. Something about him reminded me of Joshua, but I couldn't really say what. His looks were far smoother, more refined, and he had blue eyes and long, blonde hair pulled back into a braid. He bowed to my father. "Sire," he said.

"Have you examined her?" my father asked.

"Yes, Sire, and she's raving. I agree with Uistean; she definitely needs to be bled."

My father looked weary. "Do it."

Fitzrigh hid a smile. "And if she refuses to cooperate?"

"You have my permission to use whatever force you deem necessary."

Fitzrigh's smile broadened, no longer trying to hide it. "Yes, Sire." He bowed and left.

Outside two guards waited for him. Fitzrigh laughed and patted one of them on the shoulder. "He authorizes us to use whatever force I 'deem necessary.' Come on. This is going to be fun." He took off down the hall. The two guards laughed and followed him.

The scene shifted, and I saw Joshua curled up on my bed in a fetal position, muttering, "This can't be happening. Dear God, I'm a woman, and I'm in the fucking Middle Ages." No one else was in the room.

Fitzrigh and the two guards burst through the door. Joshua jumped to his feet. "I told you to stay away from me, you bastard. Nobody's going to bleed me. There's no way in hell that is going to turn me back into a man."

Fitzrigh turned to the guards. "See, gentlemen. She's definitely raving. Let's make her bleed."

The three of them laughed, and the two guards advanced on Joshua. Joshua backed away. "Get away from me. If you touch me, I'll hurt you. I swear to God."

Joshua put up quite a fight, punching, kicking, biting, and cursing, but the two guards eventually pinned him to the bed. Fitzrigh approached with the lancet and bowl. He smiled cruelly and jabbed the lancet in far harder than necessary. "Bleed, little sister, bleed."

# CHAPTER 4

I awoke thrashing in the bed. It took me a few moments to realize I wasn't pinned down. I grabbed my arm, but there was no wound. Sweet Cernuous, were my dreams real? Was Joshua being subjected to such treatment? Did that mean that Fitzrigh was responsible for my condition? Or was he just being his usual nasty self?

Worse, my father was dying, and from the look of him, he didn't have long. My father and I had never been close. He'd never been happy having a woman as his heir, and he'd get angry whenever I broke one of his 6793 rules about what princesses should and shouldn't do. Still, he was my father, and if I couldn't figure out how to get back soon, I'd never see him again. I looked at the book lying on my bed. Why couldn't it teach me what I needed? I picked it up.

I read a few minutes. Then I realized I was ravenously hungry. Good gods, this body needed a lot of food. I went to the kitchen and got out the box of Frosted Flakes. I took them back to Joshua's bed and ate them out of the box while I continued reading.

Uncle Gilly walked in. He rolled his eyes when he saw me. "Came over to see if you found out anything in that book of yours, and I find you eating from the box again. Don't you ever eat anything other than Frosted Flakes? Not a very balanced diet, if you ask me."

"I can't go to Meemaw's house for every meal," I protested.

"Of course, you can't. You might find your mind being taken over by Oprah, same as the old lady, but you could go to the grocery store and pick something else up, but I don't suppose they have grocery stores where you come from either." Uncle Gilly sighed. "Let me draw you a map." He took out his pad and pencil and drew. He ripped it off and handed to me. "You do have money, don't you?"

"I don't know. Where would Joshua keep it?" I'd never paid for anything in my life. As a princess, if I'd wanted something, I'd merely mentioned the fact, and someone had provided it.

"In his wallet," Uncle Gilly said, as if I were stupid. "It's not like we've computerized everything with credits and such."

I ignored the part of his statement that made no sense. "Where is his wallet?"

Uncle Gilly shrugged. "How should I know?" He left.

I decided I'd just have to look for it. Despite the trailer being so small, it took me nearly an hour of searching to find Joshua's wallet. The trailer held the oddest assortment of objects. Across from the bed was a TV thing larger than the one in Meemaw's kitchen. I had no idea how to make it work, and I wasn't sure I wanted to. Pictures simply shouldn't move. On the bedside table was a black box like Jocelyn had threatened to use to summon Uncle Braeden. In a closet, I found several odd sticks made mostly of wood with round metal barrels attached. I couldn't image what they were. Amazingly, there was also a bow and arrows. I was relieved to see something familiar. I picked up the bow even though I didn't know how to use it. Weapons training was on my father's list of things princesses didn't do.

Finally, between the bedside table and the bed, I found a leather wallet. It was black—everything of Joshua's seemed to be black—and had another picture of a bucking bull tooled into it. I opened it to see Joshua's face, staring back at me. Like the picture of Joshua and his mother, the picture didn't appear to be painted, but at least, it stayed still. The picture was on something called a driver's license. I also found three green pieces of paper decorated with large pictures of men's heads. Two said twenty dollars and one said ten. In small writing were the words, "This note is legal tender for all debts, public and private." Could this be money? Who were these men that people would consider simple pictures of them valuable? I decided not to puzzle it out at the moment.

I went out to Joshua's truck. I felt a shiver of fear as I put the key in and it roared to life. By Cailleach, it was loud! I eased it onto the street in the direction that, according to Uncle Gilly's map, led to the grocery store. I started to think driving wasn't that hard when I heard a horrible wailing noise. I looked behind me and saw a carriage with flashing red and blue lights on top. What kind of strange magic was this? I gripped the steering wheel hard and reminded myself there was apparently no magic in this realm. Still, that didn't mean the lights weren't dangerous. I considered pushing harder on the go pedal to see if I could outrun it. But I saw the word "sheriff" written across the front of the carriage. Dear gods, what I had done to get a sheriff's attention? In this realm, what could the sheriff do to me? In mine, sheriffs had a lot of power in rural areas. It was difficult for the crown to make sure they didn't abuse their power. Visions of all the horror stories I'd heard about local sheriffs beating, robbing, maiming, and raping flashed through my head. Still, I knew those who defied sheriffs fared worse than those who complied. I pulled Joshua's truck over, and the sheriff's carriage stopped behind me.

The sheriff got out of his carriage. As soon as I saw him, I knew I was in trouble. I don't know how, but I knew this was Sheriff Wilson and he hated Joshua.

Reminding myself that a princess was always brave, I got out of the truck.

The sheriff's eyes narrowed. "What do you think you're doing, Killenyen? Get back in your truck before I have to hurt you."

Dear gods, I'd already done something wrong. I hurriedly got back in the truck and grabbed the steering wheel to steady my hands.

Hitching up his pants, the sheriff swaggered over. "You moron, it isn't like we haven't been through this dozens of times. Close your door, and roll down the window."

I could close the door, but what did he mean by roll down the window? Uncle Gilly's instructions hadn't covered that. "Um, the window's broken."

The sheriff spat on the road. "You know, you're a real piece of work, boy. If you're not being drunk and disorderly or poaching deer, you're up to some other mischief." Poaching? You could be hung for poaching, but I hadn't poached anything. There was not a single dead animal in the truck. "You know the drill. Let me see your driver's license and registration."

Grateful I understood at least part of what he was talking about, I got out Joshua's wallet and handed over the driver's license. I didn't know what he meant by registration. "I don't know where my registration is," I said, hoping this wouldn't mean I was in deep trouble.

The sheriff didn't look amused. "Did you try your glove box?" He pointed to the far side of the truck, where a door of some kind was built in to the front panel. I opened it, and a mountain of objects, most of which I had no idea what were and none of which were gloves, cascaded out. It was so full I didn't know how Joshua had gotten it closed. In the midst of the mess were a few pieces of paper, one of which said "registration." Breathing a sigh of relief, I handed it to the sheriff and tried to stuff everything else back in.

The sheriff looked at the driver's license and registration. He asked, "Do you mind telling me why you're going thirty-five in a fifty-five?"

I stared at him, having no idea what he was talking about. He was waiting for an answer, so I had to say something. "I must have made a mistake," I said.

The sheriff spat again, a dark brown liquid staining the road. "You never make the mistake of going too slow. You better have some excuse for the way you're driving, or I'll find something to charge you with."

What possible reason could Joshua have for going too slow? "The truck doesn't seem to go any faster. There must be something wrong with the magic."

The sheriff's nostrils flared, and I wished I could take back the last word. Somehow horseless carriages weren't magical. "Have you gone off to la-la land with Uncle Gilly, you no-account bastard?"

I stiffened. I was the true born daughter of a king. "You have no right to insult me!"

The sheriff leaned closer. "Your mother gets knocked up by some asswipe who doesn't even stay around long enough to give you his name, and you think I don't have a right to call you a bastard? I'll call you a lot worse if I have a mind to."

Shocked, I drew back. Was Joshua a bastard like Fitzrigh?

"You know what, boy? I don't care why you decided to turtle it down this road. I find driving twenty miles under the speed limit to be reckless, so I'm giving you a ticket for reckless driving, and I'll be watching you. Never forget that, bastard." He gave me a nasty smile as if daring me to object again. He got a pad of paper out and starting writing on it.

I didn't know what a ticket was, but it didn't sound too bad. At least, he wasn't arresting me or putting me in stocks. Trying not to provoke him further, I kept my mouth shut and my hands on the wheel. He finished writing, ripped off the piece of paper, and handed it to me. I'd ask Uncle Gilly what it meant.

When the sheriff let me go, I slammed the door and sped out of there. If he wanted me to go faster, by Cailleach, I would go faster. The speed hit my system, and I felt a rush of elation. I remembered riding Ghost Rider over the fields at top speed jumping fences along the way. Gods, what a rush! Why had I been so afraid?

\* \* \*

I made it to the grocery store without any further difficulty. I parked the truck, walked in, and stopped short. There were more different kinds of food in here than in the largest market in Asteria. Why had Joshua confined himself to Frosted Flakes when there were so many choices? Not that anything was wrong with Frosted Flakes.

Most of the food in the store needed to be cooked. But I loaded up in the produce section on fruits and vegetables that could be eaten raw and got some prepared food from the deli and bakery. I got a couple of bottles of wine and several boxes of Frosted Flakes and beer for good measure.

When my buggy was full, I watched the other buyers. Apparently, I should join a line. After a few minutes, it was my turn, and I put my food up on the moving counter like I'd seen the other shoppers do. My food traveled by the woman in starts and stops, my Frosted Flakes, beer, everything emitting a beep as she waved it over a flashing light. I pretended not to find this alarming.

The clerk announced the total of $214.83. I got out the green pieces of paper and handed them to her.

She stared at them, and maybe the papers weren't money after all. "Got any more?" she asked.

I looked in the wallet, but that was all there was. I shook my head.

She sighed and rolled her eyes. "Joshua, this is only $50. The total is $214.83. Do you need to go back to kindergarten math?"

I started when she used Joshua's name. If she knew Joshua, why didn't I know who she was, like I'd known the sheriff and Jocelyn? Not sure how to handle it, I asked, "What can I buy for $50?"

"What you always buy." She rolled her eyes, hit some buttons on her machine, picked out the Frosted Flakes and beer, and made it beep again. "$45.63," she said.

She put the $50 in the box in front of her and gave me change. I put the paper in the wallet and the coins in my pocket because it seemed like they ought to go there, grabbed the bags, and left. I almost cried as I left the fresh fruits and vegetables and potato salad behind, but of course, princesses never cried.

When I got back to Joshua's trailer, I put the beer in the ice box and the Frosted Flakes in the cupboard. I collapsed on the bed. What was I going to do for food when what I bought was gone? How was I going to get more books about parallel realms so I could figure out how to get home? If I just had one of the jewels from my jewel box—the silver and diamond brooch, perhaps—I could buy all I needed.

I needed to find out how Joshua got more money. Surely Uncle Gilly would know, and while I was at it, I could ask him about the ticket the sheriff had given me.

I found Uncle Gilly in the barn, mucking out some stalls. "Did you find Joshua's wallet?" he grunted.

"Yes, but there wasn't much money in it."

Uncle Gilly shrugged. "Doesn't surprise me. He's been having a dry spell. Hasn't won in a rodeo in a few weeks."

"How am I supposed to get more money?"

"I guess you'll have to win the rodeo this weekend."

I gaped at him as I thought of the picture of the bucking bull on Joshua's wall. "I can't do that."

"Can't, huh?" Uncle Gilly smiled. "Then you can start in on the list of chores I have piling up for Joshua. To begin with, you can muck out the rest of these." He pointed at the long line of stalls.

I blinked. "You can't possibly expect me to shovel . . . You know, that stuff."

Uncle Gilly's eyes widened mockingly. "Oh, yes, I guess where you come from they probably vaporize it or something. Not that you'll explain any of your technology to me." He turned back to the stall, shoveled up a huge pile of crap, and brought it around to the wheelbarrow, but instead, he dropped it on my boots. "Oops! I guess you'll smell like the rest of us now."

I grabbed Uncle Gilly's shirt. "If we were in Asteria, I'd have you hung."

Uncle Gilly pulled loose. "We're not in Asteria, princess. Things work a little different around here. Not my fault aliens put you in Joshua's body. You have a problem, go take it out on them."

"Maybe I will." I turned and stomped out of the barn. I'd ask about the ticket later. I took off my boots at the trailer door, but there was no servant to take care of the mess for me. I picked the boots up, carried them to the bathing stall, and washed the shit off.

For the first time, I understood Clenyeth's complaints about shoveling horse shit. I remembered when I first realized how unhappy he was in the stables. I'd been in my rooms, absently staring in the mirror and combing my hair. Small pebbles sounded against the window. I raced to the window and opened it. Clenyeth was standing on the ground, two floors below. He saw me and rapidly climbed the trellis.

"Clenyeth," I said, as he entered through the window. I threw myself into his arms. His lips met mine, and we tore at each other's clothing. We didn't talk much until after.

He lay beside me in the firelight. I rested my head on his chest, and he played with my curls. "Beynon asked me where I was going again tonight," he said. Beynon was the Master of the Horse.

I lifted my head. "What did you tell him?"

"Told him about a girl in the village, but I don't think he believes me. I think he knows, and he doesn't like me much."

I laid my head back down. "He's just a snob. Thinks you're acting above your class. You aren't worried, are you?"

Clenyeth got up from the bed and poked at the fire. "It will be my neck if the king finds out."

"Beynon won't tell. My father won't live forever. Beynon knows his future lies in pleasing me."

Clenyeth poked a log savagely. "He doesn't act like it. He's always riding me. Giving me the worst chores. I think he hopes I'll quit. I would if I had somewhere else to go. I'm tired of smelling like horse shit."

I got up, put my arms around him, and pushed my breasts against the strong muscles of his back. I breathed in the scent of his hair. "You smell just fine to me." I kissed the side of his neck.

He stiffened under my touch. "You think being a stable groom's enough for me? You can't offer me anything better?"

I drew back. "When my father dies, it will be different."

He whirled to face me. "And what then, Daul?" he snarled. "What then?"

I took a step back. "I don't know. We'll figure something out. What does it matter as long as we can be together?"

Clenyeth threw the poker on the hearth and left through the window without saying another word.

\* \* \*

Thinking of Clenyeth, I collapsed on the bed and rolled up in a ball. Despite our occasional problems, I missed him so badly it physically hurt. He had to be okay. But why would those who had done this to me leave him alive?

# CHAPTER 5

The next day, despite his antics with the shit and the boots, I had no choice but to approach Uncle Gilly. I found him in the barn. First, I asked him about the ticket the sheriff had given me.

"It means you got to pay a lot of money or go to jail," he said. "What were you driving recklessly for anyway?"

"I wasn't driving recklessly, but that's not the point. I don't have any money. Do you really think I can win a rodeo?"

"Sure, Joshua was pretty damn good at it, and he wasn't good for much. Besides, as an alien, you have that genetically enhanced DNA."

"I'm not an alien!" I snapped. "And I have no idea what you're talking about most the time."

"Trying to get me to let my guard down? Like you did when you abducted me back in the day?"

"I'm not trying to do anything but get back home." I felt suddenly overwhelmed with the hopelessness of my condition. I collapsed on the barn floor and struggled not to cry. "Nothing makes sense here. We don't have any of this technology."

Uncle Gilly squatted down beside me and patted me on the shoulder. "The aliens take you from a more primitive planet, did they?"

I wanted to shout that aliens had nothing to do with it, but I knew Uncle Gilly wouldn't believe me, so I nodded without looking up. My shoulders started shaking from repressed sobs.

To my shock, Uncle Gilly sat, put his arm around me, and drew me to his chest. "Don't worry, girl. It will be okay. The aliens brought me back, after all. I'm sure they bring you back when they're done with their experiments."

The kindness of his touch was more than I could take. I burst into tears and cried like I hadn't dared since I was a child. After my initial burst of emotion had passed, I pulled away and hurriedly wiped my eyes. "Princesses aren't supposed to cry."

"Supposed to be like a man, huh? Only emotion you can express is anger. Did you ever think what such rules do to the masculine psyche? Cost me my wife, they did."

I didn't know what to say, "I'm sorry."

Uncle Gilly shrugged. "That was a long time ago. Look, since you need the money and all, I'll show you how this bull riding is done. I rode a bull or two in my day. Before the aliens abducted me, that is. Tell you what, I'll even go over to Pontotoc with you. Get you all set up. I always did like rodeos."

I felt sick when I thought of tumbling from the bull's back onto its horns. "Did Joshua ever get hurt?"

Uncle Gilly shook his head. "Hardly ever. Well, that scar there"— he pointed to the scar beside my right eyebrow—"is from when a bull kicked him in the head. Gave him quite the concussion, and he had to have twelve stitches. But other than that, and bumps and bruises, Joshua led a charmed life. All the other bull riders are always breaking their ribs or dislocating their shoulder or tearing their ligaments, but not Joshua."

This wasn't what I wanted to hear. But surely, if this peasant Joshua could do it, I, the crown princess of Asteria, could. After all, I was an expert horsewoman. That was kind of the same, wasn't it? You just had to show the horse who's boss. Certainly, you could do the same with a bull, right?

Uncle Gilly stood and helped me to my feet. "First, you need to look like a cowboy. You've got the jeans, boots, and hat, but we need to do something about your shirt." I followed Uncle Gilly back to Joshua's trailer. He looked in Joshua's clothes closet, which was empty. "Where are all Joshua's clothes?"

I showed him the bag of clean laundry that I hadn't unpacked. He picked through it and drew out a black, long sleeved shirt with white embroidery on the shoulders. "Ah, here's a western shirt for you."

While I changed the t-shirt I was wearing for the shirt Uncle Gilly picked out, he continued to search through the clean laundry. He picked out a less ornate western shirt, this one black and white plaid. "You'll need a different one for tomorrow night. Rodeos almost always last two days," he explained.

He searched through Joshua's drawers and pulled out a belt with a huge buckle on it. The buckle had a picture of a man riding a bucking bull and the words "Rodeo. #1 American Sport" etched around the edges. I put it on.

"Now, where's your gear bag?" Uncle Gilly asked.

"How would I know? What does it look like?"

"It's black, of course, and about so big." He indicated dimensions with his hands.

"I think I saw something like that in the closet." I opened the closet containing the bow and arrows and took out a bag.

"Yeah, that's it," Uncle Gilly said. "Should have a smaller bag somewhat like that in there with his toiletries. You can put the other shirt, some clean boxers and socks in there."

I found the second bag. Inside was a razor and shaving foam, a small brush and something called toothpaste, soap, a comb, and a few other items. I put in the things Uncle Gilly suggested.

Uncle Gilly nodded like he was satisfied. "Bring the gear bag outside, and I'll show you how to mount a bull." I followed Uncle Gilly outside, and he led me over to a black metal barrel, placed sideways and propped up off the ground on a single metal leg. It had a metal pole sticking out the back of it like a tail. "This is Joshua's practice barrel." Uncle Gilly opened the gear bag, which was clean and well organized, unlike everything else in Joshua's trailer. First thing he pulled out were a pair of jeans with what looked like ground-in dirt and a pair of beaten up black boots with spurs attached. "Your riding pants and boots," Uncle Gilly said.

"The ones I have on are much nicer," I protested.

"Of course they are, and you want them to stay that way, don't you? What do you think will happen to them when you got thrown off into the dirt?"

"Oh," I said. I guessed that made sense. But what stuck in my mind was the thought of getting thrown off. Surely, I should just humble myself and shovel horse shit.

He pulled out a bunch of other items and showed me how to put on the protective vest, chaps, and a single glove. He got out what he called my bull rope. He showed me how to get the rope around the bull and how to mount the bull. Sitting on the barrel felt familiar. "You'll have a helper pull the rope tight." He pulled on what he called the rope's tail to tighten it and gave it to me. "Of course, the bull might not just stand there all quiet like. You might need to—" He stopped abruptly. "What the hell are you doing?"

I stopped what I was doing and looked at the bull rope. I'd been wrapping the rope's tail around my hand. "I don't know. It felt like the right thing to do."

"Hmm," said Uncle Gilly. "Must be muscle memory. Joshua's only done this about a thousand times."

I'd heard warriors talk of muscle memory, when you'd practiced so much that you didn't have to think any more because the body just knew what to do. It might be useful, but having Joshua's muscle memory scared me. I didn't want to be Joshua. "Did I do it right?" I asked.

Uncle Gilly shrugged. "Looks right to me. But it was about a thousand years ago when I did this. I never was any good." Uncle Gilly shook his head and went on. "Once you got your hand wrapped, you slide up toward the bull's head and nod. They'll open the chute. You only have to stay on for eight seconds. How hard can that be?"

I looked at him dubiously. I was taking advice from a man who'd admitted he wasn't any good.

"And one more thing," Uncle Gilly said. "You can't touch yourself or the bull with your free hand, or you'll be disqualified." I wanted to practice the procedure several times, but Uncle Gilly insisted it wasn't necessary. "You got that muscle memory. You'll be fine."

I wasn't so sure, but Uncle Gilly said we had to get going if we wanted to make the rodeo. We packed Joshua's gear bag up like he'd had it.

"Get your keys," Uncle Gilly told me. "You'll want to drive your own truck."

"No, I don't. I'll ride with you."

Uncle Gilly looked disgusted. "You aren't still scared of driving, are you?"

I shook my head. I couldn't admit that I was afraid to drive so far because, of course, a princess is always brave.

"Good. You put that camper shell on the back of your truck so you can sleep in there in-between rodeos. Got a nice set-up back there—mattress, sleeping bag, and everything. You won't want to drive back here Friday, just to go back to Pontotoc on Saturday night, and I can't hang around for two days. Besides, you'll want to go out drinking with your buddies after the rodeo. You always did say riding builds up quite a thirst."

"Maybe Joshua said that, but I certainly didn't." I argued with him, but he was adamant about going in separate trucks. I put the gear bag in the back of Joshua's truck and fetched the smaller bag and Joshua's keys from his trailer.

"You can follow me, but you got that GPS on your phone in case you lose me."

I stared blankly at him.

He hit himself in the forehead. "Yeah, I forgot. You're from one of those primitive planets, probably don't even know what GPS is. Let me get you a map." Uncle Gilly took a folded paper map out of his truck, unfolded it on the front part of his truck, and drew on it to show the route.

I took the map and got in Joshua's truck. Uncle Gilly pulled out, and I followed him. Fortunately, there weren't too many other carriages on the road; the route to the rodeo was through rural areas full of comforting cows, horses, and crops that wouldn't look out of place in Asteria. The houses were of a different style and about the same unusual size as Meemaw's—too large for a peasant, but too small for a nobleman. I guessed peasants lived much better in this world than they did in mine. Except Joshua, that is.

* * *

By the time I arrived at the rodeo grounds, I thought I'd gotten pretty good at driving. We parked in a grass lot with a couple of dozen other trucks and a couple of cars. I got Joshua's gear bag out of the back of his truck, and we walked toward the arena. The atmosphere was like a fair or a joust back home. Vendors were setting out their wares. There was a pony ride for the children, a big dirt area with stands on two sides, a corral for horses, and another corral with about a dozen of the biggest bulls I'd ever seen. My stomach clenched; they must have weighed close to a hundred stones, hardly a riding horse. "I'm supposed to get on one of them while it's bucking and stay for eight seconds?" I asked Uncle Gilly. If I got myself killed, whoever had done this to me would win.

Uncle Gilly patted me on the shoulder. "No sweat. We'll go pay your fee and see which bull you've drawn. Then you can change your pants and boots."

I stopped short. "You didn't say anything about paying a fee. I don't have any money."

Uncle Gilly hit himself in the forehead. "You didn't save enough money for your fee? What were you thinking, girl? I guess I can float you the $50, but I expect you to pay me back out of your winnings." I thought about the $50 that had been in Joshua's wallet. It had probably been meant to pay his fee.

As Uncle Gilly led me to what he called the rodeo office, we passed a host of vendors' booths. I paused at one that sold t-shirts. The same symbol was on more than half the shirts, and I remembered seeing it on the shirt Jocelyn had worn the first time I'd seen her. I pointed at it. "What does that mean?"

"That's the Confederate flag. Folks around here don't seem to realize we lost that war more than 150 years ago. The aliens were on the Union side. That's why they won, of course." Uncle Gilly shrugged and walked on. I followed more slowly. I caught up with Uncle Gilly at a trailer, little bigger than Joshua's, at the far end of the arena. There he paid my $50 fee, and we looked at what Uncle Gilly called the draw. For tonight, Joshua had drawn a bull named Sorrow's Edge and would be riding first. Tomorrow night he'd drawn Hell's Angel.

As we left the office, Uncle Gilly smiled. "Sorrow's Edge is a fine bull. He'll give you a hard time, all right," he said, like this was a good thing.

My palms were sweating. I wiped them off on my jeans. Surely I wasn't going to do this.

Uncle Gilly showed me where to change, and I put on Joshua's riding pants and boots. He led me back to the bull pen and the chutes. He told me where I could put my bag down. There were about a dozen other men sitting or standing around. About a half dozen of them greeted me.

I said, "Hi," back, trying not to look as lost as I felt. Names for three of the men flashed into my mind: Cody, Austin, and Nash. These, I realized, were Joshua's friends. Why didn't I know the others' names since they seemed to know Joshua?

A lot of the men were wrapping white strips around various body parts: ankles, wrists, elbows, knees. "What are they doing?" I whispered to Uncle Gilly.

"There just taping, you know, for where they've dislocated their shoulders or pulled their backs or broken their ribs or strained their wrists or . . ."

"Okay, okay, I get it!" If I heard any more, I'd never be able to get on the bull's back, but maybe that wouldn't be a bad thing. Bull riding was certainly only engaged in by the insane.

Uncle Gilly patted me on the shoulder. "You don't have to worry about taping. Like I said, Joshua leads a charmed life. Come, check out your bull." He walked over to the bull pen, and I followed reluctantly. "That brown and white one is Sorrow's Edge." He pointed to the biggest of the bunch. I stared at it, and it stared back with mean, little eyes. "The pure black one is Hell's Angel, your draw for tomorrow. Bull riding's always last. But you're the first rider tonight, so make sure you're ready."

A voice boomed through the arena. "Testing. 1, 2, 3. Testing."

"Dear gods!" I dropped to the ground. I darted my eyes around, expecting to see one of the gods towering above us.

Uncle Gilly looked down at me in disgust. "What are you doing? It's just the microphone. It's that guy over there." He pointed to a man in a booth. "And the sound comes out in speakers all around the arena." He pointed to the pole near us that had a box attached to the top. "You really are from a primitive planet, aren't you?"

How could a voice sound so loudly without magic? Without the very force of the gods?

I got to my feet, but before I could ask Uncle Gilly any more questions, a man clapped me on the back so hard I staggered. "Hey, Josh. Good to see you, buddy."

I turned. A young man, a little taller than Joshua with a blond mustache and beard, stood there. Joshua's best friend, Dan. "Hey," I said.

"See you got a good draw. With a bull that fierce, tonight just might be the night you end your losing streak."

I shook my head. No, it wasn't. I was not going to get on the back of that bull. I didn't know what I'd been thinking to even contemplate the idea. Dan saw Uncle Gilly and nodded. "Uncle Gilly, right? Dan Williams." He stuck out his hand.

Uncle Gilly grabbed it, and they shook hands. It seemed to be some kind of greeting ritual. "You the one always getting Josh here in trouble?"

Dan laughed. "More like the other way around." He clapped me on the back again. I laughed because it seemed expected of me.

Dan smiled and looked off into the distance. "There's one mighty fine bunny, and it looks like she's coming this way."

I followed the direction of his gaze, and Linda walked toward us. I didn't know why he'd called her a bunny, but I couldn't stop staring at her. She was wearing a top that bared more skin than a whore's corset, incredibly short jeans, and a belt with a buckle as big as Joshua's.

"Hi." She smiled and stepped far too close.

"You came?" I took a step back. Of course she came. She was standing in front of me, and it was obvious she had a thing for Joshua.

"Uncle Gilly." She nodded toward him; apparently everyone called him uncle. "Did you enjoy that book on parallel realms?"

"Parallel realms," Uncle Gilly scoffed. "What a bunch of nonsense! Joshua didn't say that book was for me, did he? I've got a reputation to uphold."

Linda looked at me curiously. "Well, he . . ."

Fortunately, Dan saved me. He stepped forward and held out his hand. "Hi, I'm Dan."

They shook, and Linda said, "Pleased to meet you. I'm Linda."

"A pleasure, ma'am," Dan said, tipping his hat and winking.

Linda smiled uncomfortably and looked back at me. "Thought maybe we could go have a drink afterwards."

I glanced over at the bulls. "If I'm still alive."

Linda laughed as if I'd made a joke, but hers wasn't the only laughter. I turned to find another man, carrying a gear bag like Joshua's. Ben Walker, I thought, wanting to punch him in his stupid face. I blinked, surprised by my violent intentions. Usually, I wasn't the vicious sort. It struck me that maybe I was tapping Joshua's emotions and I only knew the names of those Joshua had strong feelings for.

"Scared of a little ol' bull, Killenyen?" Walker said. "You've been hitting the ground hard a lot lately."

Something I didn't understand surged through me. How dare he laugh at me? I got in Walker's face. "I'm going to flatten you tonight."

"More like the bull will flatten you." Walker laughed again and walked off toward the rodeo office.

I fought the urge to run after him and smash my fist through the back of his head. Dear gods, what was causing me to react so intensely. I unclenched my fists. Linda scowled after him. "What an arrogant ass! You'll show him, won't you, Joshua?"

Uncle Gilly clapped me on the shoulder. "Of course he will."

Bull riding was absolutely insane, but the same force that made me want to beat Walker to a bloody pulp wouldn't allow me to back down now. I nodded. "He'll regret he ever met me."

"Should I meet you back here afterwards?" she asked, running a finger down my arm.

Thinking I might well need a drink by then, I agreed.

Uncle Gilly and Linda went off to watch the rodeo. The rest of Joshua's friends came up to me, and they all watched Linda saunter off. "Not bad, Josh," Dan said.

"Hell of a nice ass," Cody agreed. "I guess you've got something better to do after the rodeo than go drinking with the rest of us losers."

"I guess so," I said, but my pulse was racing, and my mind was focused on Sorrow's Edge. How could I show the bull who was boss before he bucked me off, and I broke my ribs or strained my back or got my head kicked in again or . . . I rigorously cut off the list of potential injuries. If I was going to do this, I couldn't be thinking like that, and by all the gods, I was going to do this. It hit me—my magic! I didn't have to worry about the bull bucking. I could calm it. Yeah, I'd have to make a poppet, so the magic would hurt, but surely not as much as getting bucked off would. I looked around for something to make a poppet out of. I hit myself in the forehead. Of course! I could use my sock again! I waited until Sorrow's Edge's back was turned and plucked out a couple of hairs. I nearly dropped them when the voice boomed again from the microphone. "Welcome to the Pontotoc Rotary Club Rodeo." Dear gods, how could that not be magic?

I turned to go back to Joshua's truck. "Where you going?" Dan asked. "It's almost time for the Drill Team." He wiggled his eyebrows at me like this was something I definitely wanted to watch.

"I forgot something," I said, and hurried off. With the hairs and some string I found in Joshua's glove box, I tied the sock up into the semblance of a bull. I used two small nails I found for horns.

When the sock bull was ready, I looked for some mud. There wasn't any, so I bought a beer with what little money I had left over from buying groceries and made my own in the dirt near the front tire of Joshua's truck. I carefully thrust all four of the sock bull's legs into the mud. I sank them deeply, making sure they were stuck fast. I whipped a knife out of the glove box, cut my left thumb, and bled a drop on the bull. I breathed on it, braced myself for the pain, and willed a connection between the sock bull and Sorrow's Edge. It felt like a knife thrust through my hand. I breathed a second and a third time, gritting my teeth against the increasing pain. Finally, I felt the magic coalesce, and the pain drained out of me. When it did, I smiled. That bull wasn't going to be doing any bucking. It would have to work hard enough just to walk.

Feeling more relaxed, I went back to the arena. I found Dan, standing with Joshua's other friends, watching as a host of people rode horses into the arena.

Dan said, "Where you been? It's the grand entry now. You missed the whole drill riding team."

Nash laughed. "I'd say Killenyen's missed little about Southern Expressions. Just how many of the ladies have you entertained in the back of your truck?" He thrust his hips crudely.

When I didn't answer, Dan starting putting up fingers. "Let's see. There was Suzy, Cindy, Mary Beth, Alicia, Haley, and let's not forget Jane."

Cody smiled. "Who could forget Jane? She has quite a nice ass."

"I leave anyone out?" Dan asked.

I just stared at him. Dear gods, what kind of man was Joshua? I no longer felt sorry that Fitzrigh had bled him.

Nash clapped me on the shoulder. "It might not have been in the back of his truck, but Josh here told me he bagged Sheryl Weston out behind the concession stand three rodeos ago and that she rode him like a crazy bitch in heat."

I gasped. "I most certainly did not!"

Nash looked at me like I was the alien Uncle Gilly thought I was. "I don't know why you'd try to deny it. I had to console Sheryl myself when you ignored her at the next rodeo."

"This . . . this isn't right."

"What isn't?" Dan asked, and they all looked around as if trying to spot a problem. "You're right. It certainly isn't," Austin said, and my opinion of him instantly went up. Not all of Joshua's friends were pigs. "Rick shouldn't be riding without a helmet. He had a concussion two weeks ago." He was looking at one of the men climbing up in back of the chutes.

Dan shrugged. "You can't tell Rick anything."

The other two nodded, and all of them seemed to have forgotten that they'd just been discussing Joshua's various conquests.

I certainly couldn't give them all a lecture on the proper way to treat women without them getting suspicious, so I drifted over to watch what the men were doing. Uncle Gilly had told me that the bull riding was last. Now, there seemed to be horses in the chutes. I hadn't known riding horses was an option. Horses were certainly more sensible than bulls.

One of the men climbed onto a horse's back, leaned back, and nodded. They opened the gate, and his horse charged into the arena, bucking wildly with the man thrashing about. It obviously hadn't been broken. The man came off the horse, did a flip in mid-air, and hit the ground hard. The next rider out of the chute got his hand caught when he was bucked off. I was certain he was going to be dragged under the horse's feet and trampled before he got his hand free. Was I really about to do the same thing on a bull? This was insane. I reminded myself of my spell. Sorrow's Edge would not be bucking like this. At least, dear gods, I hoped not.

I stood there, staring in horror as rider after rider went flying. Dan came up to me. "You look like you've never seen bareback broncs before."

I turned to him, having a hard time comprehending what he was talking about. Somehow, I needed to get myself together and act more like Joshua. Reminding myself that I was now a man, I grunted. "Just thinking."

"About?" Dan asked, then sat down and started tying leather strips around his boots.

Before I could stop myself, I blurted out, "By all the gods, what are you doing?"

"What does it look like I'm doing? I don't like my boots flying off. Do you?"

Having my boots fly off did seem like a bad thing, so I went to Joshua's bag and found similar leather strips. I tied my boots on like Dan had his.

The other bull riders got out their ropes and used their gloves to rub something on them that looked like amber, although it crushed rather easily in their hands. Uncle Gilly hadn't mentioned this either, but all the riders were doing it so it must be important. I went to Joshua's gear bag, and sure enough, he had a bag filled with those amber-like rocks. Places on the rope had clearly been covered with this amber-like stuff before. I watched what the other men did and tried to do the same. The stuff made the rope very sticky, which made sense if you wanted to hang onto the bull. Preparing to ride a bull seemed to take a lot of work for something that no sane person should be doing and would be over in eight seconds anyway.

As the rodeo went on, I tried not to act as out of place as I felt. I laughed at the others' jokes even though I rarely understood them.

Then, to my complete horror, the other riders started putting on their chaps and vests. It must be almost time. Two riders—Dan and Walker—exchanged their hats for some strange variety of helm that looked like it would offer a lot more protection than a simple hat. Unfortunately, Joshua didn't appear to have one.

The bulls started running into the chutes. Remembering that a princess is always brave, I took a deep breath and, clinging tightly to my bull rope, climbed up behind the chute. I got the rope around the bull, pulled on my glove, then eased onto the bull's back. I could feel its lethargy. A big smile spread across my face. Everything would be all right.

The man who held the tail of my rope acted like he expected me to do something with it. Was there another step Uncle Gilly forgot to tell me? I tried to ignore his expectant gaze and positioned the handle of my rope so that my little finger was in the middle of the bull's back and told my helper to pull it tight. "You aren't going to warm it up?" he asked.

I had no idea what he was talking about, so I said, "No."

He gave me a strange look, but pulled the rope tight and handed me the tail. Working quickly so I didn't have to think about it, I wrapped the rope around my hand and threw the tail in front of me. I slid up toward the bull's head, got my balance set, and reminded myself not to touch the bull or myself with my left hand. I nodded, and they opened the chute. Sorrow moseyed into the arena. Every step seemed like a tremendous effort, and as I hoped, he didn't bother bucking. He walked a few steps, stopped, and snorted. He stood still, looking at the crowd. I thought I'd really shown the bull who was boss, but the crowd started booing and throwing trash into the arena. This was apparently not how bull riding was done. The 8-second horn sounded, and my ride was over. I slid off the bull's back. One of the men in the booth with the microphone threw a red flag into the arena. I had no idea why, but I guessed it couldn't be good.

Some of the bull riders were laughing as I climbed over the fence. "Looked like you and Sorrow were getting real cozy. Do I hear marriage bells?" Cody said. I got hot.

A rodeo official approached me. "Never seen Sorrow's Edge so damned docile. He's usually a really rank bull. Looks like you got yourself a re-ride, son."

"A re-ride?" I stuttered.

"Of course, if the bull doesn't even buck. You'll want it, of course."

"I have a choice?" I asked.

"It's not much of a choice, son. You'll ride Pure Poison for your re-ride."

"No." I shook my head, as out of the corner of my eye I saw Austin go sailing over the bull's head.

"What do you mean no?" The official looked at me like I was mad.

"I don't want a re-ride."

"A thirty-five isn't going to win any rodeos!"

"I don't care," I said, and turned away. Joshua had to have been mad to do this.

As I watched the rest of the riders, I became further convinced of the absolute insanity of bull riding. Only two of the other riders lasted the full eight seconds: Walker, who was disqualified because he touched himself with his free hand, and Dan, who rode last. Dan made eight-seconds and scored a 79, more than twice my score.

When Dan came out of the arena, he grabbed my arm. "Why the hell didn't you accept the re-ride? The stock contractor can't get away with foisting lame-ass bulls on us."

Walker walked by. He was swearing fiercely, I guessed because he'd been disqualified. He got in my face. "At least I didn't let the bull do me in the ass."

Dan grabbed my arm. "I know he deserves it, but don't start anything on rodeo grounds."

I hadn't been about to start anything, but now I felt like I should. "We'll see who takes it in the ass tomorrow," I said. Dear gods, had I lost all decency?

Walker sneered and walked away. Dan tried to go back to the subject of my re-ride. "Forget it, okay!" I snapped.

Dan put up his hands like he was fending off a blow. "Whatever, Killenyen." He walked off.

I wanted to get well and truly drunk and forget the whole thing. A terrible realization hit me. I couldn't. I didn't have any money, and I wouldn't ask Uncle Gilly for more. I already owed him $50 that I had no way of paying.

I changed my boots and started packing Joshua's gear bag. Uncle Gilly trudged up. "Too bad about Sorrow. You know half your score is based on how hard a time the bull gives you." I hadn't known, but that made sense of why I'd scored so low. "Aliens must have beamed an Asterian bull in his place since your bulls don't buck and all."

I didn't know where he'd gotten that idea, but I didn't tell him about the spell. He wouldn't have believed me anyway. He said, "Good night," and walked off.

Linda arrived, and I told her about my money problem. "I haven't won a rodeo in a few weeks. I guess I'll have to take a rain check on that drink." Rain check? What by all that was holy was a rain check?

Linda's face fell, seemingly at the idea of missing out on a date with Joshua. "I could buy."

"You could?" I said, surprised. "I'd love to go for a drink then."

I finished packing and walked with Linda back to my truck. I put the gear bag in the back, and she went off to get her car. As soon as she was gone, I pulled the bull poppet out of the mud and removed the hairs to free Sorrow's Edge from my magic. I tossed the muddy sock into the back of the truck.

I followed Linda to Lucky Joe's Bar and Grill. They had a green sign over the door with a big clover. Inside, there was a dance floor and a stage where a band played a weird kind of twangy music. The band was singing about having friends in low places. We sat at the bar.

The bartender came up, and Linda asked, "Can you make a Mai Tai?"

"Anything for you, little lady," he said.

It was attitudes like his that made it hard for me to get the respect I deserved in my father's court. "She's an adult, not a child," I said.

"What?" The bartender looked like he didn't have a clue what I was talking about.

"Linda"—I gestured toward her—"is not a child. She's not particularly little, and neither is her brain. She's a librarian."

I expected the bartender to be impressed, but he rolled his eyes. "Do you want something to drink or not?"

I wasn't used to people ignoring me. If I corrected them, they always apologized. To my face at least, they were unfailingly polite, except Fitzrigh, that is. I guessed this bartender was like my bastard brother, and it would do no good to try to teach him respect. I didn't know what to order, so I snapped, "I'll have the same."

The bartender sneered like I'd said something ridiculous, and said, "Okay, cowboy, two Mai Tais coming up."

Linda beamed at me and scooted closer. "It's nice to have a gentleman stick up for a lady." She ran her finger down my chest.

Uh-oh. I'd given Linda the wrong idea. She'd expect me to take her back to Joshua's truck. I found myself growing hot at the idea of having the type of intimacy with Linda that I'd only shared with Clenyeth. Besides, I wasn't attracted to women.

The bartender delivered our Mai Tais, which were a pretty orange color with a fruit garnish and an umbrella. I was about to take a taste of mine when Walker walked up. Curse him, why had he come to the same bar? Walker laughed and pointed at my drink. "What a pansy! Not only can't you handle a real bull, but you drink frou-frou drinks."

My hands formed fists. I would not be laughed at. I stood, but Linda grabbed my arm. "No, Joshua. Why do you care what he thinks?"

I wasn't sure why I did, but I felt a hatred so strong I could almost taste it. Still, I settled back on my stool.

"Total pansy," Walker said, and ordered a couple of pitchers of beer for a table over by the dance floor where two other cowboys sat. Walker returned to the table and said something to them; they all looked at me and laughed.

I turned away and downed half my drink without tasting it. I couldn't allow Walker to belittle me. I'd have to show him tomorrow. The thought terrified me, so I downed the rest of the drink and ordered another.

"What happened with your bull?" Linda asked.

I shrugged. "Happens sometimes. They don't want to buck."

She stirred her drink. "Not very exciting. Why didn't you take the re-ride?"

Damn the re-ride! I drank deeply. I finished my second Mai Tai and ordered another. Linda had hardly taken a sip of her drink.

I had to get home, get my own body back. When Joshua was back in this body, he could take all the cursed re-rides he wanted. It all seemed so absurd, I wanted to cry. No, I wanted to punch someone in the face, especially the someone who was responsible for me being here. The more I thought about it, the angrier I got, and the angrier I got, the more I drank.

Linda chattered on about something. Fortunately, she was the type that didn't require much in a conversational partner. I grunted and nodded every now and then, and it was enough for her.

The world had begun to spin when Linda asked, "You want to dance?"

I tried to say no, but she didn't wait for an answer. She just grabbed my hand and pulled me onto the dance floor.

# CHAPTER 6

I woke up under the shell of Joshua's truck in the parking lot of Lucky Joe's. From the sky outside, I judged it to be mid-afternoon. Thankfully, I was alone, but I had one killer of a hangover. I didn't remember much about what had happened after Linda pulled me onto the dance floor, but I did remember my dreams.

Joshua, in my body, paced the tower room. The east tower was used to confine prisoners of special importance. My grandmother had occupied it for most of my life. My grandmother had been a powerful witch, and my father hadn't trusted his own mother. He thought she was the reason he hadn't been able to sire legitimate sons, and he might have been right. Granny had been eager to prove the power of women. It was because of Granny he hated witchcraft so badly.

I was five when my mother first brought me to my grandmother, and my mother had just caught me playing with a poisonous snake. I'd twisted a piece of cloth into a snake and had been causing the real snake to dance around me. My mother had screamed and called for the guard. The guards had come running, startling the snake. It'd reared and began shaking its rattle. A guard had decapitated it with his sword.

"No!" I cried. "Why did you kill my friend?"

My mother hadn't answered, but grabbed my hand and marched me straight back into the palace and up the long tower stairs. She'd thrown open the door at the top, and I saw an old woman bent over a cauldron. She didn't look up when we entered, and later I learned she was hard of hearing.

"Zinna, what have you done to my daughter?" My mother demanded. "She is bewitched. She was playing with a snake."

"Bewitched?" The old woman's eyes met mine and seemed to see into the very depths of my soul. "No, she isn't bewitched, but she is a witch like her granny before her." She beckoned to me. "Come here, child."

I tried to hide behind my mother's skirts. But my mother pushed me forward. "Is there any help for her?"

Granny had closed her eyes and touched me on both shoulders. I'd wanted to run and hide behind my mother, but I'd remembered that a princess is always brave. "You must send her to me every morning" Granny had said. "She must learn to control her talent, or it will control her."

She'd only had three years to teach me before she died, and my father refused to find me a new mentor when she was gone. He never wanted a witch for a child. I tried to learn more on my own, but there was so much I hadn't been able to figure out without someone to show me. I'd always wondered how powerful I might have become if Granny had lived longer.

When my grandmother had occupied the tower room, it'd been full of books, cauldrons, scrying mirrors, and herbs. Now, the room was bare except for a small cot, a dressing table and chair, and a chamber pot. Two large windows let in light. Joshua wore a tunic and trews that looked like they'd been borrowed from a stable hand. He gestured wildly as he paced. My maid Sylvia stood by, holding a peach silk dress. "You've got to get me out of here. I'm going crazy locked up like this."

"Your Highness, if you'd just put on a dress and—"

Joshua stopped pacing and put his hands on his hips. "I ain't wearing no dress. I may have boobs and have lost my dick, but I can at least maintain my dignity."

Sylvia sighed. It was obvious they'd had this conversation before. "Your Highness, what's wrong with being a woman? Haven't you always told me that women are just as smart and capable as men?"

Joshua threw up his hands. "Nothing's wrong with being a woman. Some of my favorite people are women, but there's definitely something wrong with being in the wrong fucking body! And I told you not to call me, 'Your Highness.'"

Sylvia shook her head sadly. "If you won't put on a dress, I don't know what I can do for you, Your . . . what was it you said you wanted me to call you?"

"Joshua. My name is Joshua."

\* \* \*

I cringed at the dream. What had Joshua done to get himself locked up? Serves him right for the way he treats women, part of me thought. But it couldn't be good for my position at court.

As I lay there with my head pounding, I thought through my options for money. There had to be a way I could do this bull riding thing without killing myself. I tried to think of a spell that would allow me to stay on the back of a bucking bull. The trick was somehow to stick my butt to the bull. Glue, I thought, I needed glue, and I'd thought I'd seen some in Joshua's glove box. I staggered out of the back of the truck, opened the front door, and searched the box. Sure enough, there was a tube of glue; "superglue," it read. I smiled. If the glue was truly super, I couldn't fail to stay on.

Back at the rodeo grounds, I scouted around for some sticks to make poppets of me and the bull. I figured sticks would be better than my socks. Using the super glue, I whipped up some poppets. I glued the butt of my poppet to the bull poppet. I plucked a couple of my hairs to link the poppet to me magically. All that I needed to make the spell complete was my will, my blood, and a couple hairs from the bull.

\* \* \*

Walker was standing around the bull pen when I walked up. "Well, if it isn't Princess Killenyen."

I froze. "What did you say?" Did he somehow know who I was? Was he in league with my enemy?

Walker put his hands on his hips and thrust out his lip. "You heard me, Princess. Right before I banged her, Linda told me all about how you claimed you were a princess trapped in a bull rider's body. Shit, Killenyen, even I never thought you were a fairy, you pervert."

I didn't know what princesses, fairies, and perverts had in common. But dear gods, what had I said last night, and how many people had Linda repeated it to? Did everyone now think Joshua was a fairy pervert? What did they do to fairy perverts in this realm?

While I was trying to think my way out of the situation, Dan walked up. "You got a problem, Walker?"

"I was talking to the fairy, Williams. Or are you a homo, too?"

"Don't be an ass, Walker. We all know Killenyen's not a homo. He takes a different girl back to his truck nearly every damned rodeo."

Walker sneered. "Killenyen thinks he's a god-damned princess."

I had to say something. One thing I learned at court was that letting someone else defend you made you look weak. The perfect thing came to me. "You're just mad you got disqualified last night because you couldn't stop touching yourself."

Walker lunged toward me. A rodeo official walked up and clapped Walker on the shoulder. "Problem, boys?"

Walker glared at me, but he said, "No problem, sir," and walked away.

Dan was laughing. "Walker has to touch himself. He can't get anyone else to." He sobered. "Not that I have an easy time of that either."

"I'll show Walker I'm no fairy tonight." I prayed to all the gods I could think of that I could give a decent ride. Even though I wasn't sure what a fairy was in this realm, I was certain that a good ride would disprove Walker's theory. The spell had better work.

Dan laughed again. "Show Walker, but don't beat my score."

I felt a flash of guilt. The spell I was about to do would help me beat everybody. Was what I was doing fair? I repressed my conscience. I had to win. I needed the money if I was ever going to find my way home.

Dan said he was hungry and went off to get something to eat. I sneaked up to Hell's Angel and got a couple of hairs. I took the hairs back to my truck where I tied them to the stick bull. I cut my thumb, bled on the poppets, focused my will, braced myself for the pain, and breathed on the poppets until the magic coalesced and the pain drained away. I hid the spell in my truck and went back to the arena.

As I walked up to the other cowboys, one of them pointed at me and said, "Well, if it isn't the princess."

"Can I get you a drink with a nice little umbrella, Your Highness?" another added, and they all laughed.

Dear gods, what was I supposed to say? I had to somehow deflect the blame. An idea came to me. I smiled. "Did Linda tell you that? Well, if that lying bitch ain't good enough for a man like me and had to settle for Walker, they can both just kiss my princess ass." Following a compulsion I didn't understand, I turned and gave myself a slap on the rear.

The cowboys erupted in laughter, and I knew I'd saved myself, but at what cost? I had just sunk to Joshua's level. Could I ever look myself in the mirror again?

But as the rodeo progressed, I got more and more nervous about my spell. What if I hadn't gotten it right? This is insane, Daulphina, I told myself. Swallow your pride, and go shovel horse shit for Uncle Gilly. But as I looked at Walker, I knew I couldn't back down. No one laughed at a princess and got away with it.

By the time it was time for the bull riding, my nerves jangled, and I was afraid I'd vomit. But I wiped my sweaty palms on my jeans, got ready, and climbed on Hell's back. I could feel his anger. He wanted to be free of the constraints of the small chute, and he wanted the irritating flank strap—and irritating human—off. I prayed to all the gods I could think of. I wrapped my hand, slid up on the bull, and nodded. They opened the chute. Hell took off into the arena and bucked up a storm, rearing and kicking, spinning this way and then the other. The adrenaline hit my blood stream, and I laughed. No matter which way he moved, my butt stuck to his back. But it was more than just the spell. Joshua's body knew how to move to accommodate the bull's movements. Joshua's body knew how to ride bulls. It was by far the wildest ride I'd ever had and the most exciting.

I felt a rush of absolute jubilation when the horn sounded, telling me I'd made the eight second mark, followed immediately by mind numbing panic. I had no idea how to get off. Uncle Gilly hadn't covered that, and I hadn't thought to ask. Somehow, I must have believed that the bull would just miraculously stop bucking when the horn sounded. I was going to die. I thought I should just let Joshua's muscle memory get me off, but now that I was thinking about it, I couldn't seem to access it. Think, Daulphina, think! I knew how to dismount a horse while riding side saddle. How much different could dismounting a bull be? I tried to ignore the voice that insisted my horse was always standing still when I dismounted, didn't have horns, and loved me as much as I loved her. But I couldn't stay on the bull all night. Attempting my typical graceful dismount, I threw my right leg over the bull, loosened my grip, and immediately went sailing off. I landed face first in the dirt with the bull still bucking around me. Terrified of getting stepped on, I scrambled to my feet and ran for the fence. Fortunately, there were two other men in the arena to distract the bull, so it didn't follow me. I learned last night they were called bull fighters.

When I was safely on the other side of the fence, I collapsed to the ground, panting. Dan came running up. "You hurt?" he asked.

"No." I smiled, getting to my feet. "Dear gods, what a rush!"

Dan smiled back. "Don't I know it?" His face fell. "I'm sure you beat me with that ride."

I felt another tinge of guilt, but I rigorously repressed it. Dan hadn't had his body stolen from him.

I ended up scoring an eighty-nine and taking top prize money of $1052. My guilt was further assuaged when I learned that Dan, placing second, would get money as well, although not as much.

As we were packing up our gear, Dan asked, "Want a beer while we wait for our checks? I have a cooler in my truck."

I didn't know what a cooler was, but by Cailleach, I wanted a beer. I decided not to puzzle about my sudden desire for something I'd found repulsive just two days ago. I went with Dan back to his truck, and he got out two beers and handed me one. All the while, I couldn't stop talking about the ride of my life. Would I ever be content with a mere horse again?

Dan laughed. "You act like you've never done this before."

I sobered. I needed to act more like Joshua.

# CHAPTER 7

On Sunday, I couldn't wait to tell Uncle Gilly about my ride, but when I started talking about how the bull roared out of the chute, he waved me off. "Yeah, yeah, we've heard it all before. We've had it up to here with it." He indicated the top of his forehead with his hand.

I wilted. "But this is the first bull I ever rode!"

"If I start listening to you go on about bulls now, I'll never hear the end of it."

Disappointed, I got out the check the rodeo officials had given me. "Can I buy stuff with this?"

"No, you'll need to cash it first." Uncle Gilly sighed. "I suppose you'll want me to show you how to do that. I'm going into town anyway. You've got Joshua's debit card, don't you?"

I got out Joshua's wallet and handed it to him.

He looked behind the driver's license and pulled out a card. "That's the ticket. Don't worry about his PIN. I'm sure he used his birthday. It's just the kind of bonehead move Joshua would make."

I had no idea what he was talking about, but since he'd told me not to worry, I decided not to.

We went in his truck to a bank and walked up to a TV on the front. Uncle Gilly said, "This here is an ATM." He showed me how to use it.

I gave him the $50 I owed him and held out the remainder of the cash. "Would this be enough to get some books at that Barnes and Noble Linda talked about?"

"Oh sure," he said. His eyes narrowed. "You are planning on wasting your money on that parallel realms nonsense, are you?"

I looked away. "It's my money to waste."

Uncle Gilly shook a finger at me. "Don't spend all your money. Remember you need your fee for next week's rodeo. Don't forget to call in to register, or you won't be able to ride."

"Call in?" I asked.

Uncle Gilly sighed. "I suppose I'll have to teach you how to do that as well." He went back to his truck, grumbling about getting Joshua back.

Sulking a bit, I followed. I was used to people at least pretending to want me around.

When we got back to Uncle Gilly's farm, he led me into Joshua's trailer. "First, you need to find Joshua's copy of *The Chute Gate*." He opened the drawer in the bedside table. "Ah, there it is," he said, withdrawing a very thin book and opening it. "Joshua circles the rodeos he's planning on attending." He pointed to a circled listing for what he said was next week's rodeo in Carthage, Mississippi. "Here's the call-in number and time. You just call in and say you want to ride. That's all there is to it." He shoved *The Chute Gate* at me and started for the door.

"Now, wait a minute. How do I call in?"

He rolled his eyes and picked up the small black box from bedside table. "You really are primitive, aren't you? This is Joshua's phone." He pushed a button, and nothing happened. He sighed again. "Like a bonehead, you've let the battery go dead. You'll have to charge it." He picked up a white cord from beside the picture of Joshua and his mother and plugged it into the phone. I jumped as the phone made a noise and a picture appeared on it. He showed me how to push buttons to make a phone call.

"And I can summon people just like that?" I asked.

"No, you just talk to them. You don't have to worry about the important numbers. He'll have them programmed in already." He pushed a button labeled contacts, and a list of people's names appeared. Most were women. "He's got every woman he's ever dated in here: Amy, Cindy, Debbie, Sheryl." I blushed at the last name, wondering if this was the Sheryl who'd rode Joshua "like a crazy bitch in heat." "He never cleans out his phone, so there's a ton of them. Still, he's got the numbers of the important people as well. See, here's me." He pointed to his name. "You just push that if you want to call me. But don't do that too often. I don't like getting interrupted. You'll have to leave the phone plugged in for about half an hour, then you can unplug it and take it with you." He shoved the phone at me.

I stared in wonder at this marvelous technology. Just what kind of world was I in? Before he could leave, I asked him how to get to the Barnes & Noble in Tupelo. He took me out to our trucks and had me get out the map he'd drawn on to show me how to get to the rodeo and drew on it again.

* * *

After riding a bucking bull, driving seemed downright tame, even though Tupelo, Mississippi, was a larger city than Hamilton by a long shot and had a lot more carriages on the road. When I walked into the bookstore, I stopped short. The place was wall to wall books. My father's library didn't even contain a tenth that number. I looked around stupidly, and a clerk with a thin nose came up to me. "May I help you?" he asked.

I told him I was looking for books on parallel realms. I was afraid he'd tell me they didn't exist and think me mad, but he showed me to a section on the paranormal. "You might also want to check the fantasy fiction section, which is up front on the right." He walked off.

I searched the shelves and found about a dozen books that might be promising, including several books of fiction. In this realm writers might try to pass off a fantastic truth like realm-traveling as fiction. I decided I was going to buy them all so I could study them in more detail.

On my way up to the counter, I caught sight of a book titled *Bull Riding for Beginners.*

Thinking it might be able to teach me how to get off the bull without getting killed, I grabbed it, too, and carried the huge stack up to the counter. The clerk totaled them and announced they came to $253.49. Nearly a quarter of my prize money. They'd better have the information I needed.

I brought them back to my place—did I say "my" place? Dear gods, I meant Joshua's place. I started reading them for any hint on how to get back where I belonged.

I'd just barely gotten into the first book when a knock sounded on the door. Swearing under my breath, I answered it. Jocelyn stood there, wearing an obscenely short shirt. Dear gods, it was almost as bad as what Linda had been wearing. But she was the one who asked, "You're not going like that, are you?"

"Going where?"

Jocelyn closed her eyes as if praying for patience. "Don't tell me you forgot. Jayleen's graduating. You promised Meemaw you'd come."

"I can't." I didn't want to leave the books now that I'd found them.

She put her hands on her hips. "And why not? Just what demands do you have on your oh-so-precious time? Get ready now. I'll wait for you."

She turned her back, as if expecting me to change my clothes. I wanted to protest, but if I told her I had to read, she'd think I'd gone mad, and I'd have Meemaw to answer to. Groaning at the necessity, I dumped Joshua's clothes out of the bag onto the bed, wondering what would be appropriate to wear to a graduation. Joshua didn't have much variety, so deciding wasn't too hard. I put on the nicest pair of jeans and a western shirt. I told myself I'd get away as soon as possible.

I joined Jocelyn. "I'll drive my own truck. I'm not squishing my legs into that carriage of yours again."

"Carriage?" She looked at me like I'd lost my mind.

"Car," I said. "I meant car." Geez, I'd have to make sure I called things by the right name.

"Suit yourself," she said.

I followed her over to a place called a high school, even though it was located at the bottom of a hill. We walked in and were greeted by a whole host of people who had to be Joshua's family since they all looked so much alike. Just how many relatives did Joshua have? There were so many I wondered if I'd be missed if I just slipped away. But Meemaw caught my eye and shook her head as if she'd known what I'd been thinking. I decided I'd have to endure it.

A graduation turned out to be some kind of bizarre ceremony where young people in scholar's robes and odd hats walked across the stage as their names were called and were given a piece of paper. I couldn't imagine the significance. As name after name was called, I nearly went mad with boredom. I thought of how much better I could be spending my time.

After the ceremony, all the Killenyens headed over to Meemaw's for a party. Though I wondered if it was wise, I decided to go because I thought there'd be better food than Frosted Flakes; maybe Meemaw had made more of her potato salad. When I drove up, a man stood on the front porch like he had a ramrod stuck up his ass. I couldn't believe I'd just thought "ass." My mother would have been appalled at what was happening to my language and in so short a time.

"Good of you to come, Joshua," he said, speaking with quite a different accent than Joshua or the other people around here.

Listening to his accent, I felt the urge to slam my fist into his stomach. Then I knew: this was Uncle Braeden, the very man Jocelyn had threatened me with.

"Are you going to bless us with stories of your latest rodeo triumph?" He sneered. "Think you're some kind of rock star, don't you?"

I didn't know what a rock star was, but I didn't like his attitude. "So what if I do? Scored an eighty-nine yesterday. I'd like to see you try that."

He didn't look impressed. "Unlike you, I'm not a moron."

A girl—I guessed she was Jayleen because she still had the odd hat on—squealed when she saw me, "Josh!" She gave me a big hug. Evidently, she didn't share Uncle Braeden's sentiments. Maybe she'd want to hear about how I'd ridden Hell's Angel and even got off without dying.

Before I could ask her, we had to move out of the way because the men were coming out carrying tables and a whole herd of children followed with chairs, trailed by the women with the food. Meemaw's house was big, but not big enough for all the Killenyens. Besides, it was nice out.

Last of all, Meemaw walked out with her cane. "Good to see you, Josh, darling." She put an arm around my waist, and I leaned down to give her a kiss on the cheek because that seemed like the thing to do.

After living on Frosted Flakes, I couldn't wait to dig into the food. There was plenty of fried chicken, ham, and yes, potato salad, plus a bunch of other things I didn't know what were but smelled delicious. There was also a cooler full of beer. I loaded up a plate, grabbed a beer, and found a place at one of the tables. As soon as I sat down, one of the older men sat down across from me. I didn't know his name. Did this mean Joshua had no strong emotions toward him? "Got something for you," he said. "7-11 is hiring."

Not knowing what he was talking about and didn't want to look crazy by asking questions, so I just stared at him.

"They have health benefits and a steady paycheck. You know you're not getting any younger."

"My paycheck's steady enough."

Acting like he hadn't heard a word I'd said, the man got to his feet. "I'll put a good word in for you."

He scrambled away, and a boy of about sixteen took his place: Braeden, Jr., Uncle Braeden's son. "Uncle Joe still trying to get you to get a job?" Braeden asked. I nodded because I guessed that was what he'd been doing. "Don't listen to him. Bull riding's cool." Braeden's eyes practically glowed. "Can I come with you next week?"

I didn't know the right answer. Would Joshua allow this boy to come? It was probably safer not to, but he looked like he'd be willing to listen to my story about riding a bull. Before I could answer, though, Uncle Braeden and a woman sat down on either side of Braeden, Jr.

Braeden, Jr. turned to the woman. "Momma, can I—"

"No," Uncle Braeden answered. He must have heard us talking.

"But—"

"Your daddy said no, Junior," the woman said. "You need to get up Sunday morning for church." The woman looked straight at me, and I could tell she shared Uncle Braeden's distaste for Joshua. Her name came to me, Aunt Lou Ann. "Is it going to take another person dying to get you back inside the holy walls, Joshua? How do you think your momma feels looking down from heaven and seeing that her boy hasn't set foot inside a church since her funeral?" She looked at me like she expected an answer.

"I honor the gods in my own way," I tried.

"Gods!" Aunt Lou Ann put a hand over her heart. "Joshua David Killenyen, have you become some kind of a heathen? There's only one God, and that's Christ Jesus. How dare you spout blasphemy in front of my son!"

I blinked. Only one god? Wouldn't that make him a bit overburdened?

Aunt Lou Ann got up and put her hand on Braeden, Jr's shoulder. "Come on, Junior. I won't have you associating with someone on the fast track to hell."

Sulking, Braeden, Jr. got up. "See ya, Josh," he said, following his mother and father over to a table where the people apparently weren't going to hell, wherever that was.

Jocelyn sat down next to me. "Are Uncle Braeden and Aunt Lou Ann giving you a hard time again?" she asked.

My head still reeling from the idea that these people worshipped only a single God, I hardly knew what to answer. "Apparently I'm on the fast track to hell," I said.

Jocelyn glared over at Aunt Lou Ann. "That sanctimonious bitch! She'd put everybody in hell if she had her way." Jocelyn glanced at me. "Although it wouldn't hurt you to come to church once and awhile. I know you blame God for your momma's death, but he must have had a good reason for taking her when he did."

A half dozen more people around our age joined us. One of them belched and said, "Your Royal Highness." James, I thought. He and Joshua were close. He broke down in giggles, as did most the others. Had my drunken prattle travelled this far? Would they think Joshua mad and get Uncle Braeden to lock him up? Or would they think him a fairy pervert like Walker did? I really shouldn't have come. I didn't know why I thought I could get away with pretending to be Joshua around his family.

I tried to think of something to say. "Linda sure is vindictive when a man tells her no."

James laughed again. "When have you ever told a woman, no? I bet you've banged half the damn county."

I wanted to give Joshua a piece of my mind. Tell him to keep it in his pants once and awhile.

James looked thoughtful. "But maybe you've finished with the women and decided to start in on the men."

"James, that is more than enough!" Jocelyn glared at him, and he shut up.

\* \* \*

Later, when I fetched my fourth or maybe my fifth beer, I heard Braeden, Jr. arguing with Uncle Braeden. "I said no." Uncle Braeden's voice got louder. "I'm not going to let you go watch a bunch of grown men playing around with dumb animals. Besides, as momma said, he's become a heathen."

I clenched my fist and had to fight with myself to avoid punching him in the gut. I didn't know why I was so mad. Why should I care what a backwoods peasant thought? If he'd been in my court, he'd have been bowing and scraping to me. I gulped down the beer and grabbed another.

\* \* \*

I woke up the next morning on Meemaw's sofa. I didn't remember much about what happened after overhearing Uncle Braeden disparage Joshua's profession. When I stretched and opened my eyes, I heard a loud, "Humph!" and turned to see Meemaw glaring at me. She turned and tottered toward the kitchen. Uh-oh. Besides getting stinking drunk, I wondered what else I'd done to earn Meemaw's disapproval.

I crept after her. Meemaw was getting eggs and bacon out of the ice box and muttering, "Parallel universes, princesses, magic."

Crap! I sat down at the table. I vowed to stop drinking. I couldn't seem to keep my mouth shut when I did. How much trouble was I in? Fortunately, Uncle Braeden was nowhere to be seen.

Meemaw slammed the griddle down on the stove, and I winced at the noise. "I know Lou Ann's husband can be a right pain in the behind, but that doesn't excuse your behavior. Do you mind explaining?"

"Er . . . Sorry, ma'am. I don't remember much. Sounds like this book I've been reading."

Meemaw stared at me. "Since when have you read a book?"

"I read sometimes," I protested. "Got a whole bunch of books at Barnes & Noble just yesterday."

Meemaw shook her head. "You're acting mighty strange this last week, Joshua. You sure you haven't fallen off a bull one too many times? Besides, you weren't talking like it was a book. When Lou Ann's husband said there was no such thing as magic, you slugged him in the belly. You claimed you healed Uncle Gilly's horse with magic."

Meemaw gave me a half-smile and cooked as she talked. "I can't say Lou Ann's husband didn't have it coming, calling you a loser and all. But Josh, darling, some of us were wondering if you're cracked in the head."

"I'm not crazy, Meemaw. I was just drunk," I said, praying she'd believe me.

"Humph. Something you are all too often, Josh, darling." Dear gods, that was true, especially since I couldn't keep my mouth shut.

She sat a big plate of food in front of me and dished up a smaller one for herself. She poured us both coffee, adding cream and sugar to mine. "Seriously, Josh, darling, I know it hurt when your momma died. The Good Lord knows I miss her like the dickens, and I know it was tough on you growing up without a daddy. But isn't it time you put that behind you and moved on? I know you don't want to hear about God anymore, but as Oprah says, praying can really help you through your grief."

She paused, evidently waiting for some response from me, but I didn't know what to say, so I kept my eyes on my food.

"This bull riding you do. It's dangerous, and it's getting you nowhere." She touched the scar beside my eye. "It isn't too late to go to college like you'd planned before your momma died. It's what your momma always wanted for you. She didn't want you to remain stuck in this small, little town. She saw big things coming for her little prince." Meemaw patted my arm. "Just think about it. Okay?"

I mumbled, "Yes, ma'am." That seemed to satisfy her, at least for now.

# CHAPTER 8

I stared around me in disgust. With no servants to clean up after me, the mess kept piling up. I'd thought it had been bad when I'd first come awake here, but now, a month later, it was ten times worse. Everything not covered by empty cereal boxes and beer bottles was stacked two to three feet high with books—books that had been no help in figuring out how to get my own body back.

I tried to push away my big problem and focus on the immediate one. With no secretary to keep track of my affairs, I was running late, and I couldn't find my belt. You would have thought with its huge buckle it would have stood out a bit more, but no matter how many empty cereal boxes I moved around, I couldn't find it. If I showed up without it, people would notice, and they were noticing too many strange things about me already.

There was a knock on the door. I swore under my breath. I didn't have time for Uncle Gilly and his endless prattle about aliens. "Come in," I shouted, while I grabbed a bag and started shoveling empty beer bottles into it.

The door opened, and, to my surprise, in walked Jocelyn. I hadn't seen her since I announced to Joshua's entire family I was a princess. She crossed her arms. "Good Lord, where did you get all these books?"

I ignored the question and continued searching. "Help me find my belt. I have a three-and-a-half-hour drive to Lafayette. I've got to get going."

She picked up books from one of the stacks. "Jim Butcher, Barbara Hamby, Mercedes Lackey, *Parallel Universes, Guide to the Supernatural for Dummies.* Why on earth would you be reading fantasy? If you're going to read, shouldn't it be Louis L'Amour or something?"

I stopped what I was doing. "Who in tarnation is Louis L'Amour?" And who in tarnation says, "tarnation"?

"You ride rodeo, and you don't know L'Amour? Only the greatest Western writer of all time."

Cowboy stories weren't likely to contain the answers I needed. Not that any of these books had been much use. I snatched the books out of her hands. "Help me find my belt or go on your way."

Instead, she picked up *Bull Riding for Beginners.* "Why do you have this? You've only been riding bulls since you were like twelve."

I snatched it out of her hands, too. "I was having trouble with my dismount. I thought it might help." The book had at least taught me the proper way to dismount, and I'd been practicing on Joshua's practice barrel whenever I could get Uncle Gilly to help me, which wasn't very often. According to Uncle Gilly, Joshua was never good at dismounts, and I still hadn't quite got the hang of it and usually ended up eating dirt. Still, the rush of the ride was well worth the fall.

Jocelyn leaned against the trailer wall. "Meemaw sent me by to remind you James's birthday is Sunday, and you'd better be there with the rest of us." I groaned. "If you answered your phone, I wouldn't have had to come all the way over to tell you. I called about a hundred times and left dozens of messages."

Although I'd starting carrying Joshua's phone in my pocket, the truth was I left it off almost all the time since James had called two days after the fiasco at Meemaw's wondering if I wanted to "go huntin'." I didn't know how they hunted in this world, so I had to make up some excuse. It seemed safest after that to avoid Joshua's family. I couldn't tell Jocelyn this, though. "It's broken," I said, instead.

Jocelyn sighed and rolled her eyes. "Get it fixed or get a new one. I don't know how a person with a lick of sense can get on without one. Of course, that probably doesn't apply to you."

I looked up and glared at her.

She ignored the glare. "Meemaw says you've stopped by only once since Jayleen's graduation, and that was because you needed your laundry washed. James and Eddie say they haven't seen you down at Charlie's Place. Are you avoiding us? Just what are you doing with all your time?"

What was I supposed to say? I've been reading, trying to figure out how to get my own body back? "I've just had things to do. That's all."

"Wayne says you haven't even been to the gym. Haven't you always said you need to stay fit to ride? Are you depressed or something?"

"Of course I'm not depressed," I snapped, wanting to sink through the floor, curl up in a ball, go to sleep, and never wake up again.

"You're acting pretty strange."

"There it is!" I finally found the belt under *Dragon Riders of Pern* and *Spells for the Clueless and Inept*. I buckled it on and grabbed my gear bag and the new hat I'd bought with last week's prize money. I couldn't afford such frivolous purchases, but Joshua's hat had gotten pretty ragged, and while I might not be a princess in this world, I could at least maintain appearances.

Jocelyn stood between me and the door. "Excuse me," I said. "I really need to go."

She put her hands on her hips. "Not until you promise to be there on Sunday."

"I'll be there, all right. But I've got to go win a rodeo first."

"How do you know you'll win?"

I grinned. "I always win." It was true. In the month I'd been riding rodeo, I'd won every time. The superglue really worked.

On the drive to Lafayette, I cranked up the air conditioning, another marvelous piece of technology Uncle Gilly had introduced me to. Despite starting late, I made it to the rodeo in plenty of time. First thing I did was pay my fee and see which bull I'd drawn. It was a bull I'd never heard of named Man Killer. I hoped he had a buck worthy of his name. If I was going to win tonight, I needed a good bull, especially since I'd drawn He-Man, the daisy-muncher, for tomorrow night. No one could win on that bull.

Walker walked into the office as I was leaving. "You're going to get flattened tonight, Your Highness." He called me "Your Highness" all the time now. The more I beat him the nastier he got. I went to push past him. "You better prepare your will. Man Killer comes from out West. They got rid of him because he killed a couple of riders. Smashed them to death after he bucked them off."

"I can't see what the problem is. Unlike you, I don't fall off."

Walker laughed again. "Tonight you do. Tonight your momma's going to weep."

"My momma's dead! Worry about your own." I knew it was a lame comeback. Walker always made me look like an idiot. I didn't know why I let him get under my skin. I shouldn't have been caught in this stupid male game of one-upmanship, but dear gods, every day it seemed I became more like the man whose body I wore.

I left the rodeo office, changed into my riding pants and boots, and headed over to the bull pen. Dan, Cody, and Austin were sizing up the bulls. "Hey," I said, and they turned.

"If it isn't the guy that's driving all of us to the poor house," Cody said. I froze. I'd tried not to think what my winning streak was doing to the other bull riders. I didn't care what it was doing to Walker, but these other cowboys were Joshua's friends. If they were anything like Joshua, they didn't have much money, and I was horning in on their livelihood. I felt guilty as hell, but I really needed the money, and I didn't know any other way to get it.

Dan rolled his eyes. "You know he's been beating us fair and square. His rides have been incredible."

Austin and Cody grudgingly agreed, but the problem was I wasn't beating them fairly. Should I stop working the spell? Compete with them on equal ground? If I did that, I'd surely be killed by the huge beasts. "Which one is Man Killer?" I asked to change the subject.

"The big white one." Austin nodded toward a bull that did look like it wanted to stomp someone's head in. At least it wouldn't be mine.

The stands went quiet, and the announcer gave a prayer, something they did at the start of every rodeo. The other bull riders took off their hats and closed their eyes. I used the opportunity to grab a few of Man Killer's hairs. I sneaked back to my truck and finished the spell that would allow me to win yet again.

When I rejoined the other bull riders, Cody shook his head. "Always sneaking off during the prayer. What do you have against God?"

Their god didn't make much sense to me. They only had one, and somehow, they still believed he was concerned with a little thing like rodeo injuries. Surely a single god would be too busy to worry about such things. I couldn't say that though, so I gave what I thought would have been Joshua's answer. "He killed my momma."

"Now, now, Killenyen." Cody shook his finger at me. "You know—"

"That I'm on the fast track to hell," I interrupted him. "Yeah, my aunt tells me all the time, and frankly, I don't care."

"You should care." He looked serious, but abruptly, his eyes moved away from me. I turned and followed his gaze. As usual, it was focused on a woman's rear. "Mighty fine ass," he breathed. I was glad that the woman had distracted him from his concern over the fate of my soul.

When it came time for the bull riding, Dan rode first. I was riding last. Dan got bucked off just after leaving the chute. Walker rode next and, to my annoyance, managed an impressive ride, scoring an eighty-two. Man Killer had better be as fierce as Walker claimed.

When my turn came, I climbed onto the chute and onto Man Killer's back. When my helper held up the rope's tail for me, I rubbed my glove up and down it several times. I'd learned from my book you do this to heat up the rosin (the amberlike rocks) and get it sticky. I did the same with the rope's handle. I got the rope pulled tight, wrapped my hand, and slid up on the bull. I nodded, and the chute opened. Man Killer roared into the arena and began bucking fiercer than any bull I'd ever been on. I laughed as adrenaline filled me.

Suddenly, my riding hand exploded with pain, like it had been struck by lightening or something. My hand spasmed and lost its grip on the rope.

I flew off and slammed into the ground, knocking the wind out of me. The bull's hoofs crashed down inches from my head before the bull fighters could distract the beast. As soon as I could gasp in a breath, I scrambled to my feet, ran for the fence, and vaulted over it. I fell to the ground shaking and panting.

Dan ran over. "You okay?"

"I don't know." But I did know, and I wasn't okay. Walker was nearby. I got up and grabbed his shoulder. "What the hell did you do to me?"

Walker laughed. "I'd say I beat you, Your Highness. Man Killer's more bull than you can handle."

"Like hell he was." I stopped myself before I could say someone had just used magic to try and kill me. Walker couldn't have done it. If he'd had any magical ability, I'd have been able to feel it. Besides, magic didn't exist in Joshua's realm.

Someone must have come from my realm to finish me off.

I turned every which way, but I couldn't tell a witch from sight alone. Surely it wouldn't be someone I knew. I closed my eyes and reached out with my magic, but I couldn't feel a thing.

Dan caught my shoulder. "Josh, what's going on?"

"Later," I said, and tore off for the other side of the arena. Halfway there I caught a whiff of something and stopped. Charging down a witch of unknown power wouldn't be the brightest thing I'd ever done. Before I could decide what to do, I lost the witch's scent. I closed my eyes to pick it up again, but I sensed nothing. I prowled all around the stands and the vendors, but I couldn't catch the scent again.

I stood by the entrance as the crowd milled out. Dan joined me. "You care to tell me what's going on?"

"No," I said, trying to concentrate on the crowd.

"Whatever," Dan said. "Me and some of the boys are going down to Mac's for a few. Want to join us?"

I wished he would just shut up so I could concentrate, but he was waiting for an answer. "I don't have any money," I said.

Dan snorted. "You can't be that hard up. You've won the last four rodeos. You can crash at my place afterwards. It's only a couple blocks from the bar, so we won't have to worry about a DUI."

"Not tonight," I snapped, certain by now I'd missed the witch.

"Whatever, Josh. When you're ready to tell me what's gotten into you the past few weeks, I'll be here." Thankfully, he walked off.

I hung about the rodeo grounds until the lights had been turned off and nobody was left, but it was wasted effort. I didn't catch another scent of the witch. Still, since the spell hadn't harmed me, the witch would surely try again.

I fetched and packed my gear and went back to my truck. I curled up in my sleeping bag in the back. As I tried to go to sleep, I started shaking. What little sleep I got was full of dreams that nearly made me vomit; picturing the effect a 1,500-pound bull would have had on the human head wasn't pretty.

Near morning, I drifted into deeper sleep. Baron Ysbail slithered into my father's room. "There are rumors, Sire. Rumors that Daulphina has gone insane."

My father grunted. "I will not dignify such rumors."

"Call her back to court. Let her prove her sanity. If she can't, Fitzrigh must be named heir."

"She's in religious retreat, and as I've said. I'll speak when I'm ready and not before. Leave me."

"Yes, Your Majesty." He bowed and left.

Pain crossed my father's face. He reached to the side of the bed and rang for a servant. Sean, my father's personal servant, arrived. He bowed. "Your Majesty."

"Bring me Daulphina."

Sean's jaw dropped. "Sire, she's still raving."

"Bring her through the servant's corridors so she's not seen by the court."

"Of course, Sire. But the servants will talk."

My father was racked by coughs before he could answer. "It can't be helped. I'm dying."

Sean bowed his way out.

A little while later he returned with Joshua in my body. Joshua wore the same none-too-clean tunic and trews I'd seen him in before. His hair was disheveled, and he was struggling against Sean's hand on his arm.

"I told you to get your goddamn filthy hands off me." Joshua pulled his arm free of Sean's grasp. "God, I hate being a woman!"

My father turned red, and a vein in his temple throbbed. "Daulphina, you are a lady and a princess! You will not comport yourself like a stable hand!"

Joshua put his hands on his hips. "I told you, old man, I ain't no goddamned princess. I don't belong here."

My father turned redder and tried to sit up in bed, but he was racked by coughs again. Sean hurried forward to support him until the fit passed. My father lay back on the bed. "Daulphina, Baron

Ysbail has just been here to see me. He wants me to name Fitzrigh heir. Do you want me to promote your bastard brother over you?"

No, Joshua! Say no! Don't you dare lose me my throne!

Joshua jutted his chin forward. "I don't give a flying fuck what you do! Just as long as somebody gets me back into the right goddamn body!"

My father's eyes narrowed. "Have you considered what Fitzrigh's first act as king will be? He'll execute you. Do you think I want my only remaining legitimate child beheaded?" Only legitimate child? What about my little sister, Jenna?

Joshua opened his mouth to make some retort, then seemed to reconsider. Finally, he said, "He'd cut my head off?"

My father nodded. "He couldn't afford to leave around a rival claimant to the throne." My father's forehead creased with concern. "My daughter, I'm dying, and if you don't want to die with me, you must give up your delusions, dress like the princess you are, and present yourself at court again. If you can't or won't do this, I'll have no choice but to seal your death warrant by naming Fitzrigh heir."

"But—"

Rage filled the king's eyes. "Do you think I want Fitzrigh to take your place? He cares for no one but himself. He will be a tyrant. He can't wait to crush the people under his heels. As soon as I name him heir, I have no doubt he'll find some way to hurry my death along."

Joshua's insides seemed to crumble. "Old man, you've got to believe me. I'm not your daughter. I don't know how it happened, but there's been some mistake." Joshua looked so pathetic I almost wanted to give him a hug.

The king apparently didn't share my feelings. He looked away in disgust. "You have until tomorrow to change your story. If you don't, we'll both be dead by the end of the week."

Damn them all to Cailleach! I wanted to shake Joshua. Couldn't he pretend to be me? What was I going to do? What would happen to me if Joshua died in my body? Would I be stuck in Joshua's body forever? Or would I die along with him?

My dream shifted to Fitzrigh and Baron Ysbail. "Your father is still refusing to name you heir, but our agent is in place. Considering his history, are you sure he will be loyal?"

Fitzrigh laughed. "He'll be loyal. I've promised him a barony when I'm king. She'd never do anything like that for him."

"Killing her would make for a more permanent solution. I've never known you to be this squeamish about a corpse or two."

Fitzrigh's eyes went deadly. "I have my reasons for keeping Daulphina alive, and they don't concern you. Question my judgment again, and you'll see how squeamish I am."

* * *

I spent the next day pacing the rodeo grounds going over and over my dreams and everything I'd read, looking for some clue I might have missed. But I had a hard time concentrating. Where was Jenna? Of course, my father would never name her heir if he had any choice. Not only was Jenna only sixteen, she was flighty, and she never even tried to understand court politics. But my father had said I was his only child. Dear gods, what had happened to my sister?

I remembered the last time I'd seen her truly happy. I'd been sitting at my dressing table, and Sylvia was just finishing with my hair. The door opened, and Jenna bounced in. She always seemed to be bouncing. "It's a gorgeous day!" she said in her perkiest voice.

"What's so gorgeous about it?" I snapped; Clenyeth and I had had a fight the night before about him working in the stables again. I wasn't sure what he wanted me to do about it. It wasn't as if he had other skills, and we couldn't allow my father to get suspicious.

"Oh, don't be such a sourpuss, Daul. The sun's shining. The wind is perfect, and we're going kite flying! Mother said we could. We're going to make an outing of it."

"Eilwen is not our mother. Our mother died so Eilwen could be queen." I'd always believed my mother falling down the palace stairs and breaking her neck had been no accident. The king wanted a male heir, and my mother had only given him two daughters and numberless miscarriages.

"Let's not get into that again, Daul. I know you don't like Eilwen, but that is no reason to think Father capable of murder."

Jenna grabbed my hand and nearly skipped out of the palace. On the palace lawns about fifty lords and ladies and about twice that number of servants were gathered. One of the servants bowed and handed me a kite. Another servant did the same for Jenna.

Jenna and I walked to the center of the green. Two young men approached. One of them was Duke Tearlach, of course. Duke Tearlach was almost like my lapdog. The other was Tearlach's best friend, Lord Murdo. They bowed, and Duke Tearlach said, "Your Highnesses, may we have the honor of flying your kites?"

I accepted graciously and handed my kite to Duke Tearlach, but Jenna looked behind Lord Murdo and met eyes with Lord Bowen, who'd crept up without me noticing. No wonder Jenna had been so bouncy. "Lord Bowen, will you fly my kite?" she asked him.

Lord Bowen blushed deeply. "I'd be honored, Your Highness," he said, stepping forward and forcing Lord Murdo behind him, a serious breach of rank.

I suppressed a desire to beat my sister to a bloody pulp. I warned her again and again that she shouldn't show preference for Lord Bowen in public. Father would find out, and he'd make life difficult both for Jenna and Bowen. But Jenna was only sixteen and refused to let reality interfere with the fantasy she'd created for herself. Lord Bowen's father, Earl Cargan, was an important member of my father's court, but Bowen had six older brothers. He would inherit nothing. I'd told Jenna that she'd never be allowed to marry him, but she insisted that Father would die before he forced her into a marriage with someone else and that when I was queen, I'd let her marry whoever she wanted. While the second might be true, I had great doubts about the former. The only reason Father hadn't married us yet was that he was still hoping for a male heir from Eilwen before he sorted us out. Of course, I'd made sure Eilwen would have no children. I wasn't going to be replaced by an infant.

Duke Tearlach and Lord Bowen ran, getting our kites aloft. They returned the strings to us so that we could fly them. Dressed as we were, we couldn't possibly run without tripping over our dresses. By Cailleach, why did women have to dress so ridiculously? No wonder men wouldn't take us seriously. While the other members of the court got their kites flying, Tearlach and Bowen stayed close to us, directing us how to keep the kites aloft. Duke Tearlach kept smiling and touching my hands to correct my grip. I didn't know what to do about him. He actually thought he had a chance with me.

At the moment, I was more worried about the spectacle Jenna was making with Lord Bowen. She smiled and laughed far too loudly as she made her kite do an aerial dance. Bowen gushed about her every gesture. There was no way news of this wouldn't reach Father.

Despite her complete lack of common sense, I loved my little sister. If anything had happened to Jenna, I didn't think I could stand it. It was my job to protect her. I needed to get home so I could make sure everything was all right. This agent that Baron Ysbail had mentioned must be who'd attacked me last night. If I could just find him, I'd make him tell me how to get home.

When people started to arrive for the rodeo, I bought a chicken-on-a-stick and some roasted corn. While I ate, I browsed the booths.

A cowboy I didn't know, but maybe Joshua did, stopped beside me. "You ought to check out the roping horses," he whispered, as if telling me some big secret.

"Why? I'm a bull rider."

"You just ought to do it," he said, and walked off.

I stared after him, wondering what to make of the odd suggestion. I loved horses. I used to ride Ghost Rider every day. Uncle Gilly wouldn't let me ride his horses because "of what happened last time." He wouldn't tell me what that was, and when I reminded him that whatever it was had been Joshua's fault, not mine, he just shrugged and said, "You're in Joshua's body. That's enough for me."

I thought about ignoring the cowboy, but my curiosity won out. I went to the horse corral, climbed over the fence, and went in among the horses. As I patted shoulders and scratched noses, I came upon a horse with its head drooping. "What's wrong, buddy?" I asked. "You not feeling good?"

The horse whinnied softly and nuzzled into me as if for comfort. Something was definitely wrong. Maybe I could figure out what by making a poppet. Since I didn't have anything better to use, I whipped off my boot and sock. I plucked two hairs from the horse's mane and used them to tie up the sock into the semblance of a horse. I used Joshua's pocket knife, which I'd taken to carrying, to cut my left thumb and bleed a drop onto the poppet. Preparing myself for the pain, I breathed on the sock horse and willed it to be one with the suffering horse. With a jolt of agony, the magic coalesced, and a wet spot formed on the rear of the poppet, indicating something that shouldn't have been there. I couldn't see how someone could have gotten a foreign substance into the horse back there, but I didn't have time to puzzle it out. I used my knife and cut a hole in the poppet where the moisture was most dense. I put my mouth to the hole and sucked out the liquid. Something spewed forth out of the horse's rear. I spat the liquid onto the ground. I sucked and spat until nothing more would come out. I swayed a little and steadied myself with the horse. "You'll be fine now," I told it.

"Hey! What the hell are you doing to my horse?" a voice yelled from behind me. I turned to find the same cowboy who'd told me to look at the horses barreling toward me with a sheriff's deputy in tow. "You see, deputy? I told you he was up to something."

I shoved the poppet in my pocket.

The cowboy searched on the ground. "Look!" He pointed to some kind of tube. "I bet he used this syringe to give my horse a roofie or something." He whirled on me. "Trying to sabotage me? Tired of seeing me win?"

"Why would I care if you win?" I said. "I'm a bull rider."

The deputy put on a glove and picked up the tube. It had a sharp needle attached. "Care to explain this, son?"

"I swear by all the gods I never touched that."

"Which gods would those be?" the deputy asked.

Damn it! I racked my brains trying to remember what Aunt Lou Ann had called her god. "Christ Jesus, of course. I swear by Christ Jesus I had nothing to do with that thing."

"Humph," he said. "What are you doing in the horse corral?"

"He told me I should check out the horses." I pointed to the cowboy who was accusing me for reasons I couldn't imagine.

The cowboy puts his hands on his hips. "I said nothing of the kind! Deputy, you have to arrest him."

The deputy raised an eyebrow and looked back and forth between us. I couldn't tell if he was buying what the cowboy told him or not. "What was it you shoved in your pocket when we walked up, and why do you have only one boot on?"

I looked down at my bare foot and took the sock out of my pocket. By Cailleach, how was I going to explain this? People in this world tended to think you were crazy if you talked about magic. "It's just a sock." I held it out to the deputy. "It had a hole in it so I took it off."

The deputy took the sock and examined it. "And tied it up with horse hair?"

Dear gods, how much trouble was I in? "Look! I haven't done anything wrong. There's nothing wrong with the horse." At least, now there wasn't. "I never touched that thingy."

"You liar!" the cowboy said. "I ought to—" He started toward me.

The deputy grabbed his arm. "Mr. Parrish, don't start anything. We'll have a vet check out the horse, and we'll check the syringe for prints." He turned to me. "Don't leave the rodeo grounds until you hear from me." He handed me my sock back.

Even though I didn't have a clue what he was talking about, I heaved a sigh of relief. I shoved the sock back in my pocket, slipped on my boot, and started to walk off. The deputy grabbed my arm. "You leave without my say-so, and you'll find yourself in a load of trouble, son."

"Got it, sir," I said. He let me go.

"You can't just let him walk off," Parrish protested, as I climbed back over the fence. "He's dangerous."

The deputy shook his head. "I can't see why a bull rider would want to sabotage your horse, and he's not going anywhere."

When I joined the other bull riders, Walker walked up. "I'll show you how it's done, Your Highness," he said. I swore I smelled a whiff of magic on him. Not as if he had magic himself, but as if a subtle spell had been placed on him. I wondered whether I ought to warn him, but what would I say?

Since there was no way in hell I was going to beat Walker on He-Man's back, I turned to Dan. "Beat Walker for me."

Again during the prayer, I got He-Man's hairs, went to my truck, and fixed up the spell. I thought about doing one for Dan, too, but it could be dangerous doing a spell on someone without their knowledge and permission. I returned to the bull pens to get my rope ready and talk and relax with the other cowboys.

Finally, they ran the bulls, and we went to our chutes. Dan rode first and got bucked off again. Damn it! He wasn't going to beat Walker. When it was my turn, I climbed on the chute and onto He-Man's back. I got my rope ready, slid up on the bull, and nodded. The chute opened, and He-Man moseyed into the arena. He gave a few bucks I could have probably ridden without the help of the spell. Thankfully, nothing weird happened, but I scored a whopping fifty-five. No red flag granting me a re-ride was thrown into the arena. Still, on this circuit, staying on a bull usually guaranteed you at least some money.

When it was Walker's turn, I held my breath as he climbed onto Man Killer's back. I prayed to my gods, Christ Jesus, and any other god who might have been listening that he fell off. My conscience tugged at me. I'd feel guilty if he died, but I'd get over it. He nodded, and the chute opened. I waited for him to fall. Instead, he gave the best ride I'd ever seen.

I scowled at Walker as he climbed back over the fence, and he smiled like he knew something I didn't. Had he known about the spell? Was someone helping him beat me? Why would anyone come all the way from Asteria just to make me lose at rodeo? That couldn't be Fitzrigh's plan.

After the rodeo, the deputy found me and told me that although the syringe held traces of poison, there didn't appear to be anything wrong with Parrish's horse and there were no prints on the syringe. "But stay away from the horses in future rodeos, why don't you?"

I told him I intended to. After I picked up my paltry check for $234, Dan invited me out for beers with them again, and after being so abrupt with him the night before, I thought I'd better go. Immediately upon walking in, I wished I'd come up with an excuse not to. The place was crawling with Buckle Bunnies. The rodeo groupies couldn't stay away from Joshua.

Joshua's friends and I sat at the bar, and we ordered beer.

"Hey, cowboy." A brunette Bunny settled herself on the stool next to mine. She wore skin-tight jeans and a white T-shirt that left her breasts popping out. She licked her lips in what was obviously supposed to be a seductive way. Dan surreptitiously gave her the once-over. "You gave a mighty fine ride today," she said, batting her eyes at me.

I laughed. "The only fine thing about it is I managed to stay on."

"That's more than most of the others. Buy me a drink?"

"I'm sorry, but I'm broke. Dan here seems right interested, though."

Dan smiled at her, but the Bunny was no longer smiling. "I'll find my own second choice." She went off in a snit.

Dan shook his head. "I don't get it, Josh. You used to take any old Bunny back to your truck. What's made you so picky all of a sudden?"

"I'd have banged that one," Nash added.

"She has a nice ass," Cody said, watching her walk away.

I didn't know what to say, so I took a swig of beer and pretended I hadn't heard. I downed more than a couple beers, all the while dodging Bunny come-ons.

I was just about ready to call it a night when Walker walked in with a blonde wearing a ponytail, a short skirt, and a low-cut blouse. I smelled something—magic.

It had to be her—the witch who'd tried to kill me.

I stormed up to the witch, grabbed her arm, and shouted, "Who are you? Why are you in bed with that bastard Fitzrigh?"

Walker got in my face. "Keep your filthy hands off my woman, Killenyen."

"Stay out of this, Walker. It's between me and the witch."

"How dare you call my girlfriend a witch?" He sucker punched me in the face, knocking me over backwards, my balance being none too good to begin with. Rage surged through me, and I came off the floor, determined to beat him to a bloody pulp.

Mac stepped between us, and a couple of the guys grabbed me. "Take it outside, boys," Mac ordered.

The entire bar emptied outside—Bunnies, witch, and all, and they formed a circle with Walker and me in the middle. For half a second, I thought this was stupid. What did I know about fist fights? But I had to get at the witch who was standing behind Walker. Besides, I'd wanted to punch Walker since I first met him. I rushed him, ready to crush his ugly face. When I threw a punch, he sidestepped it and gave me a good one in the gut. I doubled over, gasping, and he brought his knee up into my face. I heard the crunch of my nose breaking, and blood started to pour out of it.

I'd like to say I got some good punches in, but I don't remember them, although I'm sure I did an excellent job of bruising Walker's knuckles. As well as breaking my nose, I thought he broke a couple of ribs. When I couldn't get up any more, he proceeded to kick me half a dozen times until someone finally dragged him back, saying I'd had enough. I'd thought I'd had enough about fifty punches ago, but at least they stopped him from beating me to death.

Walker grabbed the witch's hand. "Come on, Eileen."

Dan squatted down beside me. I don't know where he'd been during the fight. "We need to get you to a doctor."

"No," I moaned. "I can't afford a doctor."

"Don't have any insurance, huh?" He nodded sympathetically. "I'll take you to my place. My brother's an EMT. He'll come check you out."

"I'm okay," I protested, coughing up blood. I knew I would be okay because witches heal faster and easier than normal people.

"Like hell you are," Dan said, and he and the rest of Joshua's friends loaded me in Dan's truck. I tried to tell them it wasn't necessary, but I hurt too much to argue. However, if this EMT tried to bleed me, that would change.

On the short drive to Dan's house, which turned out to be trailer a little bigger than Joshua's, he called his brother.

"Mike will be over in a few minutes," Dan told me as he helped me out of his truck and into his trailer. He led me to a saggy, worn floral sofa with cat hair all over it. Two cats meowed around our feet as we made our way across the trailer.

"I wouldn't have figured you for flowers," I said, as I collapsed onto the sofa.

"Shut up, Killenyen," he said. "It was my grandmother's. You have something nicer, I bet."

"I don't even have a sofa," I groaned, my ribs killing me.

"I'll get some water and wash that blood off your face," he said, going into his small kitchen, which didn't have dirty dishes over every surface. He came back with a cloth and a bowl of warm water and began washing the blood off.

It wasn't long before the door opened, and a man walked in, carrying a box. "Hey, Dan," he said, and he and Dan slapped each other on the back. "This is Joshua, I guess."

"Thanks for coming, Mike," Dan said. "He says he can't afford a doctor. You know how that is."

Mike nodded. He opened my shirt and poked at various places on my chest and abdomen, asking me if it hurt.

"Holy Cernuous, yes!" I gasped.

"What?" Dan said, and the two brothers exchanged looks.

"I meant Christ Jesus, yes!"

That seemed to satisfy them. Mike finished poking me, grabbed my wrist, and held it while looking at his watch. He opened his box and did a bunch of strange things to me with the items in his box, but he didn't suggest bleeding me.

When he was finished, he looked up at Dan. "Pulse, blood pressure, and temperature are all okay. He shows no sign of shock or a concussion. But his nose is broken, and I'm pretty sure a couple of ribs are, too. As sore as he is, he could have internal bleeding. He really should go to a hospital to check it out."

"No," I insisted. "I'm fine."

Dan looked at his brother, and Mike shrugged. "There's no obvious signs he's in trouble, but these things don't always show themselves at first. With the punishment his torso took, I can't promise he doesn't have a bleeder."

Dan looked down at me. "They'll work out a payment plan with you. I don't want you to die on my couch."

"I'm not going to die."

"Is he?" Dan asked Mike.

"Probably not," Mike said. We argued for a few more minutes. Mike shrugged. "You can't take him against his will, but I'd have him sign a statement that he refused treatment, just in case something does happen and his relatives want to make a stink about it."

"I'll sign whatever you want. Just let me get some sleep."

They had me sign something I didn't bother to read. Mike gave me a little round thing he called a pain pill and told me to swallow it. Mike said to Dan, "Wake him every couple of hours just to make sure." When they finally left me alone, I drifted to sleep and dreamed of Asteria again.

Joshua, in my body, sat at my dressing table in my shift with Sylvia combing his hair. He grimaced as Sylvia pulled at a tangle. "Your Highness, you know this would have been a lot easier if you hadn't refused to let me do your hair for the last month."

"You know I'm not Your Highness," he snarled.

Sylvia sighed like they'd been through this a million times. "Whoever you claim to be you are going to start acting like Her Highness, aren't you?"

"I'm letting you do my hair and put me in a dress, aren't I?" His face twisted with disgust. "What would the other cowboys think if they could see me now? Fuck them. They're not about to get their heads chopped off."

"Yes, Your Highness, fuck them."

Joshua looked at Sylvia, and I was equally shocked. I'd never heard my maid use such language. "I've been a bad influence on you.

I guess I've never been anything but a bad influence on anyone. That's what my Uncle Braeden would say, anyway."

"You have no Uncle Braeden, Your Highness."

The dream shifted, and I saw Fitzrigh sitting with that treacherous bastard, Baron Ysbail.

Baron Ysbail said, "Daulphina is returning from her spiritual retreat. She's expected later today. What are we going to do?"

Fitzrigh's lip curled. "Don't worry. I have the situation in hand."

"How can you be sure? Your sister does have some firm supporters, people who do not want to see you king. They call you, 'The Bastard.'"

Fitzrigh snarled, "They will come to regret that, just as Lord Bowen did."

I remembered when Lord Bowen had died. I'd always known Fitzrigh had deliberately murdered him.

The day had started with Jenna giggling with Lord Bowen behind the jousting stands. Jenna hadn't told me she planned to meet Bowen until after we'd nearly arrived at the rendezvous spot, or I'd have tried to talk some sense into her, not that it would have helped. After the kite flying fiasco, Jenna had been sternly lectured, and Lord Bowen's father had sent him to the family estate for six months. Jenna had moped the entire time Bowen was gone. He'd been back less than a week, and already she was acting like an idiot.

"Hurry!" I hissed. I was standing watch, making sure father didn't catch them together. I caught sight of our father's advanced guards. "He's coming."

Jenna looked fearfully over her shoulder. She hurriedly removed something I couldn't see from her pocket and gave it to Bowen. "I love you," she whispered, and pressed a quick kiss to his lips.

Jenna turned to stand beside me as Lord Bowen faded into the background. She gasped. I followed her gaze. Fitzrigh was standing nearby with a smirk on his face. He was so close he had to have seen the kiss. Damn it, I'd forgotten to be on the look out for him as well.

"He saw!" Jenna wailed. "What am I going to do?"

"I'll take care of it," I promised her, but I wasn't sure how. After Lord Bowen had called Fitzrigh "nothing but a bastard" yesterday in the Hall of Games, I didn't think anything would prevent Fitzrigh telling Father.

"Thanks, Daul." Jenna smiled and squeezed my hand. "You're too good to me."

I certainly was, especially if she didn't develop more sense.

Father arrived, and we curtseyed. "It's a lovely day for the joust," he said, leading the way into the royal box. Jenna and I followed. The crowd cheered when we appeared. Father made a speech and signaled for the joust to begin.

Jenna kept biting her lip through the first contests. "Oh, I hope he wins today," she whispered. "He feels ashamed that he loses so often." I had no idea who Bowen was up against, but I very much doubted he'd win. Bowen was just developing his manly strength, and he was usually too busy showing off for Jenna to pay attention to his opponent.

Jenna gripped my arm tightly, as the herald announced, "Fitzrigh, illegitimate son of King Tormaid, and Lord Bowen, seventh son of Earl Cargan!"

Good gods! How had this happened? Fitzrigh usually arranged his matches against nobles of greater consequence and greater skill than Bowen. Bowen didn't stand a chance. Despite how I felt about my bastard brother, Fitzrigh was an excellent jouster.

Fitzrigh and Lord Bowen entered from opposite ends of the jousting list. I bit back a scream of frustration when I saw the turquoise scarf tied to Lord Bowen's lance. Jenna had given him her favor, and she'd hadn't had enough sense not to use her usual color. I prayed that Father hadn't paid enough attention to Jenna to know turquoise was her color.

Fitzrigh didn't immediately take his place at the end of the list. Instead, he slowly rode by the crowd, eyeing the ladies as if deciding whose favor to request. A flurry went through the crowd. Fitzrigh only rarely accepted a lady's favor. The ladies leaned forward hopefully as he approached their position and sank back in disappointment as he passed without tilting his lance. Many of the fathers frowned at their daughters. The men at the court had mixed feelings about my brother, but he was almost universally admired by the ladies, at least by the young and giddy ones. Fitzrigh, for all the viciousness, was extremely attractive and knew how to be charming when he wanted to be.

The crowd gaped as Fitzrigh stopped in front of the royal box and tilted his lance toward Jenna. A knight rarely requested a favor of his sister, and the animosity between Fitzrigh and Jenna was well known. I prayed Jenna had had the sense to bring more than one scarf. "Sister." Fitzrigh smiled nastily. "Would you bestow your favor upon me?"

Jenna's eyes widened in horror, letting me know that, of course, she hadn't had sufficient sense. It was unthinkable for a lady to come to the joust without being prepared with a favor. Father would notice if Jenna claimed not to have one with her. Of course, a lady could always deny a request for her favor, but it was rarely done, and our father would be furious if Jenna denied Fitzrigh in front of the entire court. She looked at me in panic. I quickly slipped my favor from my pocket and handed it to Jenna as surreptitiously as possible. I didn't know what I was going to do when Duke Tearlach requested mine, as he inevitably would. I'd have to plead a headache and leave before that could happen.

I berated myself for having no more sense than Jenna as I watched her tie my emerald scarf on the end of Fitzrigh's lance. Fitzrigh smirked in my direction, drawing everyone's attention to the fact that the scarf was the same color as my dress. Our father's eyes narrowed. He glanced toward Bowen, and his eyes narrowed further at the sight of the turquoise scarf flying from Bowen's lance. Jenna would pay for this, as would Bowen, which was surely Fitzrigh's plan.

When Jenna finished tying the scarf on, Fitzrigh trotted back to his end of the list. Jenna leaned forward to watch, completely oblivious to the fact that Father knew what she'd done.

The two knights faced each other, their horses snorting and prancing, eager to be off. The referee at the side of the field dropped the flag, and Fitzrigh and Bowen thundered toward each other. Jenna's nails dug into my arm. Fitzrigh and Bowen crashed their lances against each other, and Bowen flipped over the rear of his horse, landing heavily on the ground.

Jenna screamed and ran to the rail. She overhung it, looking down at Lord Bowen. "No!" she shrieked. "No!" Tears streamed down Jenna's cheeks. Attendants and a physician descended on Lord Bowen, but it was clear long before the physician declared it: Lord Bowen was dead. I hurried to Jenna's side and put my arm around her. She buried her head in my shoulder, sobbing uncontrollably. "No, Daul, no!"

"Jenna!" my father bellowed. "How many times have I told you princesses don't cry?"

Instead of calming, Jenna sobbed out Bowen's name.

Earl Cargan rose from the body of his son and approached the royal box, his eyes gleaming with rage and grief. "Your Majesty, I demand redress."

Looking at Jenna in disgust, Father ordered a servant to fetch Fitzrigh to the royal box. Shortly, the bastard appeared. Jenna launched herself at him, beating him with her fists. "You killed him! You did it on purpose!"

My father motioned to a couple of nearby guards, and they restrained Jenna. She struggled to get back at Fitzrigh. "Take her to her room until she can control herself," Father ordered.

The guards dragged Jenna away, screaming, "Murderer!"

I glanced at Bowen's body. Fitzrigh's broken lance still protruded from his chest, my emerald scarf flying above the wound. This shouldn't have happened. The lances were supposed to be blunt. They caused bruises certainly, but not puncture wounds. This had to have been deliberate, something that Earl Cargan would be well aware of.

Father narrowed his eyes at Fitzrigh. "Explain yourself."

Fitzrigh looked thoroughly unconcerned, even bored. "It was a tragic accident, Sire. I don't know how my lance broke with such a sharp point. The manufacturing must have not been as it should have been. Shall I have the lance maker disciplined?"

Father's eyes darted to the turquoise scarf on Bowen's fallen lance and the emerald one on the lance protruding from Bowen's chest.

"The lance maker! Surely, Sire—" Earl Cargan protested.

But Father cut him off. "See to it," he ordered Fitzrigh, and Fitzrigh bowed his head in acknowledgement.

I gasped. The king was no fool and had to know that Fitzrigh had sabotaged his own lance and killed Bowen on purpose. But because of Jenna's preference for an unsuitable candidate, he'd allow Fitzrigh get away with deliberate murder.

Fitzrigh turned to me as he was leaving the royal box. The corners of his mouth were turned down in sorrow, but his eyes twinkled with amusement. "Tell our sister how very sorry I am for this tragedy. The sight of her favor streaming from my lance will always haunt me."

I glared in impotent rage at the bastard. My little sister's heart had been crushed, and I'd been unable to protect her. The bastard bowed mockingly to me and left. Earl Cargan glared murderously at Fitzrigh's back. My brother had just made an enemy, and I a new friend. Cargan had previously distanced himself from the conflict between my brother and me.

Still, Fitzrigh had just shown the entire court no one was going to insult him and get away with it. He'd shown them he was a force to be feared; he could kill without consequence.

# CHAPTER 9

Between my dreams and Dan waking me every couple hours, I slept terribly, but by morning I could tell my injuries were beginning to heal. We witches are hard to kill. I joined Dan at a small rickety table that was still more than anything I had. It, too, was clean. He got out bowls, spoons, milk, and a box that resembled my Frosted Flakes but said Captain Crunch. Instead of eating them straight from the box as I always had, he poured them in the bowl and poured milk on top of them. Marveling, I did the same. It was actually much better this way. I'd try it at home if I had any clean bowls.

"Do you know that girl Walker was with?" I asked Dan.

"She's his girlfriend, Eileen something. She goes to Auburn like he does."

I nodded as if this meant something to me. "How long has he been seeing her?"

Dan shrugged. "About a month or so. Why?"

Just about the time I got into this body. "I need to find her."

Dan put his spoon down. "Walker didn't beat you badly enough already?"

I could hardly tell him she was a witch sent by my bastard brother. "I just need to, okay? How can I do it?"

"Besides asking Walker, how the hell should I know?"

"How would I find Walker, then?"

"His address is in the Professional Cowboy's Association directory. You got one, don't you?"

If Joshua did have such a thing, it would be back in his trailer, and I had no idea how I'd find it in the disaster. "I lost it," I said.

Dan rolled his eyes. "Is there anything you haven't lost?" He got up, rummaged around in a drawer, brought back a small paper volume, and plunked it down in front of me. "He's in there, but if you ask me, you should just leave well enough alone."

I found Walker's name and address. Dan gave me a piece of paper and a pen to write it down. You didn't even have to dip these pens in ink. More technology, I guessed. After eating breakfast, I thanked Dan and told him I'd best be on my way.

"You sure you're okay? You could crash here another day or two if you need to."

"No, I'm fine." We did the back-slapping male thing, and I left.

I arrived at about noon at Walker's place of residence. I'd learned a lot about using maps by then. Walker lived in an apartment stuck together with a lot of other apartments. I didn't see how people could live crowded together like that. Walker came out about an hour later and got in his truck. I followed him, doing my best not to be seen. As I hoped, he drove over to another group of apartments and picked up Eileen. Now that I knew where she lived, I leaned back and waited.

* * *

About two hours later, Walker's truck squealed into the lot. Eileen flung the door open almost before the truck had a chance to stop. She jumped out and screamed, "I hope I never see you again!" She slammed the door and stalked off to her apartment. Walker squealed out of the parking lot. I couldn't help smiling. Anything that made Walker unhappy was mighty fine with me.

After giving Eileen a minute to get settled, I went to her door and knocked, and she answered. Before she could stop me, I pushed my way in and grabbed her arm. I was about to ask her again what she was up to with Fitzrigh when I was hit with what felt like a sledge hammer.

* * *

When I woke up, I was on the floor with my feet tied together and my hands tied behind my back. Eileen sat on the couch across from me.

Damn it, I should have thought through this plan a little more. Knowing Fitzrigh wasn't the type to inspire loyalty based on anything but money, I said, "Why are you working for my bastard brother? If it's a barony you want, I can get it for you as easily as he can. In fact, I'll offer you twice whatever he's paying you."

She folded her arms and looked down at me with disdain. "Just what are you on, buddy?"

I struggled to a sitting position, not an easy task with your hands and feet tied. "I'm not on anything. Just tell me how to cross over, and you will be well rewarded."

"Cross over what?"

"You know, how you got here from Asteria."

"Is that in Georgia or something?"

"Don't play dumb. You know where Asteria is."

"Believe me or not, I don't care." She glanced away, looking exactly like a woman who didn't care.

Could it be that she was truly loyal to Fitzrigh? She was with Walker now, so it was possible that she was stupid enough to have fallen for Fitzrigh, as well. "Do you mind at least telling me what you plan to do with me?"

"I'm waiting for my coven to decide."

"Your coven?" I gaped at her. "There's a whole coven of you here? In Alabama?" Fitzrigh had talked of sending an agent, not a whole coven. I could be in even more trouble than I'd thought.

She shrugged. "It's not a very large coven. Alabama isn't friendly to witches. Bible belt and all. You know, Exodus 22:18: 'Thou shalt not suffer a witch to live.' Some day I'm moving to California; it's a mecca for witches."

"There are witches in other states?"

She rolled her eyes like I was the biggest dumbass she'd ever had the misfortune to meet. "Why would all witches want to hang out here?"

Just how many people had crossed over from my realm?

There was a knock on the door, and Eileen answered it. She let in a pretty black woman with her hair shaved to a fine buzz. She looked about the same age as Eileen. Eileen introduced her as Kinyisha.

Kinyisha looked down at me with her hands on her hips. "Who is this? And what did you do to him?" She pointed to the bruises on my face.

Eileen threw up her hands. "Ben beat him up, not me. He's some bull rider who seems overly interested in my sex life."

"I wasn't talking about your sex life. You're working with my bastard brother."

Kinyisha looked at Eileen, who shrugged. "I have no idea what he's talking about."

"You damned well do," I protested, but she and Kinyisha ignored me.

"Sandy on her way?" Kinyisha asked.

Eileen nodded. "And Madame Isabella, too."

Kinyisha stared at Eileen for a moment. "You called Madame Isabella?"

"Yes, or at least I think it was her, but it might have been Irene."

"Was that really necessary?"

Eileen shrugged. "We need her if we're going to perform a death ritual."

"A death ritual?" I spluttered.

Neither of them paid attention to me. "You think it's that serious?" Kinyisha asked.

"Hell, yes! He announced I was a witch in front of an entire bar full of people last night, and then he tracked me down and barged into my apartment. He's dangerous."

Another young woman, who must have been Sandy, walked in at that moment. She was tall and skinny as a rail and had pierced anything that was possible to pierce—about ten earrings in each ear, one in each eyebrow, in her nose, tongue, chin, and probably some others that I couldn't see with her clothes on. "Who's dangerous?" she asked.

"Him." Eileen pointed at me.

Sandy looked me up and down like she liked what she saw. "Looks dangerous," she said, meaning something very difficult than Eileen.

"I'm not dangerous! I've never hurt anyone." I said. "Eileen's the one that tried to kill me, making me fall off my bull Friday night. I came within inches of getting my head stomped in."

"You made him fall off?" Kinyisha asked.

Eileen glared at her. "You shouldn't have to ask. I know the rules about using magic to cause harm."

Kinyisha nodded and looked down at me. "If someone used magic against you, what makes you think it was Eileen?"

"Because . . ." I had been going to say she was the only witch around, but I found myself facing two more in this very room, and apparently, another one was on the way. "I didn't realize crossing over was so common."

"Crossing over?" Kinyisha asked.

"From Asteria!" I shouted it. I was tired of these people pretending not to know what I was talking about.

Kinyisha asked, "Where's Asteria?"

"I think it's in Georgia," Sandy said.

I stomped my foot on the floor. "Y'all damn well know it's not in Georgia! Stop acting like you don't know anything about parallel realms."

"Parallels realms?" Sandy burst out laughing. "He's cute, but he might be a little off his rocker."

"Probably," Kinyisha agreed. "Tell us about this attempt on your life." I told them about the curse that hit my hand.

"I bet it wasn't a curse," Eileen said. "I bet he just fell off."

"I know magic when I feel it. Besides, I have a spell that helps me stay on." I told them about the superglue spell.

"Ah ha! Ben was right," Eileen said. "You are cheating. Not that I care what Ben thinks anymore."

I cringed at the accusation, but before I could say anything, there was a knock on the door. Eileen answered it. In stepped a middle-aged, 200-pound woman wearing an orange robe that clashed badly with her extremely red hair. She took one look at me, screamed, and ran back out.

"Does she always have to act so bat-shit crazy?" Sandy asked.

"At least, we know we've got Madame Isabella," Kinyisha said. "Irene never screams like that." I wondered if Isabella and Irene were identical twins since the witches didn't seem able to tell them apart.

Madame Isabella charged back in, carrying a short metal tube with some kind of handle. She pointed it at me. "Die, abomination!" she screamed.

"Don't shoot!" Kinyisha shoved Isabella's outstretched hand, just as a deafening explosion ripped through the air. Something whipped past my head going faster than any arrow.

I hit the floor. "Dear gods, what was that?" Was this some kind of black magic or more of Uncle Gilly's technology? Either way I was certain it was dangerous.

"Give me that gun!" Kinyisha snatched the metal tube out of Madame Isabella's hand. "Someone will call the police. Besides, Eileen doesn't want blood all over her apartment. It would be a bitch to get out of this carpet. If we need to kill him, we'll do a death ritual."

Isabella looked puzzled. "But death rituals are so painful, and we definitely need to kill it."

Getting alarmed, I tried to stand, but ended up falling on my butt. "You can't kill me! I haven't done anything wrong. I'm the crown princess of Asteria. You help me, and I'll see you rewarded."

Kinyisha gave me the once over. "A little too much hair on your chest to be a princess, don't you think?"

But Madame Isabella nodded. "It's a princess."

Sandy rolled her eyes. "Isabella, he's a man, and where in the world do they even have princesses any more?" How would someone from Asteria not know about princesses? Was it possible these witches were from some place else?

Isabella shrugged. "I don't think this thing"—she indicated me with a wave of her hand—"is from around here. It's dripping with black magic. We have to get rid of it."

"What kind of black magic?" Kinyisha asked.

"It's black, and it's dark, and it's icky. Very, very icky." She shook her hand, as if to shake off something unpleasant. "I've never seen anything like it before."

"That must be the body switching spell, but it isn't my fault," I said. "Someone switched me with Joshua Killenyen." I told them everything I knew about my situation. "I'm the victim here. I've never dabbled in black magic myself."

The other three witches looked at Isabella. "It's telling the truth," she said.

"Really?" Kinyisha looked like she wasn't sure what to believe. "Anything more you can tell us?"

"Why do you want to know more about something so icky?" Isabella asked. "Images of such ickiness in a crystal ball would be horrid. Besides, I don't have mine with me."

Kinyisha looked me over again. "We need to know more about it before we kill it." She turned to Eileen. "Can Madame Isabella borrow your crystal ball?"

Eileen shrugged. "I guess so. It's set up in the extra room. But I agree with Isabella. We should just get rid of it."

"Would y'all stop calling me an 'it'? I'm a person, not a thing," I said.

Madame Isabella shrugged. "Can't say 'she' because the body's male. Can't say 'he' because the soul is female."

Kinyisha said, "Madame Isabella will do the ball, then we'll decide."

Sandy reached down and took a hold of my chin. "Besides, it would be a shame to destroy such loveliness."

"Whatever." Eileen rolled her eyes and got out a knife. Kinyisha pointed Madame Isabella's shooting tube at me. I flinched. "Eileen's going to cut your feet free, and you're going to go with us, but if you try anything, I will shoot you, and we'll worry about the blood later. Understand?"

I nodded, trying my best not to antagonize them. I didn't want to find out what had happened to me only to die before it could do me any good.

Eileen cut my feet free. I struggled to stand. Sandy stepped forward and helped me. Her hand lingered on my arm longer than necessary. We all trooped down the hall. It was dark when we first entered the room, and Eileen started lighting candles. Each candle was placed in a candleholder shaped like a human skull. Slowly, a table became visible in the middle of the room. It was covered with a midnight blue tablecloth decorated with silver pentacles. A blue crystal ball sat in the center. I'd never used a crystal ball before. Granny had died before she could teach me how. Placed around the table were six wooden chairs painted black. The walls of the room where also black with silver pentacles glowing on them. The overall effect was downright eerie, but it brought tears to my eyes. It reminded me of Granny.

The witches sat in four of the chairs and motioned for me to sit in a fifth. Isabella took the knife from Eileen and made small cuts on both her palms. She passed the knife to Kinyisha and put her bleeding palms onto the crystal ball. Kinyisha put down the gun, made identical cuts on her hands, and passed the knife to Sandy. Sandy did the same and passed it to Eileen. When all four of the witches had their hands on the ball, Isabella's eyes rolled back in her head, so that I could only see the whites. She started chanting in a language I didn't recognize. The other three witches joined in. I felt the magic gathering, and the air in the room became so thick it was difficult to breathe.

The witches' faces creased with pain, and thick clouds swirled through the crystal ball. Isabella's voice rose dramatically. Thunder crashed, and lightening shot through the ball. "Yes! Yes!" Isabella cried. Her eyes rolled back down, and the clouds in the crystal ball resolved themselves into the shape of a male figure. "I see . . . I see . . . I see love. The heart loves."

"Clenyeth," I said. "Is he okay? He's alive, isn't he?"

Isabella shook her head. "Hard to say. Too far away. Dark shadow over love. Very dark." Her eyes grew wide, and she screamed, "No, no, no!"

"What is it? What's wrong?" I leaned forward, as the ball turned a dark crimson.

"Darkness. Blood. Lots of blood. Sacrifice. Pain. Darkness."

An explosion sounded from the ball, throwing all four witches back. As they toppled to the ground, the image of a skull burst briefly from the ball. Then the ball resolved itself into its former, inert blue. For a moment, I feared all the witches were dead, and it was somehow my fault. But one by one, they opened their eyes and rose, holding their heads as if they feared they would fall off. Madame Isabella was the last to get up. Unlike the others, she didn't appear to have a headache. She smiled a vacant smile at me. "Did I tell your fortune, sir?" For some reason, she wasn't calling me an "it" any more.

"You said something about darkness and pain. What happened? What's wrong? Clenyeth's not dead, is he?"

She laughed. "How would I know? Madame Isabella tells the fortunes. I just collect the bills. That will be $50."

I looked in confusion at the other three witches. They righted their chairs and dropped into them. "Irene," Kinyisha groaned.

"Y'all saw something? What was it?" I demanded.

Sandy shook her head. "It's only Isabella that sees. We just lend her the strength of our magic. Unfortunately, she's not here any more."

"What the hell are you talking about?" I looked at the middle-aged woman who was struggling and failing to set up her chair.

"She's not Madame Isabella any more." Kinyisha got up and helped her with her chair.

Isabella sat in it. "Of course I'm not. That would be perfectly ridiculous." She picked up the metal tube from the table and pointed it at me. "But I need my $50. Don't think of sneaking off without paying. A woman's got to eat." She laughed a girlish laugh and batted her eyes at me, gestures completely at odds with the woman she'd been moments before.

I turned to the other witches for help. "But she saw something. Maybe something that could help. Clenyeth." I felt tears forming in my eyes and looked away so the witches wouldn't see them.

The witches shrugged. "Sometimes she's Madame Isabella. Sometimes she's Irene," Kinyisha said. "You won't get anything more out of her now."

"This isn't possible," I wailed. "I have to know what she saw."

Sandy touched my arm sympathetically. "She'll be Madame Isabella again some day."

"When?" I asked.

"You can never tell. One time she was Irene for six whole months. About drove us all bonkers, and we couldn't work any major spells."

Eileen and Kinyisha nodded in agreement.

"My $50." Irene shook the tube at me.

Kinyisha plucked the gun out of Irene's hands. "Stop that. Things are obviously more complicated than we thought. We can't kill him until we figure out what's going on. If someone's working hostile magic in our territory, we have to figure out who."

My relief that they stopped talking about killing me was overwhelmed by my fear for Clenyeth. What could all that red have meant if not that he was dead?

"I guess we need to free him." Sandy smiled, picked up the knife, and cut my hands free. "Thanks," I said, bringing my arms forward and rubbing my wrists while I struggled not to cry. Princesses didn't cry, especially when other people are watching.

"You got any plan about figuring this out?" Sandy asked Kinyisha. "Especially without Madame Isabella? She's by far the strongest of us, but who knows when she'll be back?"

"We could make a counter-curse woven from his hair to stop the curse from knocking him off the bull," Kinyisha said. "We'll go with him to each rodeo until we find whoever's casting it."

Eileen sat up straighter. "It will be a cold day in hell before I go near another rodeo."

Kinyisha raised her eyebrows. "Why? I thought you liked rodeos."

"That was before Ben turned out to be an ass." I couldn't argue with her. Walker was an ass.

"We don't all need to go, I guess." Kinyisha turned to Sandy who had no objections to the idea. They decided at least two of them should be at every rodeo.

Irene jumped abruptly to her feet. "What about my $50?"

Kinyisha looked at me. "Could you pay her? She really does need the money. Her used bookstore doesn't bring in very much. You know, with Amazon and Kindle and everything."

I had no idea what she was talking about, but I figured it was the least I could do. I took $50 out of Joshua's wallet and put it on the table. Irene snatched it up, grabbed her gun from Kinyisha, and scurried out of the room.

Kinyisha, Sandy, and I made plans for next week's rodeo. I prayed to all the gods I could think of that these witches could help me figure out how to get back home.

# CHAPTER 10

It was late when we finally got done talking, and I was too tired and emotionally exhausted to drive all the way back to Hamilton. I decided to sleep that night in the back of my truck in Eileen's parking lot despite how blasted hot it was.

When I was alone, I finally allowed myself to feel the fear and grief I'd repressed when I was with the witches. I soon found myself sobbing. "Clenyeth, oh, Clenyeth." I bawled until there were no more tears left, then lay there hiccupping until I fell asleep.

I dreamed again. When Joshua came into focus, he was riding with an escort through the palace gates. I guessed he was arriving home from his "spiritual retreat." Half the court, including Fitzrigh and Baron Ysbail, were gathered in front of the palace to greet his return. Joshua looked precarious riding side saddle. It took an entirely different balance than riding astride. Joshua arrived at the palace's front steps, and a groom took Ghost Rider's reins. Duke Tearlach, of course, came forward to help Joshua dismount. Joshua allowed Tearlach to help, but his foot got caught in the stirrup, and he pitched forward taking Tearlach down with him. Joshua landed on top and spewed a filthy word.

He struggled to his feet, stepping on Tearlach in the process and nearly falling again. The gathered nobles—with the exception of Fitzrigh and Ysbail, who were hiding smiles—stared at him in shock.

"Er . . . sorry," Joshua said, not knowing a princess wouldn't apologize.

Fitzrigh stepped forward. "Are you hurt?"

Joshua shook his head and pointed to Tearlach, who was gasping from Joshua stepping on his stomach. Tearlach rolled over, and blood seeped from a wound on the back on his head. "I think he is, though."

"My, yes." Fitzrigh knelt down next to Tearlach. He put his hand on Tearlach's head and closed his eyes. In front of the gathered nobles, the back of Tearlach's head knit together and the bleeding stopped.

Joshua jumped back and stared at Fitzrigh like he was a demon. "How in the hell did you do that?"

I wondered the same thing. Yes, Fitzrigh had magic, but he'd had less teaching than even I'd had. He shouldn't have been able to heal without a poppet.

* * *

When I awoke in the morning, I couldn't stop thinking about Fitzrigh's magic. How could he be so powerful now? Had he found someone to teach him? Maybe he could have done this to me, after all. I needed to find out, and Madame Isabella had definitely seen something. I needed to talk to her again before I headed back to Hamilton. I marched up to Eileen's door and asked her where I could find Madame Isabella.

"Why?" she asked, yawning. "I'm sure she's still Irene. She can't do you a bit of good."

"I just need to talk to her, okay?"

Eileen rolled her eyes. "Whatever. She'll be at her bookstore. It's on Gay Street." She gave me directions.

I followed Eileen's directions and found the bookstore. The sign said, "Madame Isabella's Books, Crystals, and Psychic Readings." On it was a picture of a crystal ball growing out of a petunia for purposes I couldn't imagine. I walked in and bumped my head on a mobile of green and blue crystals hanging from the ceiling, setting off a loud tinkling noise.

"You better watch your head, sir," the woman behind the counter said. She was wearing a red floral pantsuit and had a vacant smile on her face, so it had to be Irene. "You break it, you buy it." She pointed to a sign near the counter that announced this policy. The front part of the store was full of crystals in every possible color and configuration. Most of them were hanging low or perched precariously on the edge of small shelves and tables. Beyond the crystals were shelf after shelf of books.

"You shouldn't have them hanging so low," I complained. Joshua wasn't particularly tall.

She tittered. "It's one of Madame Isabella's schemes. People are always knocking them off the ceiling. She makes a lot of sales that way." She leaned toward me as if imparting a secret. "The ones on the shelves are easy to knock of, too. It really isn't fair, but we have to make money some way. People just aren't buying books like they used to, and around here the people are so hopelessly mundane they rarely buy crystals or get psychic readings."

I weaved my way toward her, being careful not to bump into anything. I noticed the price tags. Some of the crystals were outrageously expensive. "I need to talk to Madame Isabella," I told Irene.

Irene smiled that same vacant smile. "I'm afraid she isn't here."

"It's important," I insisted. "Can't you bring her out some way?"

Irene shrugged. "Afraid not, and she didn't say when she was going to be back. She's inconsiderate that way. I've lectured her about it time and time again, but it does no good."

I leaned across the counter and grabbed Irene's arm. "There has to be a way. Help me, please!"

Without meaning to, I felt my power press against hers. A jolt of agony traveled up my arm, and I snatched my hand back. The vacant smile faded from Irene's face and was replaced by an expression of fear and rage.

"Abomination!" Madame Isabel yelled and fled into the office behind her, slamming the door.

I hurried after. "Please, Madame Isabella, you know something about me. Please help me."

"Magic is too icky. Go away." She screamed through the door. "Magic that icky comes only from blood. Lots of blood. I won't have anything to do with it."

I tried to turn the handle, but it was locked. "What do you mean? Did something have to die to make this magic possible?"

"Blood everywhere. Very bloody. Pain and darkness. Go away."

I pushed against the door. "But there has to be a way to undo it, doesn't there? I have to get back where I belong."

The door jerked open, and Madame Isabella stood there, holding the thing that Kinyisha had called a gun. She'd also taken the time to pull red robes over her pantsuit. "Die, abomination!" She squeezed on the gun, and I dropped to the ground, as the roar of the gun nearly deafened me. Crystals shatter around me.

Madame Isabella started toward me with the gun. I jumped to my feet and hauled it out of there, as the gun roared and more crystals were shot to pieces.

Madame Isabella followed me outside. I jumped in my truck and took off. Good gods, that woman was crazy, and she was the only one who seemed to know anything about my condition. There had to be a way to have a rational discussion with her. I needed to get home before it was too late.

I called Kinyisha on my cell phone. She and Sandy had given me their numbers the night before. When Kinyisha answered, I yelled into the phone, "Madame Isabella just tried to shoot me."

To my surprise and annoyance, Kinyisha laughed. "Did she hit you?"

"No, she shattered crystals all over her shop."

Kinyisha laughed again. "She does that sort of thing rather often. I'm not sure if she misses on purpose or if she really is that bad of a shot."

"Can you talk to her for me? She knows something about what happened to me. I need to know what. I need to get home."

Kinyisha sighed and was quiet for several moments. "I guess I could try, but I'll give her at least a day to calm down. She won't be reasonable after shooting up her shop. She'll try to charge me for all the broken crystal."

I wasn't happy about waiting, but I could see Kinyisha's point. She told me she'd call me when she knew anything.

# CHAPTER 11

I made it back to Hamilton about midnight. Exhausted, I fell into Joshua's bed. I dreamed again of Joshua in my body.

He walked into the breakfast room, dressed in my favorite green dress. The gathered nobles rose and bowed as he entered. Joshua looked taken aback, but before he could do anything, Duke Tearlach hurried forward and pulled out my usual chair. "How are you this morning, Your Highness?" he asked, smiling.

Joshua looked at the chair and sat. "Ah, thank you. I'm doing great. You?"

Tearlach took the place next to me, as he did whenever possible. "Marvelous, Your Highness, now that you've returned to court. I'm sure your spiritual retreat did you no end of good, but you were certainly missed here."

Joshua looked completely lost. "Well, I . . . I missed you, too," Joshua said, and Tearlach beamed. I'd never said anything so encouraging to the young noble. A servant put a small plate of fruit in front of Joshua. "Is that it?" Joshua asked.

The servant looked surprised. "It is Your Highness's usual breakfast."

Joshua's face fell, and he looked forlornly over at the mounds of bread, eggs, meats, cheese, pastries and nuts on the sideboard, but he said, "Er . . . yes, of course, it is." He picked up a fork and stabbed a slice of apple. At least, he seemed to be making an effort to act like me. The servant filled Joshua's goblet with wine.

Joshua picked it up and sniffed it. "Wine for breakfast?"

The servant blinked. "Would Your Highness care for something else?"

Joshua shook his head. "No, if this is the way y'all do things, it's fine with me." He took a large swallow. He noticed Tearlach was looking at him. "Mmm, is your head okay?" he asked.

Tearlach's face brightened even more. "It's so kind of Your Highness to be concerned, but yes, I assure you, it is quite all right. I trust Your Highness took no injury from the fall."

Joshua shook his head. "I don't know how y'all expect a person to ride sidesaddle. It just ain't natural."

Some of the other nobles at the table exchanged looks, but Tearlach laughed. He laughed at almost everything I said. "I can see what you mean, Your Highness. It would certainly be more difficult to pursue a stag without the horse between your knees."

"Stag? That's the same thing as a deer, ain't it?" Joshua asked.

Tearlach blinked, but answered, "Yes, Your Highness, I believe it is."

"You like hunting, then?" Joshua asked.

Tearlach's eyes glowed. "I'm afraid I do, Your Highness. The bay of the dogs, the challenge of the sport is quite invigorating. In fact, Lord Murdo"—he gestured at the young noble sitting across the table—"and I have a hunt planned for tomorrow morning. Several particularly large stags have been sighted in the eastern forest. They should make interesting sport." He glanced shyly at Joshua. "I don't suppose Your Highness would care to accompany us?"

Across the table, Lord Murdo rolled his eyes, probably at his friend's ignorant question. Everyone knew that, according to my father, princesses didn't hunt with anything other than falcons, and a falcon certainly couldn't take down a stag.

"Oh, yeah," Joshua smiled, looking more comfortable. "I never imagined y'all doing something so normal. I'm sure you hunt with bows and all, but I'm pretty good with a bow."

Tearlach looked surprised. "I wasn't aware of that, Your Highness. I would love to witness your skill. I assure you we'd be more than happy to have Your Highness's company. Wouldn't we, Murdo?" He looked across the table at his friend.

Lord Murdo looked like he was struggling to keep a straight face, but he bowed. "Of course, Your Highness. It would most assuredly be a pleasure."

Joshua stabbed a slice of peach.

Tearlach watched Joshua eat it. "Your Highness, pardon me for saying so, but you don't seem quite pleased with your breakfast this morning. Would you care for something more than fruit?"

Joshua smile's widened. "You bet I would. I think we may well be friends."

Tearlach looked like he was going to float out of his chair with happiness. Dear gods, how could Joshua lead him on like that? Tearlach turned to the waiting servant. "Get Her Highness a proper breakfast."

The servant blinked, then bowed. "Of course, Your Grace." He dished up a large plate of food from the sideboard and placed it in front of Joshua.

"Now that's more like it," Joshua said, and dug in.

"It's nice to see a woman with a healthy appetite, Your Highness," Tearlach said.

Joshua brought the fork to his mouth, but looked uncertain. He chewed, swallowed, and took a gulp of wine. He took a smaller forkful of food for the next bite. I realized how out of his depth Joshua was in pretending to be me. He didn't have a clue on proper court protocol, and he didn't have anyone to teach him. When I didn't understand something, I went to Uncle Gilly; even if that always led to a discussion of aliens, he still helped me out, and I didn't have the entire court watching me all the time like Joshua did.

Joshua seemed to eat as carefully as he could, glancing around the room to see if he was doing all right. The other nobles pointedly avoided looking at him. He reached for his wine glass and drained it. The servant immediately filled it. Joshua ate about half the food on the plate and pushed it away. "Geez, this body gets full fast," he said, then blushed as if he knew he shouldn't have said that.

Tearlach, of course, laughed. "Lord Murdo and I were going to try our luck in the Hall of Games this morning. Would Your Highness care to accompany us?"

Joshua leaned toward Tearlach. "Card games? Gambling?"

Tearlach looked surprised. "Yes, of course, Your Highness."

"Hot damn," Joshua said, and pounded Tearlach on the shoulder. "This princess thing might not be so bad. I was afraid they'd be having me do embroidery or something."

Tearlach laughed harder than ever. "We all know Your Highness was never one for needlework. Shall we?" Tearlach rose and offered his arm.

Joshua got up and clapped Tearlach on the shoulder. "Lead on," he said, and gestured for Tearlach to proceed him.

Tearlach looked confused at this breach of protocol, but he recovered. "This way, Your Highness." They walked out of the room together. Lord Murdo hurried to follow.

When they entered the Hall of Games, all the lords and ladies stopped what they were doing and bowed. Joshua raised his hand, as if to wave, but before he could, Tearlach asked, "Would Your Highness care to play Bassett or Primero or perhaps One-and-Thirty?"

Joshua dropped his hand. "You got Poker?" he asked.

Tearlach blinked. "I'm afraid I'm unfamiliar with that game, Your Highness. If Your Highness would care to explain the rules, I'm sure we could set up a game. How many players does it require?"

"Anywhere from four to six is good." Joshua grabbed a wine goblet from a servant. "Keep it filled," he ordered.

The servant bowed low. "Yes, Your Highness."

With a clear sense of importance, Tearlach hurriedly rounded up Lord Murdo and three other players and emptied one of the tables for the game. "Will these cards do?" He handed Joshua a pack of cards. "Do we require chips?"

"Yes, chips would be great." Joshua sat his wine goblet down on the table and looked through the cards. "Wouldn't you know it? I guess playing cards are as old as James said they were."

"I beg your pardon, Your Highness?" Tearlach said.

Joshua shook himself and sat at the table. The five other nobles took their places, and Joshua explained the game.

"Somewhat like Primero, then, Your Highness?" Lord Murdo asked.

Joshua shrugged. "If you say so." He dealt the first hand and drained his wine goblet. A servant immediately refilled it.

* * *

I woke to someone pounding on Joshua's trailer door. "Your truck's out here," Jocelyn called. "I know you're in there."

I groaned and rolled over. My ribs protested. They felt much better than they had yesterday morning, but they were still tender, as was my nose.

Jocelyn pounded again. "Come open your damned door, and explain where you've been!"

Knowing she wouldn't go away, I stumbled out of bed and unlocked the door.

She took one look at me. "What in God's name happened to you?"

I let her in and sat back on the bed, wiping the sleep from my eyes. "Had a bit of trouble after the rodeo Saturday night."

She put her hands on her hips. "You mean you got in some stupid fight. Geez, Joshua will you ever grow up? If the other guy looks worse than you, he's dead."

I sighed, wondering how I could get her out of there quickly. "What do you want, Jocelyn?"

"You disappear for half a week without even the courtesy of a phone call and you wonder what I want? Meemaw's worried sick. Missing your own birthday party is one thing, but what got into you to miss James's after you promised you'd show up?"

I groaned. I'd forgotten all about James's party. Still, it was better Joshua's family thought me rude than crazy. "I had things to do."

Jocelyn's eyes narrowed. "You seem to have forgotten who was there for you when your momma died! Whose shoulder you wept your eyes out on because you wouldn't let the guys see you crying! Maybe you think you can keep secrets from me, but you're going to explain to Meemaw. Get dressed. I'm taking you to her."

"Just tell her I'm okay."

"I will do no such thing. She's been half out of her mind. Calling hospitals to see if you crashed and killed yourself. Calling police stations to see if you got yourself locked up. You at least need to have the courtesy to tell her yourself."

I couldn't see any way out of it. "Fine. Just let me get dressed."

"You got five minutes," she said, and went out, slamming the door.

As I dressed, I tried to figure out what I was going to say to Meemaw. I wished I could just tell her I was tracking down a witch.

When I came out, Jocelyn was standing by her car, fuming. "I'll take my own truck," I said.

"Fine," she snapped. "I'll see you there." She got in her car, slammed the door, and sped out of there.

Holy Cailleach, she was angry.

When I reached Meemaw's house, Jocelyn's car was parked out front, but Jocelyn was already inside. Taking a deep breath, I got out of the truck.

When I walked into Meemaw's kitchen, she had her arms around Jocelyn. "Thank the Lord," she whispered.

She let go of Jocelyn, looking so relieved to see me I felt guilty. "I'm sorry, Meemaw," I said, gathering her in a hug. "I shouldn't have worried you."

She pushed away from me and gestured at the table. "Have a seat, and tell me everything."

I sat, and told her the story I'd prepared. I pointed at my face. "As you can see, I got in a fight Saturday after the rodeo."

"A bar fight?" Jocelyn interrupted. "Over a girl probably."

I grimaced, but I said, "Yes, a bar fight over a girl." That part was technically true. "I lost, obviously, so I stayed over at a friend's house."

Meemaw frowned. "Oprah says there's no need to use your fists when you can use your words." She touched my face. "Did you go to a doctor?"

"My friend's brother is an EMT, and he came over and checked me out." I hoped that made sense to her. I still hadn't a clue what an EMT was.

Meemaw nodded. "That's good."

"On Sunday, I went up to Auburn to see a girl."

Jocelyn made a noise of disgust. "The same girl you were fighting over, no doubt."

"Yes, the same girl. Her name's Eileen."

Jocelyn leaned across the table. "You couldn't bother calling to tell Meemaw this?"

I clenched my teeth. "I told you my phone's broken."

Jocelyn rolled her eyes dramatically. "Eileen doesn't have a phone? You couldn't have used a payphone?"

I realized why Jocelyn was being such a bitch. I'd hurt her feelings. Holy Cailleach, what was I going to do now? "I'm sorry, Jocelyn. I should have called. I'm a selfish, inconsiderate bastard."

Meemaw patted my arm. "No need to be so hard on yourself, Josh, darling. Just don't let it happen again."

"And get your phone fixed," Jocelyn added, although she seemed friendlier now.

When I left Meemaw's, I seemed to have defused the tension. But things were getting out of hand. If I continued to ignore Joshua's family like I'd been doing, I'd cause ill feelings, but I feared the more time I spend around them, the more they'd notice odd things about me. It was hard enough to try to act like Joshua at the rodeos for only a few hours at a time. Damn it all, I had to get back in my own body, back into a world I understood.

When I got back to Joshua's place, Uncle Gilly gave me another lecture. "Meemaw called me two, three times a day, checking to see if you were back. I know you're an alien and all, but you need to have a little more consideration for the old lady."

"I told her I'm sorry, okay?" I said. "I'm up to my neck in problems. Joshua's relatives just haven't been on my mind a whole lot."

"Humph," Uncle Gilly said. "Neither have chores around here."

I wanted to scream. I had witches trying to kill me and my bastard brother trying to steal my throne. Yet I was supposed to worry about farm chores? "I'm trying to get my own body back! If I succeed, Joshua will be back here, and everyone will be happier, okay?" I stomped off to Joshua's trailer.

\* \* \*

Later that day, Kinyisha called me. She told me that Madame Isabella had been Irene again when she tried to talk to her. She'd let me know if and when she found out anything useful. I tried to repress my disappointment.

# CHAPTER 12

On Thursday night, I met Kinyisha and Sandy at Kinyisha's apartment in Auburn. I'd heard nothing from them since Kinyisha's call. The apartment was spotless. Hardwood floors gleamed under black and red masks on the walls. A plethora of house plants spread over shelves lined with wooden statues of animals I didn't recognize. Her couch had black and white stripes and looked firm and uncomfortable. Except for the pentacle inscribed on the floor, the place looked like an overgrown forest.

Sandy greeted me in a friendly fashion. "Hello, cowboy."

Kinyisha clipped a long lock of my hair and braided it into a ring that would fit my pinky. She must have done the hair braiding thing before because she whipped it up fast. The witches opened the curtains wide so the light of the moon shined through the window, hitting at the center of the pentacle. Kinyisha put the hair ring in the center and drew a big circle in chalk around the pentacle. The witches stepped inside the circle and left me outside. Kinyisha asked me to close the circle with a drop of my blood. I got out my pocket knife, nicked my left thumb, and squeezed out a drop. As soon as my blood touched the chalk, a surge of energy swept around the circle, almost as if an invisible wall were springing to life. I jumped back. I'd never felt magic quite like this.

The witches lit candles and incense at each point of the pentacle. They linked hands and chanted in their strange language. Still chanting, they both cut themselves and bled a drop onto the ring. I felt the power in the circle flow toward the ring. Then Kinyisha smudged the chalk with her foot, breaking the circle. She handed me the ring. "This should do it, as long as the one trying to curse you isn't too powerful."

* * *

I slept in Kinyisha's parking lot that night. When I finally fell asleep, I dreamed Joshua was in my body lying on a cot in the same tower room where he'd been locked up for a month.

Joshua groaned and took in his surroundings. "Oh, shit. What did I do?" he said. He tried to sit up, but promptly threw up and lay back down.

Before long, a key turned in the lock, and a servant entered with breakfast. Joshua looked at the food with revulsion. "Get that out of here," he ordered, and the servant withdrew.

A few minutes later, Sylvia arrived, followed by servants with a tub and bucket upon bucket of warm water. While another servant cleaned up the vomit, Sylvia helped Joshua undress and into the tub. "What happened?" Joshua asked.

"You mean besides getting drunk, cursing everyone in the game room, telling them you're not really the princess but a rodeo bull rider, and then vomiting all over Fitzrigh and the gaming tables?"

Joshua, how could you have done that? You're going to get both of us killed!

Joshua brought his hand down hard, slopping water over the side of the tub. "The old man's angry, ain't he?"

Sylvia nodded. "You could say that, Your Highness."

After Joshua was clean, Sylvia helped him dress in a midnight blue silk with stars embroidered around the edges and started combing his hair.

The door opened again, and in walked Fitzrigh. He smiled like it was Solstice and his birthday rolled into one. "You've really made this too easy, sister. Father is furious at your display yesterday. He'll announce me heir by the end of the week."

Joshua's hands formed fists. "You did this, didn't you?"

Fitzrigh laughed. "You did it to yourself."

Joshua got to his feet. "That's not what I meant. I saw that thing you did to the back of that guy's head. It was magic, wasn't it? You're the reason I'm here instead of Daulphina. You stuck me in a woman's body."

Fitzrigh's eyes widened. "I'll be sure to repeat that accusation to Father."

Joshua launched himself across the room and locked his hands around Fitzrigh's neck. Before he could even squeeze properly, Fitzrigh did something with his hand and Joshua flew half-way across the small room, landing on his butt. By Cailleach, since when had Fitzrigh had such power?

Joshua looked at Fitzrigh in terror. "You're a witch!"

Fitzrigh pointed a finger at him. "Touch me again, and I'll give you worse than that. Now I must go and console Father over the insanity of his intended heir." Fitzrigh left.

"Christ Jesus! How did he do that?"

Sylvia shook her head fearfully. "I don't know."

"Fuck them all! They're not taking my head!"

* * *

I woke feeling sick to my stomach. Things were getting out of hand. By Cailleach, I'd find the witch Fitzrigh sent, and I'd get back before it was too late.

Late that morning, I got a garbage bag from Kinyisha and cleaned the trash out of Joshua's truck so there was room for the witches, but Sandy called just before we were going to leave, saying that a friend of hers had been in an accident, and she couldn't come.

"Will you alone be enough?" I asked Kinyisha.

"What choice do we have? Eileen won't come, and Madame Isabella is still Irene."

"Where did you get this beat up rattrap?" she complained as she climbed in my truck.

"It's not my truck; it Joshua's, and I can't afford anything better."

She nodded. "That I can believe."

Kinyisha and I headed to Greenville, Alabama, about an hour south of Montgomery. On the drive down, I told her about my dream.

"So Joshua's not having an easy time being you? Doesn't surprise me," Kinyisha said. "I can hardly see you as a princess."

"But I am a princess," I protested.

* * *

When we reached the rodeo grounds, I got out of my truck and walked around to her side to open the door for her because the door handle was missing from inside the passenger side door. I helped her down.

On our way to pay my fee and check which bull I'd drawn, we ran into Ben Walker. Walker looked from Kinyisha to me with disgust. "I should have known you were one of those."

"One of what?" I said.

"A race traitor, Killenyen." His hands formed fists as if to remind me just how badly he'd beaten me.

I wasn't scared. He wouldn't start anything on rodeo grounds.

Kinyisha stepped closer. "You've got a hair on your shirt," she said to Walker, and plucked it off.

"Don't you touch me!" Walker brushed off his shirt as if to get rid of some foul substance. He turned to me. "I'm just telling you, Killenyen. Her kind isn't welcome around here." He stalked off. He took about two steps when, out of the corner of my eye, I saw Kinyisha give the hair a tug. Walker suddenly tumbled face first into a pile of horse shit.

I smiled as Walker got to his knees, sputtering. "You just made my day," I whispered to Kinyisha. "You'll have to show me how you did that."

Walker whirled off the ground. "You'll pay for that," he said, pointing at Kinyisha, but I didn't see how he could accuse her of anything. He stalked off in the direction of the bathroom.

"So that's the asshole Eileen was dating?" Kinyisha asked. "No wonder she doesn't want any more to do with him."

We reached the rodeo office, and I went in to pay my fee. Dan was checking the draw. He looked startled to see me. "What are you doing here? After last week, there's no way in hell you should be riding."

"I'm fine," I assured him. "Don't be a mother hen. I can take care of myself."

Dan grunted, as I knew he would. He wouldn't keep bugging me after being called a mother hen. Men were like that. I paid and checked my draw. I'd drawn Kracken.

Dan and I left the rodeo office, and I introduced him to Kinyisha.

Dan smiled. "Welcome to the world of rodeo. Any friend of Josh's is a friend of mine."

We talked as we walked to the chutes and the bull pen. "How long you been riding rodeo?" Kinyisha asked him.

"Shoot." Dan blew out a breath. "I grew up in rodeo. My dad was a bull rider."

I excused myself briefly to fix up the spell. When I rejoined them, they were laughing.

Dan clapped me on the shoulder. "Kinyisha was just telling me about Walker falling face first into horse shit. Damn, do I wish I'd seen that."

The rodeo was about to start, and Kinyisha went off to find a seat. Dan watched after her departing figure. "Good going, man. This is more like the Josh Killenyen I know. I haven't seen you with a girl in more than a month. I was starting to get worried, especially after you turned down that Bunny last week."

"Nice ass," Cody added.

I shrugged and decided I'd just let them think Kinyisha was a girlfriend. It simplified things.

When it came time for the bull riding, I climbed onto Kracken's back. I breathed slowly to center myself and got myself and my rope ready. I nodded, and the chute opened. Kracken roared into the arena, and adrenaline surged through me. Before hardly any time had passed, the 8-second horn blared.

I did my increasingly graceful dismount and ran for the fence. I waited for my score. The announcer announced an eighty-two, which meant that unless somebody got real lucky tomorrow, I'd walk off with top prize money. Even better, Walker lost his seat in the first second of his ride, but unfortunately, the bull's hooves didn't even come close to stomping him.

I met Kinyisha after the rodeo. "You stayed on," she said, "and I didn't feel any magic."

"I didn't either." The lack of magic was a problem. If I couldn't find who cursed me, I couldn't make him tell me how to get home.

I saw Walker coming, put my arm around Kinyisha, and smirked at him. He glared and walked by. Kinyisha shook herself out from under my arm. "Don't get too free with that arm. You aren't my kind."

As I was packing up my gear, a woman approached with a boy of about five. She was holding a black box with a short tube on the front of it, probably another piece of technology I knew nothing about. "Excuse me. Joshua Killenyen, isn't it?"

"Yes, ma'am," I said, wondering if I should know her.

"My son would like a picture with the bull rider if you don't mind." She waved the black box like it should mean something to me.

I looked to Kinyisha for help. "What's she talking about?" I mouthed.

Fortunately, Kinyisha got it. "Just stand there looking at his mother with your hand on the boy's shoulder."

It seemed a bizarre thing to do, but I followed her directions. The mother brought the black box in front of her face and said, "Smile."

I did, and a bright light flashed from the box. "Good gods." I turned my head and put my hand up to block the light.

The mother said, "Thank you," and walked off with the boy.

"What was that?" I asked Kinyisha.

She laughed. "You've never seen a camera before?"

I shook my head.

"It takes pictures. My cell phone will do it, too." She stood next to me, put her phone out in front of us, and pushed a button. "See, there we are." She held the phone up to me, and I saw a perfect likeness of the two of us.

"Holy Cailleach!" I took the phone and stared at the image. "How can it do that?"

Kinyisha shrugged. "It just does. If you really want to understand it, ask Sandy. She's a photography major." She took her phone back. "You can print the pictures out on paper if you want to." She took something out of her purse and handed it to me. It was a picture depicting Kinyisha with an older couple and two younger boys. "That's my family."

"Dear gods!" This must be how the picture of Joshua and his mother had been produced. "Can my phone do that, too?" I got it out of my gear bag and handed it to her. I always put the phone in my gear bag when I rode so it wouldn't get broken.

"Of course," she said. "All phones do it." She showed me how.

I used the phone to take a picture of Kinyisha and stared at the image. "How many times can I do that before the power wears off?" I asked.

"You can probably fit a thousand or more on there. Then you can download them to a computer and take more."

I just stared at her, deciding not to ask about downloading or computers. For now, my mind was too blown away about the idea of cameras. I look around for something else to take a picture of. Dan was walking up, so I took one of him.

"What you talking a picture of my ugly face for?" he asked. "It might break your phone."

I looked to Kinyisha in alarm. I didn't want this marvelous technology broken. She shook her head, and I decided Dan was making a joke. I laughed.

"Want to go get a few beers?" Dan asked.

I looked at Kinyisha, and she said, "Sure, why not?"

We went to a local bar and had a few. I made sure to limit my intake. I didn't want to start talking about princesses again, especially not around Dan. I kept snapping pictures of everything: the bar, the bartender, the pitcher of beer on the table, the band playing the twangy music everyone around Joshua seemed to like, even Joshua's boots. People in Asteria would never believe this was possible. It took an artist hours upon hours to paint a single portrait.

"Would you put your damned phone away?" Dan asked. "You're acting like you've never seen a bar before."

Damn it, I was acting strange again. I hurriedly put the phone in my pocket. I'd take pictures later when no one was around.

Dan, who also stayed on his bull but only scored a 75, toasted me for another great ride. "Although your boy here"—he gestured toward me—"let someone else win last week, he's been riding the best I've ever seen him. He just might be getting ready for the PBR."

"PBR?" Kinyisha asked.

"Professional Bull Riders." Dan answered, and I was glad because I didn't have a clue what he was talking about. "Josh and I ride for the Professional Cowboy Association; we're strictly local, very minor league. The PBR's like the majors for bull riders. That's how you win the big money. You get to the top of that, and some of those guys pull in $100,000 a year or more."

"Wow!" Kinyisha said, and I shared the sentiment. I didn't realize it was possible to earn more money bull riding than I'd been doing. Should I check into this PBR? I could use the money. But I was cheating, and going into the majors would just be cheating on a grander scale.

After a few beers, Kinyisha and I left.

"Have fun, you two," Dan said, as we walked out. He gave me a wink behind Kinyisha's back.

We drove back to the rodeo grounds. When we got out, I used my phone to take a picture of my truck. Was there any way I could take these pictures with me when I went back to Asteria? Otherwise, no one would ever believe me.

I let down the tail gate so we could crawl into the back of the truck. Before doing so, Kinyisha put her hand on my arm. "Just so I make myself clear. We're sleeping, and nothing else. If you try anything, I'll curse your genitals"—she used a different word here—"and make them fall off."

"Don't worry. I'm a woman, remember? I'm not interested in other women that way."

* * *

In the middle of the night, I needed to take a piss, so I crawled out of the back of my truck, careful not to wake Kinyisha. I found a convenient spot and whipped it out. Times like these, I appreciated being a man. After I was done, I heard a commotion, a horse neighing, whinnying, and carrying on. I started to follow the sound, but I stopped. Last week, the deputy had told me to stay away from the horses. Still, I couldn't turn my back on a horse in need. I continued to where the horses were being kept.

I walked up, and to my chagrin, I saw it was Parrish's horse again making the commotion. She was nipping at her belly. I told myself I should just go away. But the horse looked at me with such desperation, I couldn't just let her die. I whipped off my boot and sock, plucked two hairs from the horse's mane, and made another sock horse. I bled on it, breathed on it, and willed it to be one with the suffering horse. When the magic coalesced, moisture spread from the horse's rear end throughout the sock. I used my knife and made an incision in the sock horse at the point where the moisture was most dense. I put the knife back in my pocket. I started sucking and spitting, and poison squirted out of the horse's rear. I'd gotten a good bit of it out when something cold pressed against the back of my head. It wasn't sharp, so it wasn't a knife or a sword. I thought it was probably a gun like Madame Isabella had used.

"Don't move," a voice I recognized as Parrish's said. "Keep your hands where I can see them. What in the hell are you doing with my horse?"

I lifted my hands nice and slow, still holding onto the sock horse in my right hand and trying to think of a reasonable explanation. In a world that didn't believe in magic, I couldn't think of any, so I decided to tell the truth. "Your horse has been poisoned. I'm trying to help it."

Parrish laughed an unpleasant laugh. "How would you know my horse has been poisoned unless you did it yourself? I've already called the cops. They'll be here any minute."

"I was just trying to help."

"Liar!" Parrish drew the gun back and hit me on the side of the head. I went down hard. I struggled to my knees, but Parrish kicked me in the rear, sending me sprawling. I rolled over. He shined a flashlight in my face. "You move from there, Killenyen, and so help me God, I will shoot you."

I believed him, so I stayed still with my hands plainly in sight. I hoped I'd gotten enough poison out so the horse wouldn't die, but I was certain it would still be ill. "Look, your horse is ill. Just let me suck on my sock, and it'll be—"

He kicked me in the ribs, aggravating my injuries. "Shut up, Killenyen. I don't know why you've decided to sabotage me, but this is the last time." He snatched the sock horse out of my hand and threw it aside.

A car rolled up, shining bright lights onto us and blinding me further. The door of the car opened, and a voice called out, "Put the gun down." Parrish backed up from me a few steps and did as he'd been told. "Now step away from it." Parrish did, and a sheriff's deputy walked forward with his gun drawn. "You mind telling me what's going on here?" The deputy positioned himself so he could keep an eye on both of us.

"This worthless piece of shit"—Parrish gestured toward me—"is messing with my horse again. I think he's poisoned it."

"Did you?" the deputy asked me.

"No, I didn't. Can I get up?"

The deputy nodded, and I got slowly to my feet. But the blow to the head in combination with my weakness from healing sent me face first into a pile of horse shit.

* * *

When I woke up, my hands were cuffed behind my back, and the deputy was wiping my face off with a handkerchief. I didn't think I'd been out long. A hand grabbed me by the shoulder. "Come on, Killenyen," the deputy said, and I struggled to my feet, a harder accomplishment than you might have thought with your hands cuffed behind you, especially since I was wearing only one boot. Besides, I was still dizzy.

The deputy dragged me away and shoved me in the back of the police car, muttering, "You have the right to remain silent. Anything you say can and will be used against you in a court of law. You have a right to an attorney. If you cannot afford an attorney, one will be appointed for you. Do you understand these rights?"

I thought I indicated I did. I put my head between my knees, hoping the world would stop spinning. I must have blacked out again because the next thing I knew, the car stopped in back of the sheriff's station. The deputy half led, half dragged me through the back door. I stumbled along on uneven legs. He took everything out of my pockets, unlocked my cuffs, dipped each of my fingers in ink for some odd reason, and put me in a room with plain white walls, a table, and four chairs.

I sank down in one of the chairs. "You don't look so good," the deputy said. "Would you like a cup of coffee?"

I nodded. "Cream and a lot of sugar."

The deputy was gone for a long time, so I put my head on the table. I must have fallen asleep because someone shook me awake. It wasn't the deputy. The sheriff was a couple of inches taller than me and broader across the shoulders. He handed me a cup of coffee and sat across from me. I picked up the coffee and grimaced as I took a sip. It was black. I didn't see how Jocelyn and Meemaw could drink it that way.

"I'm Sheriff Morris," he said, sitting down across from me. The sheriff interrogated me about what I was doing at the rodeo.

I told him I'd gotten up in the middle of the night to take a piss, heard the horses making noise, and went to investigate. He nodded like he didn't believe a word I said. "Do you recognize this?" He sat my poppet on the table. I hesitated, unsure whether I should own it. "I couldn't help noticing you're missing a sock, and I'm willing to bet the sock you're hiding under your boot is a match. Care to prove me wrong?"

"It's my sock," I answered.

"Why is it tied up with what looks like horse hair?"

If I told him it was a magic spell, he'd probably have me locked up. "Er . . . I like to make sock animals. You know, for the children."

He continued nodding. "You get up in the middle of the night, take a piss, wander to the horse stable, and use your dirty, filthy sock to make sock animals for all the children that are hanging around at three in the morning?"

I reddened as I realized I might really be in trouble. What could they do it me? I needed some advice, and I could only think of one person I could ask. I didn't know if they'd let me, but I said, "I want to make a phone call."

The sheriff scowled, but handed me my phone, which was fortunate because it was the only phone I knew how to use.

"What you doing calling at four in the blessed a.m.?" Uncle Gilly complained when he answered his phone.

I told Uncle Gilly what had happened. "How much trouble am I in? What should I do?"

Uncle Gilly sighed loudly. "I'll call Meemaw, and she'll get your Uncle Braeden down there. Don't say anything until he gets there."

"He hates Joshua," I objected.

"Yeah, but he's family so he has to help."

I was skeptical, but decided to trust Uncle Gilly. When I hung up, I told the sheriff my lawyer was on the way and I wasn't supposed to say anything until he got here.

The sheriff's scowl deepened, but he had me put in a cell. I asked that a note be taken to Kinyisha, so she wouldn't wonder what had happened to me. With nothing else to do, I took a nap.

\* \* \*

Some time later, the outer door opened, and a deputy came in to get me. I limped along to the same barren room. This time both the sheriff and Uncle Braeden waited. Neither seemed happy to see me. "Sit down, son," the sheriff said. "Now your lawyer's here, let's talk about your sock. I couldn't help noticing that it's wet, especially around the hole in the horse's ass. What's it wet with?"

I shrugged. "Could be anything."

"Guess it could be, but our guys can't figure out what. So I ask again, what's on your sock?"

I opened my mouth, but Uncle Braeden cut me off. "Don't answer that, Joshua." I gladly closed my mouth since I didn't know what I was going to say. "Despite how bizarre my client's actions may be, I don't see what they have to do with your poisoned horse."

"It's damned suspicious, that's what it is," the sheriff insisted. "What sane man makes a horse out of his filthy sock in the middle of the                                                                                        night?"

"We aren't here to debate my client's mental stability, but whether or not he has committed a crime. As far as I can tell, your evidence is circumstantial at best if not downright ludicrous."

"That horse has been poisoned, and no one else was around. Who else could have done it?"

"You said his prints aren't on the syringe. Obviously, someone else did it, and my client is telling the truth. He heard the horses making noise and came to investigate." I nodded in agreement.

This went on for some time. The sheriff continued to try to get me to admit to poisoning the horse, and Uncle Braeden kept telling me to shut up. After what seemed like hours, Uncle Braeden asked, "Is my client under arrest?"

"Not at the moment," the sheriff answered. "But we have an ongoing investigation, and he might yet be."

"I take it he is free to go."

"For now," he said, but he pushed a piece of paper across the table. "A restraining order has been issued against him going within a hundred yards of Tyler Parrish's horse Spitfire at this and future rodeos."

"Fine," I said. I'd let the horse die next time.

Uncle Braeden took the piece of paper and read it over. "I assure you my client will comply with this order." He got up, and I did, too. "Good day, sheriff," he said, and I followed him out the door.

I got my other boot back and put it on without a sock. They also gave me back my wallet, pocket knife, and keys. Uncle Braeden drove me back to the rodeo grounds in stony silence. I wasn't sure what to say, so I stared out the window. When he parked beside my truck, he turned to me. "Do you care to explain the sock to me?"

"Not really."

His face turned red, and a vein in his temple throbbed. "I don't know what you've been up to, but whatever it is, it better not happen again."

"I didn't do anything," I said, opening the door. "Thanks for coming, by the way." I hated having to thank him, but he'd probably saved me a lot of trouble.

As soon as I shut the door, he drove off. Kinyisha waited beside my truck. "Why were you arrested?" she asked.

I explained to her what had happened. I thanked the gods I had someone I could tell the truth to.

"So you think someone is trying to sabotage the roping horses, Tyler Parrish's in particular?"

"I guess. I never paid much attention to the ropers."

"Leave it to the police. I'm sure they'll figure it out."

* * *

Nothing funny happened when I rode Saturday. Dear gods, how was I going to locate the witch and find out how to get home? At least, nobody topped my score. I ended up with $1096 in prize money.

# CHAPTER 13

I got Kinyisha back to Auburn at about two in the morning. I planned to sleep the rest of the night in the back of my truck even though it was like a blazing sauna in there. Kinyisha must have been feeling friendlier toward me because she invited me to sleep on her sofa instead. Since her apartment was air-conditioned, I took her up on her offer. Unfortunately, the striped sofa was as uncomfortable as it looked, and I tossed and turned before falling asleep.

I dreamed of my bastard brother. He was in bed with a woman. I felt like a voyeur until the woman turned her head. What by all the gods' names was my stepmother doing in bed with Fitzrigh? I'd thought they'd hated each other. Had *they* conspired to give my body to another and take my throne?

They finished you-know-what-ing, and Fitzrigh rolled off of her. He smiled in a self-satisfied way. She put her head on his chest. "You look pleased with yourself."

"Shouldn't I be? It won't be long before dear old Dad proclaims me heir. The bull rider's performance was magnificent."

She threw back her head and laughed. "I wish I'd been there to see it."

Fitzrigh chuckled. "You always did like to watch. Like you did when I slit Jenna's throat."

No! If he wouldn't kill me, why kill my little sister? She'd been no threat to him. She hadn't even wanted to be queen. Damn him, I'll disembowel him for this!

\* \* \*

Kinyisha tried to feed me breakfast—toaster waffles and cold cereal, but I was so upset I couldn't eat. Kinyisha asked me what was wrong, and I told her about my dream.

Kinyisha patted my arm. "You sure it's true? You sure he killed your little sister?"

I struggled against tears. "He said he did. Why would he lie about a thing like that?"

\* \* \*

When I got back to Hamilton, I spent the rest of the day pacing outside my trailer, trying to think of anything that would help me get back and avenge my sister. But it couldn't be true. Jenna couldn't be dead. Uncle Gilly saw me and came over. "Problem?" he asked.

"Yes, I have a problem." I told him about my dreams.

"Humph! Those aliens sure do have their ways of interfering, don't they? Maybe if you apologized to them, they'd put you back."

"Just how in tarnation am I supposed to apologize to aliens?" Not that I believed aliens had anything to do with it.

Uncle Gilly shrugged. "You could try my radio."

I put my hands on my hips. "You have a radio that talks to aliens?"

He nodded. "They haven't talked back yet, but I can feel them listening. Worth a shot, isn't it?"

I closed my eyes praying for patience. "I don't think aliens are responsible. I'm from a parallel world, not another planet."

Uncle Gilly nodded again. "And people say I'm the crazy one. Come on, it wouldn't hurt to try."

He kept insisting. Finally, since I had nothing on other means of getting home, I gave in and followed Uncle Gilly into his house. He led me to a room in the back that was wall-to-wall gadgets, none of which I knew the use for. On a table by the door was the poppet I'd made to cure Whisper Willow. It seemed Uncle Gilly was still trying to figure it out.

On a desk in the center of the room was a microphone backed by two huge speakers and a panel with about a hundred switches. Uncle Gilly flipped a few of the switches, tapped the microphone, flipped a few more. He repeated this half a dozen times. Finally, he was satisfied and spoke into the microphone. "Aliens, I know you're listening. You've caused quite some trouble for my friend Daulphina here. She wants to talk to you."

Although it was nice to have someone call me by my name, I felt stupid talking into the microphone. "Er, hello, aliens. Could you please put me back?" I looked over at Uncle Gilly.

He rolled his eyes. "You've got to do better than that."

I turned back to the microphone, and I soon found myself explaining all about my dreams and Joshua and how terrible a king my bastard brother would be, how he'd killed my little sister and I needed to avenge her. "He's a monster. He cares only about himself. Please, aliens, please. If y'all can hear me, y'all have to put me back. It's far more than my life on the line."

When I was done, Uncle Gilly patted me on the shoulder. "If that doesn't do it, I don't know what will."

# CHAPTER 14

The rodeo on Friday and Saturday was in Canon, Georgia. I met Sandy and Kinyisha in Auburn. Kinyisha had a major project to do that weekend, so they told me that Sandy would come with me, and Madame Isabella would meet us there.

"She's back?" I asked. "What did she say about what she saw in the crystal ball?"

Kinyisha shook her head. "She won't talk about it."

"Does she still want to kill me?" I asked.

Kinyisha shrugged. "I don't think so," she said, which wasn't exactly reassuring.

Sandy and I drove to Georgia in awkward silence for a while. At least, it was awkward for me. She kept looking at me like she was sizing me up. Finally, she asked, "What's it like being in the body of a man?"

"The hair's the worse part, or maybe the . . ." I blushed and glanced down between my legs. "Although it makes it easier to pee."

Sandy laughed, the stud in her tongue clicking against her teeth. "What I mean is have you ever . . . you know? Is it better as a man or as a woman?"

My face heated up to about ten thousand degrees. "I don't know," I finally managed to say. "I haven't done it as a man."

"Maybe you should." Sandy gave me the once over. "I wouldn't mind volunteering."

I nearly drove off the road.

*  *  *

When we reached the rodeo grounds, I opened the door for Sandy and helped her down. She took my hand and kept it, giving me a lewd look. I snatched my hand back, and she laughed a deep throaty laugh. We went to the rodeo office, and I paid my fee and checked my draw. I'd drawn a bull named Demon.

"Demon?" Sandy said, when I told her the bull's name. "Sounds downright nasty."

I shrugged. "He's a solid enough bull, but he doesn't really live up to his name."

I took her to the bull pen to check out the bulls and meet Dan and the other guys. Her multiple piercings got a lot of less than admiring looks, but Sandy asked all kinds of questions about the bulls and bull riding in general, so the boys started warming up to her. While she distracted them, I got Demon's hair.

I took Sandy back to my truck to fix the spell. She watched while I did it.

"Interesting," she said, when the spell was complete. "You call it a poppet?"

Surprised, I asked, "Don't you make poppets?"

She shook her head. "Never have. Maybe you could teach me sometime."

I told her I'd be more than happy to as we walked back to the arena. She grabbed my arm. "Come watch with me and explain everything. I've never been to a rodeo before."

We found a seat in the stands. "I guess Madame Isabella isn't coming," I said.

Sandy shrugged. "You can never tell with her."

Sandy broke out in laughter as the horse drill team performed while the announcer talked about America, God, and Ford trucks. "Is that the Holy Trinity of the rodeo world?" she asked me, not bothering to lower her voice. I wasn't sure what she was talking about, but those seated around us glared at her as if she'd profaned a sacred name.

After watching the men's calf roping and the women's breakaway roping, Sandy frowned. "So the men have to jump off their horse and tie up the calf, but all the women do is hook the rope around the calf's neck. That says women aren't capable of competing on equal terms. I thought you wanted to be queen, and you put up with this bullshit?" Again, she didn't bother lowering her voice, and now I got the unfriendly stares. People scooted farther away from us.

Being so focused on my own riding, I hadn't paid much attention to the rest of the rodeo, but she certainly had a point. "I have to make money somehow."

"Bull riding's your only option?"

"I don't know what else to do. I don't understand your world."

She patted me on the thigh. "I'm sorry. I hadn't thought about how hard this must be for you. I guess a woman's got to do what a woman's got to do." I had to blink back tears. No one else had ever expressed any sympathy for my plight.

I got up and told her I had to get ready to ride. She grabbed my hand. "You'll have to tell me what the other bull riders say about me. They were looking at me like I was some sort of freak."

When I got to the area behind the chutes, Austin was the first one to speak up. "You've got to tell me. Does she have her nipples pierced?"

I'd thought I'd gotten used to their crude comments, but this caught me off guard. "I don't know." I was sure I was turning a million shades of red.

Nash punched me in the shoulder. "Oh, come one, Killenyen. Don't play the virgin. What I want to know is what does it feel like when she goes down on you with that stud in her tongue?"

Shocked, I exploded, "Good gods! Do y'all ever think of anything besides sex?"

"Bull riding," Dan said.

"Beer," Austin added.

"Holy hell!" Cody exclaimed. "What in God's name is that?" He pointed.

I looked, and Madame Isabella was marching toward us. She was wearing a red robe with pentacles all over it and a matching witch's hat. The crowd went nearly silent as everyone stopped what they were doing and stared. Madame Isabella seemed not to notice the attention.

Madame Isabella stopped in front of me, causing Joshua's friends' mouths to drop open. "If we can catch whose responsible for the black magic tonight, I've decided I won't kill you," she announced.

"That's good," I said, worried about what would happen if we didn't catch him or her. I tried to determine if she was carrying her gun, but her robe was so loose I couldn't tell.

Madame Isabella walked away without another word.

"Christ Jesus, Joshua!" Dan said. "Who was that?"

I scrambled to come up with an answer. "A friend of my mother's," I tried.

"But your mom's dead, and why would a friend of hers be talking about killing you?"

"Er . . . Isabella and my mom were very close friends. She went insane with grief when my mom died. Decided black magic was responsible for the car accident, and since it was on my birthday, she blamed me."

Dan and the other cowboys looked like they didn't believe a word I said, but I didn't know how else to explain Madame Isabella, so I grabbed my gear and headed for the chutes.

When I got on my bull, I spied Madame Isabella by the arena fence, holding her hands in the air and twirling in circles. Good gods! I thought Sandy was hard to explain.

I was the only bull rider to stay on. I scored a seventy-nine, which was not so high that someone wasn't likely to beat it tomorrow. More importantly, nothing funny happened, which worried me. If my enemy didn't make another attempt, how was I supposed to catch him and make him tell me how to get back to my world?

While I was packing my gear, someone screamed, "She's got a gun!"

I looked up. Madame Isabella was barreling toward me with her gun in hand. The crowd scattered out of her way, leaving her a free shot at me. Sandy ran after her, yelling, "Madame Isabella, no!"

Unexpectedly, Madame Isabella stopped and waited for Sandy. "But it's an abomination! If we can't get rid of the dark witch, we at least need to get rid of the black magic." She pointed her gun at me.

Sandy put her hand on Madame Isabella's arm, pressing it down so that the gun pointed at the ground. Madame Isabella didn't seem to resist. "Please, Madame Isabella," Sandy said. "We need to give him another chance. It's not his fault someone worked the spell on him."

Madame Isabella shrugged. "Well, if you're sure." She tucked the gun into the pocket of her robe and stalked off.

"Thanks," I told Sandy. "If it's all the same to you, I think it best if she not come to any more rodeos."

Sandy nodded in agreement, and Joshua's friends started crowding around. "I thought the crazy bitch was going to shoot you," Dan said. "How can the loony bird still be out to get you after five years?"

"Er . . . it comes and goes."

"Whatever. We're all going out from some beers. Y'all want to come?" Cody asked Sandy and me.

"You going to a cowboy bar?" Sandy asked.

"Hell, yes!" Nash said.

"I've got to check this out," Sandy said, and the guys nodded their heads appreciatively.

Sandy and I followed Dan and the others to a bar called The Flats. Once we got into my truck, she asked, "What did they say about me?"

Heating up yet again, I told her.

She laughed. "If you want to find out what's pierced, all you have to do is ask." She clicked her tongue stud against her teeth.

I tried to ignore the innuendo. We got to the bar, found a table, and ordered a couple of pitchers of beer.

In addition to the drinking tables, there were several odd tables with little balls on them that people were hitting with sticks. A woman hit a ball on a nearby table so that it bounced off the table and hit Nash in the head. Rubbing the side of his head, Nash swore. "Women can't shoot pool."

Sandy's eyes narrowed. "Sexist pig."

Nash straightened. "It's the goddamned truth."

Sandy smiled. "How about I make you eat those words?"

Nash laughed. "You don't actually think you could beat me?"

Sandy leaned toward him. "In my sleep."

"You want to put your money where your mouth is?" Nash got out his wallet and threw $50 on the table. "That says I beat you by at least four balls."

Sandy looked at me. "I didn't bring enough cash with me. Can you float me the fifty? I'll pay you back if I lose, but I won't lose."

"Sure," I said. I got out my wallet and matched Nash's $50.

They got up, and Nash gathered all the balls on one of the tables into a plastic triangle. "I'll even let you break," he told her. Cody, Austin, and I all grabbed our beers and got up to watch the game.

"That's your first mistake." Sandy smiled. "You won't get a second." She seemed pretty confident, and I hoped her confidence wasn't misplaced.

Nash shook the balls around inside the triangle, then removed the triangle. Sandy placed the white ball at the other end of the table and used her stick to shoot it toward the remaining balls. She hit them with such force the balls bounced around a lot. Three of them went into the pockets on the side of the table.

"Lucky shot," Nash said, which made me believe this was a good thing.

Sandy ignored the jibe, lined up the white ball behind a solid green ball, and said, "Solids. Number six into right side pocket."

"We never said anything about calling shots," Nash objected.

Sandy ignored him again and hit the green ball with the white ball, and it rolled into the right side pocket. Sandy kept calling shots and putting balls into the pockets.

After the third time she'd done this, Cody jabbed Nash in the ribs. "She's not even going to give you a turn."

Sandy smiled nastily. "I don't plan to." She hit a fourth ball into a pocket. She kept doing this until the only solid ball left was the black one with a number eight on it. "Still want to call it luck?" Sandy smirked at Nash.

Nash glowered back, but didn't say anything.

Sandy said, "Eight ball in far left pocket." Sure enough, she hit the black ball with the white one, and it fell into the pocket she'd called.

"Hot damn!" Cody said. "Just what were you saying about women and pool?"

Nash swore under his breath.

Sandy threw back her head and laughed. She picked the $100 up off the table and handed my $50 back to me. She put the rest in her pocket. "Want to give it another try? I'll let you break this time."

Nash threw his stick on the table. "I don't play with no goddamned sharks." He stomped off in the direction of the bathroom.

"Sore loser," Austin called after him.

"Anyone else want to give it a try?" Sandy asked the rest of us.

The other guys responded with a chorus of "no's."

We went back to the table. I patted her on the thigh. "Well done. You'll have to show me how to do that some time."

"For you, lover, any day of the week."

The other guys hooted and hollered. I picked up my beer and downed about half of it before reminding myself I didn't want to get drunk.

Before much longer, Sandy and I headed to my truck. We crawled into the back. I tried to get to sleep, but I kept thinking about the roping horses and how someone was most likely going to poison one of them tonight. Sandy noticed my restlessness. "What's wrong?" she asked.

"If I do nothing to stop it, I'm pretty sure a horse is going to die tonight," I told her.

"What can you do with the restraining order against you?" she asked. "Besides, shouldn't Parrish protect his own horse?"

"He probably should, but he hasn't been doing a very good job of it. Surely if I'm careful, I won't be seen."

Sandy tried to talk me out of doing anything. I knew the only thing interfering could do is get me in more trouble, but I couldn't just lay there, thinking about a horse dying. Finally, I said, "Screw it. I have to at least go check."

I put my boots back on, and I stole out, real quiet like. I kept to the shadows as I sneaked to where the horses were kept.

When I got close, I saw they'd put guards on the horses—Tyler Parrish and another cowboy whose name I didn't know—and left the bright lights on. I almost went away, figuring they would stop anything from happening.

Then the lights went out. Parrish and the other cowboy swore. I was close enough to hear them talk. "It's Killenyen, I bet," Parrish said, getting out a flashlight.

"I still don't see what Killenyen would get out of it," the other cowboy said. "It's not like he's our competition."

"Somebody turned the lights out," Parrish insisted. "Go check on it, and I'll watch the horses."

The other guy walked off. As soon as he did, someone emerged from the shadows on the far side of the horses. He walked up to

Parrish. "You have it?" Parrish asked. The second man nodded. As he walked into the light of the flashlight, I nearly fell on my butt.

I was staring at the same face I'd seen in the mirror every day for the last two months.

Parrish giggled as he took a syringe from the other me. "You must really hate your brother to set him up like this." Brother? Joshua didn't have a brother. As I looked closer, I realized he didn't look exactly like Joshua. His nose was a little bigger. His eyes were wider apart. But the resemblance was uncanny. He even had the same scar by his eye. Who could he be?

Other Me scowled, "Just get on with it." He didn't sound like Joshua, but his voice seemed familiar.

"Testy, testy," Parrish said, but he plunged the syringe into Spitfire and turned back to Other Me. The lights came back on.

"Ready," Other Me said.

Parrish nodded, and Other Me punched him in the face. Parrish went down groaning. He yelled, "Help! It's Killenyen!"

The second cowboy came running back. Other Me waited until the roper had a good look at him, then ran off into the darkness. After he disappeared, I realized I should have done something to stop him, but I'd been too shocked to think.

"Are you all right?" the cowboy asked, helping Parrish to his feet.

"Blake, he got my horse. He hit me and stuck the needle in before I could stop him."

Blake cursed me in ways that made the princess within me blush. Meanwhile, the poison was starting to move within the horse. If I didn't do something soon, it was going to die. If the horse died, surely they'd come looking for me. When their backs were turned, I crept silently forward to pluck a couple of hairs from Spitfire. Parrish got his cell phone out and called the cops. I got the hairs and retreated as far away as I could and still have the spell work. I took off my boot, whipped up another poppet, and started sucking and spitting.

Although I could no longer see them, I could still hear them. "What in God's name would make it squirt like that?" Blake asked. "This just ain't natural."

"Killenyen!" Parrish swore. "He's got to be around here somewhere."

Just as I finished, I heard the police arrive. I put on my boot and hurried away. Sandy was still awake when I reached my truck. "You weren't gone long," she said.

"Long enough," I said, and told her what happened.

"The other guy really looked like you?" she asked.

"Close to identical."

"Do you think he's a witch?"

I shook my head. "I don't know. I couldn't feel any magic coming from him. I think it's some kind of glamour."

"Why would anyone want to frame you?"

I shrugged. "If I end up in prison, it will be hard to figure out how to get home."

"Why not just kill you?"

I shook my head again. "I don't know. In my dream, Fitzrigh says he can't kill me. I can't imagine why. I think he killed my younger sister."

"It doesn't make sense he'd do that and then be squeamish about killing you. And why would Parrish want to kill his own horse?"

"How should I know? I'm sure it won't be long before the sheriff comes looking for me. Do you think we should get out of here?"

Sandy shook her head. "You'd probably be caught doing it, and it would look like you were trying to make your getaway. Probably best to stay here and claim you were asleep. I'll back you up."

We heard footsteps approaching and quickly feigned sleep.

Soon, bright lights shone all around us, and someone pounded on the side of my truck. "Joshua Killenyen, it's the sheriff. Come out. We know you're in there."

I groaned and turned over, trying to make it seem like they'd awakened me. I stumbled out the back of the truck. A whole herd of deputies surrounded me. "What's this about?" I asked.

One of the deputies grabbed me and slammed me into the truck. "Put your hands above your head." I complied. "Joshua Killenyen, you're under arrest for assault, violating a restraining order, and the poisoning of a horse belonging to one Tyler Parrish." After checking me for weapons and removing my pocket knife, he cuffed me and rattled off the same rights the last deputy had.

"What's going on?" Sandy asked, crawling out after me.

"Your boyfriend's been out poisoning horses, ma'am," he said, as he led me toward a cop car.

"He can't have been. He's been here with me."

"You can tell them that at the station," he said.

In a process that was becoming far too familiar, they took me to the station, took my things, put ink on my fingers, and placed me in a room.

The sheriff came in. He introduced himself as Sheriff Watson. He was about Uncle Braeden's age, balding with sandy gray hair around the fringe. He was about fifty pounds overweight. He had a cup of coffee, but he didn't offer me one. He set the poppet on the table. Damn it, I must have dropped it in my hurry to get back to the truck. He set a syringe next to the poppet.

The sheriff stared at me for an uncomfortable minute, then asked, "Want to tell me why you poisoned the horse? I can't see what you have to gain."

"I didn't do it," I said.

I have two witnesses—one with quite a bruise over his eye—that says otherwise."

"They're lying or mistaken, and I'm not saying anything more until I see a lawyer."

The sheriff sighed, and I could tell he was irritated. He let me have my cell phone. Fortunately, Joshua had Uncle Braeden's number programmed in. I called him, and he didn't seem happy to hear from me in the middle of the night. "What did you do now, Joshua?" he asked.

"I didn't do anything, but they think I poisoned a horse again. Can you come?"

Uncle Braeden sighed tiredly. "Meemaw would never let me hear the end of it if I refused, but I'm running out of patience with you." He hung up. I guessed that meant he was coming.

They put me in a holding cell. I was tired, but I couldn't sleep. I kept cursing myself for not going after the Other Me. He had to be from my realm. If I'd caught him, maybe I could be home by now. I paced the small cell, waiting for Uncle Braeden.

After what seemed like forever, Uncle Braeden strode into my cell. His nostrils flared, and the vein in his temple throbbed. "Thank you," he told the guard, and as soon as the guard left us alone, he rounded on me. "What in the hell is going on with you, Joshua? You violate the restraining order, and you've added assault to your list of offenses."

"I didn't hit Parrish. I didn't do anything."

"Beside Parrish himself, there's another witness who saw you hit him. Were they in fact seeing illusions?"

Something like that, I wanted to say. Instead, I said, "I have an alibi this time."

"You expect them to believe some floozy you picked up? If you want any more of my help, you'd better tell me the truth."

I tried to loom over him. "I didn't punch Parrish or do anything to the damned horse, and that's the truth."

"If you go down for this, it isn't my fault." When Uncle Braeden was done haranguing me, they hauled me back into the interrogation room. The sheriff was waiting for us. I sat next to Uncle Braeden on the opposite side of the table.

The sheriff picked up a piece of paper from the table. "The toxicology report is back on the horse Mr. Parrish claimed you poisoned. There doesn't appear to be anything wrong with it."

"That's because I didn't poison it," I said. "I never went near those horses."

Uncle Braeden looked at me like he was telling me to keep my big mouth shut. He turned to the sheriff. "You can't charge my client when no crime has been committed. I take it he's free to go."

"Hardly," the sheriff said. He pointed to the syringe. "It's tested positive for T61 and succinylcholine, the same compound Mr. Parrish's horse was poisoned with last week. Perhaps your client could tell us how he got a hold of such a lethal cocktail."

"I had nothing to do with that."

"Are his prints on the syringe?" Uncle Braeden asked.

The sheriff shook his head. "It's been wiped. Doesn't mean he didn't do it. We also have the matters of violating a restraining order and the assault on Mr. Parrish."

"I didn't hit him. You can ask Sandy. I was with her from the time the rodeo ended up until I was arrested."

"I have asked Ms Lane, but I have two witnesses who put you at the scene, and I take it you aren't sleeping with either of them. Did Mr. Parrish prevent you from carrying out your plan to poison his horse? Is that why you hit him?"

"I didn't hit him. I wasn't there." I swore inwardly. If I ended up in jail, there was no way I'd get home in time to stop Fitzrigh.

The sheriff kept asking me the same questions, and I gave the same answers. Finally, the sheriff sent the case to the district attorney. After I'd spent several hours in the holding cell, the district attorney decided to charge me with aggravated assault, a felony, because the assault had been committed in an attempt to commit a second felony of killing an animal. Uncle Braeden finally got me up before a judge who set bail so high Uncle Braeden flatly refused to pay.

"You are in serious trouble, boy," Uncle Braeden informed me. "You better start being honest with me so I can mount a decent defense. Otherwise, you could be going to prison for a long time."

"I've told you everything that happened," I said.

"Like hell you have. Take the time you spend in jail to think about what you want the rest of your life to be like." He left me there.

Dear gods, was this Fitzrigh's plan? If I was in jail, I certainly couldn't figure out a way back and make trouble for him. But what did this have to do with whoever was making me fall off bulls? The two tactics seemed at odds with each other. Did I have two enemies? Holy Cernuous, god of life, help me get out of this.

They took all my clothes and subjected me to a humiliating total cavity search. I tried to tell them I didn't have anything up my butt, but they checked anyway. They gave me a jail jumpsuit to wear and put me into a cell with a man with tattoos all over his body.

Trying to be polite, I stuck out my hand. "Joshua Killenyen."

He looked at my hand and grunted, "What you in for?"

I dropped my hand. "I didn't do anything."

He grunted again. "What you in for?"

He looked at me with mean eyes, so I said, "Assault."

"Me, too. I took a tire iron to my ex-wife. The bitch deserved it. All bitches do. You can't trust a one of them."

Mr. Bitch-Deserved-It spent the next two days regaling me with stories of how all the bitches of the world had done him wrong and how he'd gotten even. Finally, on Monday, Meemaw put up her house as collateral and got me out of jail.

Sandy had taken my truck home to Auburn, so she came and picked me up. I had to say it was mighty nice of her. I was starting to really like Sandy.

On the way back to Auburn, we talked about how much trouble I was in and what I could do about it. "I can't tell them about the Other Me, can I?" I asked.

Sandy shook her head. "Who would believe you? Since the horse didn't die, do you think whoever did it will try again?"

I nodded. "I would think so."

"What we need to do is get a video of the two of you together."

"A video?" I asked.

"Yeah, you know. Moving pictures."

"Your magic can make pictures move?"

Sandy laughed. "Not my magic, but my cameras can. I'm a photography major. I got a whole host of cameras."

Dear gods, what could this technology not do?

When we got to Sandy's place, she touched me on the thigh again. She tilted her head to the side. "Want to come inside? I know a perfect way to work off some of your stress."

In the dark, I felt the heat begin to rise in my face and stirrings of that thing between my legs. Embarrassed, I picked up her hand and placed on her own thigh. "Remember, I'm a woman."

Sandy leaned toward me and put her hand on my shoulder. "You don't feel like a woman," she whispered in my ear, while running her hand up and down my arm. "You've got to try it as a man. If you don't, you'll always wonder, and it's an awfully attractive man's body you're wearing."

Suddenly, my jeans felt about three sizes too small. I didn't say anything, and Sandy took my silence for assent. She leaned closer and pressed her lips against mine. Deprived of touch for so long, I responded. She tugged my shirt out of my jeans and placed her hand on my bare skin. I broke the kiss and pushed her gently away. "I can't do this to Clenyeth. We've been each other's only lover."

Sandy sighed and sat back. "I'll leave you alone, but I still say you'll regret not finding out. Want to sleep on my sofa? I promise not to jump you in the middle of the night."

I hesitated, but I was too tired to drive home, and it was blasted hot out. "If you promise."

"Cross my heart." She made an x over her heart, which must have been some sort of swearing to their God.

I got out of the truck and helped her out. She led me up three flights of stairs. "You'll have to forgive the mess," she said, unlocking the door.

She turned on the light. I walked in. "Dear gods, it's worse than my trailer." This wasn't quite true, but it was close, except it smelled a lot better. There was a dining area to the right. The table was covered with cameras, camera parts, pictures, and dirty dishes. Every chair was draped with discarded clothing, including a pair of boxer shorts too big for Sandy. The sofa and coffee table were covered with more of the same. The floor in front of the sofa had more clothes and open fantasy novels placed face down.

"I really should clean up, I guess." She started taking stuff off the sofa and piling it on the coffee table and a nearby easy chair. "My mother says I'm a slob and will never land a husband, but I don't know if I want one. Men are fun and all, but far too much of a bother if you let them get close. Start thinking they own you or something. That's when I tell them 'adios.'"

I thought of Clenyeth. "Not all men are like that."

"Maybe." Sandy got the stuff off the couch and brushed off some crumbs. "But I haven't met one yet who isn't. If I ever do, I guess he'll just have to learn to live with my mess. She fetched me a pillow and blanket. "If you change your mind, my room's right down the hall, and the bed's big enough for two." She kissed me on the cheek.

Worried about the possibility of ending up in prison, I had difficulty getting to sleep. When I finally did, I dreamed of Joshua.

He was locked in the tower room, pacing and gesturing wildly. "I can't stand to be locked up any longer," he said to Sylvia. "Did you tell the old man I promised not to drink any more? I'll give it up entirely."

Sylvia looked away. "He said the damage had been done. He said he was sorry, but he had no choice but to name Fitzrigh heir."

"That bastard." Joshua spewed forth a stream of obscenities. "He's not taking my head. We have to do something."

Sylvia put her hands up in a gesture of futility. "What?"

Joshua stopped pacing in front of Sylvia. "Can you break me out of here?"

Sylvia shook her head. "I don't know how. Fitzrigh has guards at both the top and bottom of the stairs, and they have the key."

I woke up in a cold sweat. Was I already too late to save us both?

* * *

I heard knocking and cursed Jocelyn for waking me yet again. I ignored her and rolled over—and ended up rolling off the couch onto a pile of books, papers, and clothes. A fork stabbed me in the back. I swore. Then I remembered where I was.

The knocking came again, and Sandy came out of her bedroom wearing a long T-shirt that said "War Eagle" on the front. I wasn't sure what part eagles could play in war. Sandy looked at me on the pile of stuff on the floor, laughed, and answered the door. As I pulled myself out of the pile of blankets and junk and pulled on my pants, a woman's voice said, "Sandy, you'll never believe what Ben gave me."

"I thought you hated Ben," Sandy said. She let Eileen in.

Eileen froze when she saw me. "What's he doing here?"

Sandy ran her fingers through her hair and yawned. "We got back here late, and he slept over."

Eileen wrinkled her nose as if I was the source of a foul odor in the room. "You didn't sleep with him, did you?"

"No, she didn't sleep with me." I stumbled into a relatively clean area of the floor. "I'm a woman." A woman in bad need of a shave. I scratched at my beard.

Eileen rolled her eyes. "I thought I hated Ben," she gushed to Sandy. "But I was so wrong about him. He brought me this last night." She showed Sandy a gold bracelet with a heart shaped ruby on it. Probably not a real ruby. Surely, Walker didn't have that kind of money. "He apologized and said he couldn't stand being away from me any longer. He also brought me a dozen roses. He was so sweet."

"That's. . . that's great," Sandy said. Eileen nodded enthusiastically, hugging her bracelet. "We won't have to worry about Madame Isabella. We can both go with Daulphina to the rodeo next week."

"With who?"

"Daulphina. That's Josh's real name."

Eileen looked me up and down. "I guess I could watch out for him. There's no reason for you to go, too."

"I think there is. I need to get some pictures." Sandy said, and told Eileen about the Other Me.

"You saw him?" Eileen asked.

Sandy shook her head. "No, but Daulphina did."

Eileen gave a nasty laugh. "You're not usually this naive. I can't believe you trust this guy. He's already admitted he cheats."

I jabbed a finger at her. "I didn't have anything to do with poisoning that horse."

"We'll see," Eileen said, and left.

# CHAPTER 15

When I got back to Hamilton, I collapsed on the bed. Within moments, there was knocking, and I stumbled to the door. When I opened it, Jocelyn stood there. "What?" I snapped.

She put her hands on her hips. "You could stand to be a little more polite."

"What, *ma'am*?" I snarled. I told myself I should be nicer, that I was hurting her feelings again, but I found I couldn't manage it.

"Joshua David Killenyen, you got thrown in jail, and Meemaw had to put up her house to get you out. She wants you to go over and talk to her right away."

Dear gods. Wasn't it bad enough I had to deal with people trying to kill and frame me? Couldn't Joshua's family leave me alone? I reminded myself that if it hadn't been for Meemaw, I'd still be sitting in a jail cell, so I dressed quickly and drove my truck over to her house.

She sat in her living room chair, waiting for me. "Hello, ma'am," I said tentatively.

She shook a finger at me. "Don't you 'hello, ma'am' me. You sit right down and tell me what you've been up to."

I sat. "Meemaw, I didn't do anything."
"You're facing charges of aggravated assault. I'm waiting for an explanation."

I looked away. "You wouldn't understand."

"Why wouldn't I? This doesn't have anything to do with princesses and parallel realms, does it?"

I met her eyes briefly. "I'm not crazy, Meemaw, and I didn't do anything wrong."

"You've been acting strangely. Now give me the truth."

"I've told you as much of the truth as I can, Meemaw. I'll get this worked out, you'll see."

"Just how are you fixing on doing that? Lou Ann's husband said you could be facing up to ten years in prison. Now I want some answers, and I want them now."

I closed my eyes. What could I possibly say to her? There were no answers but the truth, and she wouldn't believe that. I shook my head and stood. "I've given you all the answers I have to give. I've done nothing wrong." I opened the door and went out. I could feel the weight of Meemaw's anger behind me, and it bothered me more than I thought it would. She wasn't *my* grandmother.

Jocelyn waited for me on the porch. "You need help. Badly. The alcohol's pickled your brain or something. Telling everyone you're a princess, and now you're getting arrested. What's next, Joshua?"

I jabbed a finger into her chest. "That's my business, Jocelyn, not yours."

"We used to be such good friends, Joshua. What's happened to you? Where's the Joshua I know and love?"

"Maybe he's stuck in a princess's body," I said and stomped to my truck. I slammed the door and drove back to my trailer.

I collapsed on my bed and curled into a fetal position. Damn it all! This week I just *had* to catch the witch.

\* \* \*

On Friday Eileen and Sandy were to drive with Walker to Millbrook, Alabama, just up the road from Montgomery, and meet me there. I didn't see either of them when I arrived, so I went to the rodeo office, paid my fee, and checked my draw: Man Killer. A shiver went through me at the thought of riding the bull that had nearly killed me

I went to the bull pen and found Eileen hanging all over Walker. I set my gear bag down, and from out of nowhere, Sandy ran up, shouting, "Josh!" threw her arms around me, and kissed me on the lips. She had a large camera slung over her shoulder. I was so shocked I didn't know how to react. Nash looked on in disgust. I could tell he hadn't forgiven her for beating him at pool so badly.

Austin, Cody, and Dan arrived and greeted Sandy warmly. "If it isn't the pool shark," Dan said, smiling.

Sandy hooked her arm through mine. "Come get some roasted corn with me and watch for awhile." She turned to Eileen. "What to come with us?"

"No, I think I'll watch from here," Eileen said.

Sandy and I got some roasted corn and hamburgers and took our seats in the stands. "Eileen's boyfriend sure doesn't like you, does he?" she said.

"Did he say something about me?"

"He called you a hick with your brains up your ass and asked what I could possibly see in you."

"What did you tell him?"

She smiled and winked. "You don't want to know."

I felt myself heat up. "What did you tell him?"

Sandy took a bite of her corn and smiled. I pestered her for awhile, and she leaned close and whispered, "Let me show you what else is pierced, and I'll tell you."

I leaned away. "I guess I don't want to know."

She threw back her head and laughed. After she finished her corn, she said, "I can't see what Eileen sees in him. There's just no accounting for some women's taste."

"Isn't that the truth? I'm not sure you'd like Joshua very much either. He had a tendency to go through a different woman at every rodeo and brag all about it to the other cowboys."

Sandy put her hand on my thigh. "Maybe you could stand to be a little more like Joshua. You have to find out, and the offer's still open."

I picked up her hand and put it back on her own thigh, and she laughed again.

I left her when it was time for me to get ready to ride. Dan smiled when I walked up. "It's getting mighty serious, man. I've never seen you with the same woman two rodeos in a row."

"Sandy's just a friend," I said.

"Right," Dan said. "That was definitely a friendly kiss."

I didn't know what to say, so I turned away and readied my rope. I had drawn first ride again, so I climbed up behind the chutes, hooked my rope around Man Killer, and eased onto his back. I wrapped my hand, slid up on the bull, and nodded.

Just as I cleared the chute, my hand exploded with pain, lightening lancing through it. I went flying off, bashing my head against the gate. The bull's hooves crashed down near me, and the bull fighter tried to distract it. I told myself I needed to get up and run for the fence, but I couldn't seem to move.

Next thing I knew I was lying on a stretcher with someone shining a light in my eyes. "Do you know where you are?" a man asked me.

I stared at him. The light wasn't fire. "I don't think I'm in Asteria," I whispered.

"What did he say?" another man asked.

"Something about Asteria. That's over in Georgia, isn't it?" the first man answered.

The second man said he thought it was. "We'd better get him to the hospital right away." They started loading me into an ambulance.

"No," I tried to object. I had to stay and find whoever cursed me. But my head was reeling from the pain, and my word came out as a whisper. I must have blacked out again because the next thing I knew I was in a crowded room with people and all sorts of technology.

A woman stood over me, asking me questions. I vaguely remembered telling her my name was Daulphina, that I was in the realm of America, and that I had no idea who the president was. She asked if I knew how I'd been injured, and I told her a witch had tried to kill me.

\* \* \*

I dreamed of home again. I was in the Temple of Morrigan, the great queen of the gods. It was packed with nobles. Music started, and a casket rolled up the aisle. Fitzrigh and Eilwen walked behind it. The music playing proclaimed the presence of the king. Good gods, no! That couldn't be my father in the casket. It just couldn't be. But what other explanation was there? My father was dead. He'd proclaimed Fitzrigh heir, and he'd died as he'd predicted he would. What could I do? I was too late.

\* \* \*

When I woke up next, I heard Meemaw talking. "Will he be okay?" she asked, her voice strained with worry.

The same woman who had asked me questions earlier answered, "I'm afraid we'll just have to wait and see. He was quite confused when he was brought in, and he's been in and out of consciousness, which isn't a good sign."

"Meemaw," I croaked, and suddenly, both Meemaw and Jocelyn huddled around me.

"Thank the Lord. You're awake." Tears streamed down Meemaw's cheeks. I felt bad for being so harsh with her after my arrest.

The doctor leaned over me. "It's good to see you with your eyes open. How do you feel?"

"My head's killing me."

"We can give you something for the pain, but first, I want to see if you can answer a few questions for me. What's your name?"

I had to think for a second. "Joshua David Killenyen."

"Good. Do you know how you were injured?"

I thought about the spell. "I hit my head when I got bucked off a bull."

She nodded. "Good. What month is it?"

I tried to remember what month it said in *The Chute Gate* for this particular rodeo, but I couldn't. The names they used for months in this realm were so unfamiliar. I said, "I don't know."

She frowned. "Can you tell me who the president is?"

"What's a president?" I asked.

The physician turned to Meemaw. "The headache may be as expected, but his continued confusion isn't a good sign. We'll need to keep him under observation for at least another day, maybe longer, and I think we need to do a CT scan to make sure he doesn't have bleeding in the brain. Since he doesn't have any insurance, I was holding off on ordering the scan. The price can run up over $1000, but I don't think we have a choice now."

"No," I said, even though I had no idea what the doctor was talking about. "I don't need any scans. Is Sandy or Eileen here?"

"Sandy's out in the waiting room," Jocelyn said.

"I need to talk to her," I said.

"I'm afraid that will have to wait," the doctor said. "We should do the scan right away. If you have a subdural hematoma, which your confusion suggests you might, it could be fatal."

"I'm not confused, and I need to talk to Sandy."

"Listen to the doctor, Josh, darling," Meemaw squeezed my shoulder. "You can talk to your young lady when we're sure you're all right."

"I'm fine. I need to talk to Sandy now!"

The doctor sighed. "Maybe you should fetch the young woman. She might be able to talk some sense into him."

"I'll go get her," Jocelyn said. She left and returned a few moments later with Sandy.

Sandy hurried to my bedside. "You okay?" she asked, stroking my hair.

I turned to the others. "I need to talk to her alone."

Grudgingly, the others left. "Did you see who cursed me? Did you catch him?"

Sandy shook her head. "When you didn't get up, I got so upset I lost track of the witch."

"What about Eileen?"

"I don't know. I went in the ambulance with you, and Eileen stayed with Ben. I tried to call her a little while ago, but she didn't pick up. That's not what matters at the moment. How are you?"

"I'm fine, and the witch is what matters." I told her about my dream. "Fitzrigh could be executing Joshua any time now. I have to get back to stop him. We need to talk to Eileen now. Do you know where she and Ben were staying?"

Sandy nodded. "They got a room at the Super 8 in Prattville, but I'm sure they won't still be there. The rodeo starts in about an hour. Your buddies were here all day. They just left for the rodeo a few minutes ago."

"What?" I asked. "I was out for that long?"

Sandy nodded. "You had us all worried."

I sat up. I was wearing some very odd and awfully short garment. The world swayed around me. I grabbed the bedside cabinet for support. "Do you know where my clothes are?"

Sandy grabbed my shoulder. "Hold on now, honey. You hit your head pretty damned hard. Let me go to the rodeo and talk to Eileen. You stay here and let the doctors take care of you."

"There isn't time. If Joshua dies, I might just die along with him. Besides, you know we witches heal faster and easier than normal people."

Sandy looked hesitant, but nodded. "Okay. But you better not die on me. The clothes you were wearing are probably in one of the drawers. Your buddies said they packed up your gear bag and put it in your truck, which is still back at the rodeo grounds." She opened one of the drawers and pulled out a bag.

There was a tube attached to my arm, and a bunch of round things affixed to my chest. I pulled the tube out. I paused and put my hand to my head, which was killing me. I shook my head to clear it and started to pull all the things off my chest. Suddenly, one of the pieces of technology by the bed went from making a beeping sound to a sustained ringing. The doctor burst through the door, followed by Meemaw and Jocelyn. I could hear other people running toward the room.

"What do you think you're doing, young man?" the doctor said.

"I'm leaving," I said, grabbing my boxer shorts from Sandy and pulling them on.

"Are you out of your mind? If you have bleeding on the brain, you could drop dead before you even get out of the hospital."

"I don't have bleeding on the brain." I pulled on my jeans.

Meemaw put her hand on my arm. "Stop this nonsense, Josh, darling. Don't worry about the money. I'll take care of it. You just need to get well."

I shook off her hand. "I have to go." I pulled off the short gown I'd been wearing.

The doctor turned to Meemaw. "This is most unwise. If he walks out of here, I can't be responsible for the consequences."

Remembering what Dan's brother Mike had said, I said, "You can't keep me against my will. I'll sign whatever you want me to sign." I grabbed my shirt, put it on, and started buttoning it up.

The doctor, Jocelyn, and Meemaw all tried to argue with me, telling me I was being foolish, if not suicidal. Sandy handed me my socks and boots.

Meemaw turned to Sandy. "Young lady, if you care for my grandson in the least, you can't approve of what he's doing."

Sandy shrugged. "He has his reasons."

Meemaw glared at both of us. "What reason could be good enough to risk his life?"

"I can't tell you that." I pulled on my socks.

Jocelyn burst into tears. "If you die, Josh, I won't ever forgive you." She rushed from the room.

Meemaw tried to snatch the boots out of my hands. "I order you to stop this foolishness."

I held onto the boots. "I'm sorry, Meemaw, but I have to go." I pulled on the boots, which still had the spurs attached.

The doctor looked resigned. "I'll go process the paperwork, but remember you are leaving against medical advice."

"How do you think you're getting back to your truck?" Meemaw asked. "I'm not taking you one step from this hospital."

I looked at Sandy. "I'll call a cab," she said, and got out her phone. I wasn't sure what she meant, but she sounded like she knew what she was doing.

Meemaw glared at Sandy. "Young lady, you are helping my grandson kill himself."

Sandy looked stricken and walked out into the hallway. I put on my belt and hat and picked up a bag that still contained my glove and protective vest.

When I tried to leave the room, Meemaw stood in my way. "Don't do this, Josh, darling. Don't make me bury another one of mine."

"Meemaw, I'm not going to die." I moved her out of the way and left the room.

Sandy was talking on the phone. She hung up and said, "Cab's on the way."

"Good," I said. I signed the paperwork. Jocelyn and Meemaw glared at Sandy and me as we walked toward the elevator.

When we got to the hospital entrance, we had to wait about ten minutes for the cab to show up. I put my hand to my head. Sandy noticed. "Are you sure this is a good idea?"

"I'm sure I have no choice."

The cab turned out to be a car that will take you where you want to go for a price—an outrageous price, as it turned out. But it got us to the rodeo grounds.

The rodeo had already started by the time we arrived. My fellow bull riders cheered when I walked up. "Thank the Lord, man," Dan said. "When I heard your head hit that gate, I was afraid you were a goner. Should you be out of the hospital? When we left a little over an hour ago, you were still unconscious."

"I'm fine," I said, squinting against the pain. "Have you seen Walker's girlfriend, Eileen?"

Dan shook his head. "No, she didn't come with him tonight, and I think they had a fight because he's in a foul mood. I mean, fouler than usual."

I saw Walker on the other side of the bull pen and started toward him. Sandy grabbed my arm. "Let me ask him. He's more likely to tell me."

She was right, so I let her go. Dan looked at me. "Really, buddy, are you sure you're okay? You don't look so good. The doctor gave you a clean bill of health and everything?"

"I'm fine."

Sandy came back. "Ben says Eileen called her mother to come pick her up this morning and went back to Auburn."

"Damn it. I guess that's where we need to go."

Sandy whispered, "What about the Other You?"

I shook my head. "He can't do anything tonight. They'll load up all the horses after the rodeo and get them out of here."

I said goodbye to the other cowboys, and Sandy and I walked back to my truck. I stopped halfway there and put my hand on a car to steady myself. Damn it, my head hurt.

Sandy looked at me. "I'm driving," she insisted.

I handed her the keys.

* * *

I fell asleep on the drive, and Sandy shook me awake when we reached Eileen's apartment. The clock said 10:15. My head felt a little bit better, but it still hurt. Sandy opened the door for me, and we walked up to Eileen's apartment.

Eileen answered the door. At first, I swear she looked relieved when she saw me, but I must have been mistaken. Whatever her expression had been, it turned into a scowl. "What do you want?"

"What do you mean 'what do I want'? You saw me get bucked off the bull and bash my head in."

"I saw you get on a bull you couldn't handle."

"My ass, I couldn't handle the bull. A hex hit my hand again."

Sandy stepped between us. "You didn't feel anything? Because I did."

Eileen crossed her arms. "No, I didn't feel anything."

I jabbed a finger at her. "Maybe you were too busy snogging with Walker to pay attention to what was happening in front of your face."

Sandy shook her head. "If Eileen didn't feel anything, this could be really bad. I think we should gather the coven."

"Not Madame Isabella," I insisted. "She might try to kill me again."

Sandy hesitated, then nodded. "I'll call Kinyisha."

It didn't take Kinyisha long to arrive. Sandy told her what had happened, and Eileen still claimed she felt nothing.

The witches exchanged grave looks. Kinyisha said, "We've known all along if this were a really powerful witch, the ring wouldn't work, and Eileen might not be able to feel it. Sandy's more sensitive. We may be in over our heads."

The other witches stared at their feet and nodded. "What?" I said. "Don't tell me you can't do anything."

"We could take you to someone more powerful," Sandy said.

"You know people more powerful?" I asked. "Why didn't you tell me before?"

Kinyisha shook her head. "They aren't really people you want to mess with."

I stood. "My head's about to get chopped off. I'll take any help I can get."

"We could try Thudd," Kinyisha said. "He probably has an amulet that would protect you. But he won't sell it to you for less than $1000."

I whistled through my teeth. "I haven't got that much."

"That leaves only Erick," Sandy said. "But you don't want to mess with him."

"Why not?"

All the witches shivered. "There's something evil about him," Kinyisha said. "We think he practices black magic—sacrificing animals and maybe even more, to perform his rituals."

"Then he might know something. Isabella said black magic was used for the body switching spell. Maybe he'll know how to reverse it."

Kinyisha looked uncertain.

"Please, I'm desperate. It's not just my throne any more. Joshua's life is on the line, and I don't know what will happen to me if he dies in my body."

Sandy stood and patted me on the shoulder. "I'll take you to see Erick."

"You better call first," Kinyisha said. "Erick doesn't like surprises."

\* \* \*

Sandy called Erick, but he wouldn't agree to see us until nine the next morning. When I protested I needed to see him now, the witches all insisted if I tried to push Erick, things would be really bad.

Fuming, I drove Sandy back to her place, and I slept on her couch again. She didn't even try to seduce me, for which I was grateful because my head still hurt.

By morning, my head felt much better. Sandy fed me breakfast and insisted I call Meemaw. "She was really worried about you, and I doubt she'll ever forgive me for not trying to stop you leaving the hospital."

Sighing at the necessity, I called. Meemaw answered on the first ring. "Don't tell me you're dead," she said, before I even had a chance to speak.

"I'm fine, Meemaw. I'm in Auburn, not sure when I'll be back to Hamilton."

Meemaw started to grill me about headaches, blurred vision, nausea. "I'm fine," I interrupted. "I've got to go." I hung up the phone before she could press me further.

Sandy frowned in disapproval. "No 'I love you'?"

"Sandy, she's not *my* grandmother. Do you have any idea how hard it is pretending to be someone else?" Sandy patted my arm and looked sympathetic.

We drove my truck to a neighborhood where all the houses looked alike—red brick. She told me to stop in front of one of them. "I was expecting something a little more, I don't know, creepy," I said.

I helped Sandy out of the truck.

"He doesn't look like a witch either, but don't underestimate him." She trembled even more than she had at Kinyisha's apartment.

"He's really that scary?"

Sandy nodded emphatically. "Yes."

Before we reached the door, it creaked open. Nobody was there, so I called out, "Hello?"

"Enter," said a deep voice. We walked into a plain foyer with white walls, a white tile floor, and some kind of fern-like plant. To the left of the entrance was an office, and a middle-aged man sat behind a desk. He was wearing dress slacks, a white shirt, and tie and had plain brown hair in a standard male cut and brown eyes. He looked more like a bank manager than a witch.

I walked toward him with Sandy following closely behind. "You must be Erick." I stuck out my hand. "Joshua Killenyen."

His eyes widened, and he stood, ignoring my hand. "Marvelous," he whispered, looking me up and down. "Simply marvelous."

I dropped my hand. "You see the spell?"

"You aren't Joshua Killenyen, are you?" His eyes bored into mine. I saw what the witches meant. There was something evil, almost inhuman in his gaze.

"No, I'm the Crown Princess Daulphina from Asteria."

His eyebrows came together. "Asteria? Isn't that in Georgia somewhere?"

I sighed, my hopes falling. If he hadn't heard of parallel realms, how could he help me? "No, it's not in Georgia. It's the next parallel realm."

"Parallel realm? Really?" He sank back in his chair and gestured at the one across from him. "Sit, and tell me all about it." There was a hunger in his gaze.

I sat in the chair, leaving Sandy standing behind me. So far, Erick had completely ignored her. I told him my story. His eyes roamed over my body the entire time. It was downright disturbing. "Can you help me? Can you put me back where I belong?"

Erick nodded. "Maybe, but why would I want to interfere with such a marvelously cast spell?"

My mouth dropped open. "Didn't you hear me? Joshua's about to be executed in my body!"

He waved a hand dismissively. "What's that to me?"

"Do you want money?" I asked. "Joshua doesn't have much, but you get me back in my body, and I can see you richly rewarded."

He laughed, sending shivers down my spine. "Money doesn't tempt me. I have all I need."

"How about to prove who's the better sorcerer?" Sandy said. "You've always said you're the best. Well, prove it!"

Erick looked at Sandy, and his eyes filled with lust. "The little lady wants me to prove my talent. Perhaps I will. Shall we use her?"

"Use?" I asked.

"You don't think a spell cast with human sacrifice can be undone without another sacrifice in return." He pulled a gun from out of a desk drawer and pointed it at Sandy.

"Hold on a minute." I stood and placed myself between him and Sandy. "I'm not killing anyone."

He put the gun back in the desk drawer. "Then you're wasting my time." He picked up a paper on his desk and began to read from it.

"There has to be another way!"

He looked up at me with his creepy eyes. "If there is, I'm not interested in it. Leave now, or you'll witness what else my magic is capable of."

"But—"

Sandy grabbed my shoulder; her hand shook. "Let's go, Daul." She pulled me toward the door. I didn't fight. Before we reached the door, it creaked open on its own. We hurried out to my truck.

When we got in, I slammed my hand down on the steering wheel. "That can't be the answer. That can't be the only way."

Sandy looked over at me like she wasn't sure she wanted to be in the same truck with me. She was as white as a sheet. "What if it is?"

"I refuse to accept that. I'm going to get home, and I'm not killing anyone to do it." But I felt sick to my stomach. What if it was the only way? Was I doomed to be stuck as Joshua forever? Or would I die when he did?

In silence, we drove to Kinyisha's apartment and called Eileen over. I told them what Erick had said.

"He would've killed me," Sandy said, "if Daulphina had been willing to go along with it."

"I told you that you wanted nothing to do with him." Kinyisha patted Sandy's arm. Sandy was still white and shaky.

"There just *has* to be another way."

"Maybe," Kinyisha said. "We could all go to the next rodeo. With all of us together, maybe we could find out who's after you."

"Not Madame Isabella. She keeps trying to kill me," I said.

Kinyisha shook her head. "We may need her. I'll make sure she doesn't have her gun."

\* \* \*

The next day I drove to Hamilton and, at Sandy's insistence, stopped by to see Meemaw. When I walked into her kitchen, she threw her arms around me and squeezed me tightly, making me feel guilty yet again. She released me and slapped me across the face. "How dare you leave the hospital like that? It's bad enough you do this bull riding, but when you get hurt, you should at least let the doctors take care of you."

I rubbed my cheek. "I'm sorry, Meemaw, but there were things I had to do."

She looked at me over her glasses. "I'm waiting for an explanation."

I looked away, wishing I hadn't come. Anything I could say to Meemaw would just convince her I'd gone mad. "I'm fine. That's all you need to know."

"How can you know you're fine? The doctor said you could have a slow bleeder. You need to get to the hospital now and let them do that CT scan the doctor wanted."

"I can't afford it."

"I can, and I'm not about to have my grandson die because of a few lousy bucks. I'm taking you to the hospital now, and you're getting the scan."

I opened my mouth to argue, but I had nothing pressing to do until Friday. Why not do this CT scan if it would give Meemaw peace of mind? "I think it's a waste of money, but if you really want me to do it, I will."

Meemaw looked like she was going to burst into tears of relief. She got on the phone with the doctor who'd treated me at Prattville Baptist Hospital, and the doctor called the hospital in Hamilton to arrange for the test. When Meemaw had everything organized, she turned to me. "Don't think you're driving yourself."

"Fine, Meemaw. You can take me."

Meemaw drove me to the hospital. They made me take off all my clothes and put on one of those short gowns like I'd worn in the other hospital. The CT scan machine was another incomprehensible piece of technology, consisting of a movable bed and a huge donut-shaped thing. When I asked how it worked, the technician started talking about x-rays and radiation and other things I had no idea what were.

They had me get on the bed, moved the bed back so my head was centered in the donut, and told me not to move. I lay there for what felt like forever.

When they were finally done, they told me a radiologist would review my scans and my doctor would get back to me. I got dressed, and Meemaw drove me to her house, where she insisted on feeding me dinner.

As we were eating, Meemaw fixed me in her gaze. "When are you going to tell me what's been going on these past few weeks?"

I paused with the fork halfway to my mouth. "Nothing's going on."

"Humph," Meemaw said. "I may be old, but I'm not stupid. Leaving the hospital was just your latest. You've been acting odd since your birthday."

"I'm fine, Meemaw."

We ate the rest of the meal in awkward silence. When I got up to leave, Meemaw said, "You better tell me soon." I wished I could.

* * *

The next day the doctor called and told me that the CT scan had shown no abnormalities. I called and told Meemaw, who still seemed to be angry with me.

# CHAPTER 16

On Friday, I met the witches in Montgomery before heading down to Panama City. Kinyisha and Sandy got out of Kinyisha's car to talk to me, but Madame Isabella stayed in the front passenger seat, glowering at me. She was dressed in a purple robe with black stars this time. "She doesn't look happy," I said.

"She's not," Kinyisha said. "She still insists you're an abomination that needs to be put down." I raised my eyebrows in alarm, but Kinyisha patted my arm. "Don't worry. She's not going to do anything."

Sandy rode the rest of the way with me in my truck. Eileen drove down with Walker. Evidently, she'd made up with him again.

Kinyisha and Sandy went with me to the bull pen, but Madame Isabella marched straight to the stands without speaking to me, which was just fine with me. When we arrived, Dan, Cody, and Austin all looked at me like they were staring at my ghost.

"What the hell are you doing here?" Dan asked. "You can't actually be planning on riding so soon after you got your head bashed in."

"I have to," I said.

Dan looked over at Kinyisha and Sandy. "Talk some sense into him. You get another concussion before the first one's fully healed, and you can do some permanent damage."

"You at least got a helmet?" Cody asked.

I shook my head.

"Then use your brain, and don't ride," Dan said.

"I have to pay my fee," I said.

"Stubborn bastard," Dan muttered as I walked off.

I went to the rodeo office to pay my fee and check my draw. I smiled when I saw Kracken's name.

When I got back to the bull pen, Kinyisha and Sandy were talking to the other cowboys. "Maybe you shouldn't ride, Josh," Sandy said. "You could fall off again."

I glared at her. "You know why I have to."

That shut her up, but the other cowboys looked at me like I was out of my mind. Sandy and Kinyisha went to sit in the stands. The witches planned to spread throughout the crowd, so it would be more likely one of them would be able to pin down where the magic came from.

When they were gone, Dan looked at me in disapproval. "Both of them! Didn't know which one of them to sit with, huh? It's one thing to have a one-night stand with a Bunny, but I like Sandy and Kinyisha. Do they know you're screwing both of them?"

"I'm not screwing either of them," I said. "Sandy and Kinyisha are just friends."

"Yeah, just a friend comes with you to three rodeos in a row. Just a friend spends all night with you in the back of your truck. You really expect me to believe you didn't fuck them? That's certainly not the Josh Killenyen I know."

Cody and Austin nodded their heads in agreement. I closed my eyes and prayed this would be the last time I had to deal with people expecting me to be Joshua. Dear gods, let me figure out how to get home *tonight*. When I opened my eyes, all of Joshua's friends were still staring at me, expecting an answer. I didn't know what to say, so I turned to look at the bulls.

"Typical," Dan said, and they all walked away.

Cody sidled up next to me. "You know if you're having a hard time choosing, Kinyisha has the better ass. Sandy is just too skinny."

I ignored him. During the rodeo prayer, I got Kracken's hairs and completed the spell that would let me stay on the bull. That is, if I didn't get hexed again. Joshua's friends continued to give me the silent treatment. It seemed that everyone who had been a part of Joshua's life was mad at me.

Finally, it came time for the bull riding, but I was the last to ride. Walker rode second and scored an 89. Part of me wished I had a helmet when I climbed up on the chute, but I breathed deeply to calm myself. I climbed onto Kracken's back, got my rope ready, and slid up on the bull. I nodded, and they opened the chute. Kracken burst into the arena and began bucking up a storm, but my butt stuck tight until the 8-second horn sounded. I managed my dismount with little drama, and I scored a 90, one point above Walker. Still, I was swearing as I climbed back over the fence. If my enemy didn't act, I couldn't catch him.

Walker and Eileen were arguing as I walked by. She said, "No!" and turned to walk away.

Walker grabbed her shoulder and whirled her to face him. He hissed something at her I couldn't hear, but I didn't like the way he was manhandling a woman, even if it was Eileen.

I got in Walker's face. "Is there a problem?"

Walker clenched his fists. "It's none of your business, Killenyen!"

Eileen grabbed my arm. "Stay out of it. I don't need your protection." She let go of my arm and took Walker's hand. The two of them walked off. I stared after them, but if Eileen didn't want my help, it wasn't any of my business.

Sandy and Kinyisha met me behind the chutes as I was packing my gear bag. "Nothing," Sandy said, and I shrugged.

"There's always the Other Me," I said, and Sandy patted the camera she wore over her shoulder.

"Where's Madame Isabella?" I whispered.

"She's getting some chicken-on-a-stick, I think," Kinyisha said.

Although he hadn't talked to me since the beginning of the rodeo, Dan walked over. "You ladies want to go get a few beers? Joshua can't possibly keep you all to himself."

Knowing it would further alienate him, I had to turn him down. We needed to be on hand in case the Other Me showed up. When I said "no," he turned to the witches, who shook their heads.

"Sorry," Sandy said. "Maybe next time."

Dan and the others walked off without saying goodbye. Damn it all! Couldn't anything be easy?

* * *

We met Madame Isabella by my truck. She showed up with both hands full of the roasted meat. "This is quite good," she said, between mouthfuls. "Even an abomination like you should be able to appreciate it." She held out one of the sticks toward me.

I shook my head. "No, thanks."

She continued to wave it enticingly beneath my nose. "Come on. Have a bite. You're too skinny."

I was about to take it just to humor her, but Sandy grabbed my shoulder. "You didn't poison that, did you, Isabella?"

Madame Isabella pouted. "Kinyisha took away my gun even though there's nothing important for the blood to get on out here. The dirt would just suck it all up." She looked at me, as if asking me to confirm that Kinyisha was being unreasonable.

"That's not the point." Kinyisha grabbed the poisoned meat out of Madame Isabella's hand. "I told you that we aren't going to kill Josh. He's the victim here, not the black witch."

Madame Isabella shrugged, as if the distinction was meaningless and went back to munching on her food. I made sure to keep an eye on her.

We waited by my truck until the rodeo quieted down. Then we sneaked over to where the roping horses were kept and concealed ourselves in the shadows. Madame Isabella could move surprisingly quietly for a woman of her size. There were two guards again, and one of them was Tyler Parrish. The other held a rifle. We waited for something to happen. After a long time of nothing happening, Madame Isabella fell asleep. I thought no one was going to show and this, too, wouldn't work out for me.

About midnight, there was a sound on the far side of the horses. Parrish and the other cowboy froze. "What's that?" the other cowboy said.

"Has to be Killenyen," Parrish said, "and this time I'm not going to let him near the horses." He pulled the gun he'd used on me the other week.

The other cowboy walked toward the sound, turning his back on Parrish. Out of the shadows walked the Other Me, carrying a syringe.

"Killenyen," the other cowboy said. "I didn't believe it until I'm seeing it with my own eyes. What you doing it for?"

The Other Me laughed nastily. "Wouldn't you like to know?" Without warning, Parrish clobbered the other roper over the head with the gun. He fell to the ground.

I glanced at Sandy to see if she was getting all this on camera; she nodded. I stepped out. "Just who the hell are you?" I asked Other Me. "Why are you framing me?"

Other Me licked his lips, but Parrish said, "I can't think of a better patsy." They both laughed, Other Me somewhat nervously.

I was so mad I wanted to punch them both, but that wasn't what I wanted on film. "Why'd you want to poison your own horse?"

Parrish just laughed. "Don't you wish you knew, Killenyen? And you'll take the fall." Parrish leveled the gun at me. "I might just shoot you in self-defense for good measure. Who's to say otherwise?"

"Abomination!" Isabella came barreling out of the shadows, wielding a sharp stick. Maybe she'd only been pretending to be asleep. Thinking she was heading for me, I jumped aside and went into a defensive crouch. However, she ran past me toward the Other Me.

Other Me took one look at the crazy lady and bolted with Madame Isabella in hot pursuit. I pushed past Parrish, who didn't do anything to stop me, and took off after them. It wasn't long before I caught up to Madame Isabella leaning against a tree and clutching her side. "Get him!" she panted, as I ran by.

Unfortunately, my lack of exercise during the time I'd been in Joshua's body took its toll. Soon, I was nearly as bad off as Madame Isabella. Other Me disappeared into the trees ahead of me.

I was hopelessly lost by the time I saw a light off to the right and heard a voice chanting. There was a small, old church, and someone knelt in the graveyard, bent over a candle. His voice got louder, and I could understand the words. He called out to the goddess Cailleach, mistress of death.

I stepped out of the trees. "Who are you and why are you doing this to me?"

The man looked up. He held a stone of black obsidian in his hands. I saw his face in the light of the candle. "Clenyeth!" I cried. "No, Clenyeth! It can't be you! You have no magic."

He stood, still holding the black stone. "Fitzrigh gave me an amulet with the glamour on it."

"How could he make such an amulet? He doesn't have that much power."

Clenyeth laughed. "The blood bond has given him more power than you ever dreamed of. He even made a Traveler's Stone to open the void." Clenyeth held up the black rock. "I'm sorry, Daulphina. We can't have you coming back."

Questions raced through my mind. Blood bond? Traveler's Stone? What was he talking about? Instead, I asked the question that troubled me most. "Why would you be working with Fitzrigh?"

"He's going to make me a baron, whereas you saw me as fit only to shovel horse shit." He threw the stone to the side, and a hole in reality burst to life beside him. Darkness and the nothingness pulled against me. "Goodbye, Daulphina," he said, and jumped into the void.

"No!" I cried, and leapt to follow him. But the void closed, and nothing was left but the darkness of the night.

Sandy found me sobbing next to the candle that Clenyeth had used to complete his ritual. She knelt next to me.

"What happened?"

I collapsed against her shoulder. "It was him. It was Clenyeth!" Through my tears, I told her what had happened. "How could he do this to me? I thought he loved me."

Sandy let me cry for a moment, but the flashlights and calls were getting closer. "We called the cops," she said. "They've arrested Tyler. Now everyone is looking for you and the other you."

"He's gone," I said. "He jumped back through the void into Asteria. Damn him, why couldn't he take me with him?" I pulled myself together and wiped my eyes on my shirt sleeve.

Sandy called out, "Over here. I found him."

The flashlights turned in our direction, and soon the small churchyard was crawling with cops. They drew their guns. "Step away from him," the sheriff said to Sandy, and she did.

"I'm the real Joshua Killenyen," I said. "The one who was pretending to be me got away."

"Humph," The sheriff said. "We'll see about that." He cuffed me and led me out of the woods by the arm.

They took me to the sheriff's station where they asked me a lot of questions and replayed the video Sandy took half a million times. I told them again and again I didn't know who the other man was or why he looked so much like me. Seeing us on camera together, you could tell he was a little taller and more slightly built, as well as slightly different in facial features. It was like someone had copied Joshua from memory and hadn't gotten it quite right.

In the wake of the evidence against him, Taylor Parrish broke down and confessed everything, including how he and a man he'd believed to be my brother paid him a million dollars worth of gemstones to help set me up to take the fall. In the end, the police had no choice but to let me go, although they didn't seem any too happy about it. They knew I was hiding something, but I could hardly tell them that the other me had been my lover from a parallel realm using a glamour.

The witches, including Madame Isabella, were waiting for me. She seemed oddly subdued. We went to Waffle House for some breakfast. Madame Isabella got a lot of stares when we walked in, but she didn't seem to notice. Over breakfast, I repeated to them everything I'd told Sandy. I had to fight to stop the tears.

"Why did he do it?" Sandy asked. "What would putting you in jail here accomplish, especially if Fitzrigh's already been named heir? Why not just kill you? Or kill Joshua?"

I shrugged. "I don't know. I just don't know."

"There's something unusual going on here," Isabella said, as if she were stating a startling fact.

"Really?" I said.

She nodded, seeming not to hear the sarcasm. She turned to Kinyisha and Sandy. "I know it's an abomination, but I don't think we should kill it until we figure this out."

"How are we going to do that now that C—" I bit back a sob. I couldn't say his name. "Now that he's gone back to Asteria?"

Sandy patted my thigh. "We'll figure something out."

"I don't see how. I suppose there isn't any reason for you to stay for tonight's rodeo."

"We're here," Kinyisha said. "We might as well. The worst that can happen is nothing."

Part of me didn't care what happened tonight. After Clenyeth's betrayal, what could a little thing like making me fall off a bull matter?

Then I got mad. I was the crown princess of Asteria, and I wasn't going turn into some helpless female mooning over some man! I would face this problem like someone born to rule.

\* \* \*

When the witches and I arrived at the rodeo grounds, Madame Isabella split off and went straight to the stands. Kinyisha and Sandy continued with me to the bull pens. Dan glared at me. "Have fun last night?"

I heaved a sigh and turned to the witches. "Kinyisha, Sandy, tell him that we're just friends, that I haven't been screwing around with you."

"He hasn't," Sandy said.

"He's not my type," Kinyisha agreed.

I turned back to Dan. "See, I haven't done them wrong."

"Whatever," Dan said.

"Whatever to you, too." I knew it didn't make much sense, but I didn't know what else to say. I grabbed some of Man Killer's hair and stomped away with the witches to watch the beginning of the rodeo. I sat with Sandy again, and Kinyisha and Madame Isabella sat in other parts of the arena.

I mostly stared ahead and saw nothing but Clenyeth's face in the light of the candle. Sandy kept patting me on the shoulder and didn't make any suggestive moves. She didn't say anything, but what was there to say?

When it was time, I went back to my truck and made up my spell. I went to the area behind the chutes to get my rope ready, but I could hardly concentrate on the simple task. Dan came up next to me. "Don't insult my intelligence. You're hanging around with two good-looking women, and you actually expect me to believe you haven't screwed either of them? The Joshua Killenyen I know never talked to a woman without at least trying to get into her pants."

I rubbed more rosin on the rope. "People do change." Some more than others. Surely I'd missed my chance, and I was destined to be Joshua Killenyen forever.

Dan didn't say anything more while I finished up with my rope. When I started stretching, he asked, "How's your head?"

Surprised by the question, I stared at him. I realized this was his way of apologizing. Men never seemed to be able to do that directly. "It's fine," I said. "Not even a little pain." My heart, on the other hand, was completely battered and bruised.

He nodded. "Good. I still think you ought to get a helmet."

"It might not be a bad idea," I agreed.

Finally, it came time for the bull riding. Walker rode first and managed a ride even better than the night before, scoring a 91. To beat him, I was going to need one hell of a ride. When it was my turn, I climbed onto the bull's back and got ready. I nodded, and they opened the chute. For the first few seconds, I thought everything was going to be fine. Then the curse hit my hand, and I flew off.

"Cailleach curse you!" I tried to say, but my wind had been knocked out of me. I scrambled to my feet, and the bull fighters tried to get me to go over the nearby fence, but I wasn't going to risk losing the witch's scent this time. I ignored the danger of the bull and charged across the arena to the stands where I'd felt the curse coming from. I vaulted over the fence.

I gaped in disbelief. Right in the middle of the stands sat Eileen. Kinyisha, Sandy, and Madame Isabella ran up to me, and they gaped at Eileen, too. The rodeo ended, and the crowd started to clear, walking wide around us and staring at Madame Isabella. Eileen came down to meet us. "What are all of you looking at? I didn't do anything."

I pointed a finger at her. "Like hell you didn't."

"Eileen, we all felt it," Kinyisha said.

"It wasn't me. It had to have been someone near me."

"Come with us," Kinyisha said. "You can tell your story to the council of the coven, and we'll learn the truth." Eileen looked a little green.

"Just who is this council?" I asked.

"Us," Kinyisha said.

"Where are we going to have this council?"

"*We* aren't." Kinyisha said. "It's private. No outsiders involved."

"But she nearly killed me. Just try to stop me from coming." Kinyisha hit me with one of those sledgehammers.

\* \* \*

When I woke up, I ached all over, and the witches were nowhere in sight. I cursed them by all the gods I could think of, but it didn't help much. I looked all around the rodeo grounds for them, but I couldn't find them. Finally, I waited at my truck, figuring they'd come fill me in when they were done with their coven thing.

I fell asleep waiting, and about three in the morning, Sandy crawled in the back with me. "Hi," she said. From the sound of her voice, I could tell she'd been crying.

I sat up. "Why did you let Kinyisha sledgehammer me?" I asked.

"Could she have kept you from coming any other way?" Sandy asked.

"No. I had a right to be there."

Sandy shrugged. "Maybe. But that's not how the council of a coven works."

"What happened?"

Sandy looked at her hands. "Eileen finally admitted it. Breaking all our codes, she sent the curse against you. If it helps any, she wasn't trying to kill you, just make you fall off so Ben could win. She said you were using magic, and that wasn't fair."

"Well . . ." I started to defend myself, but I knew she was right. I wasn't about to admit it, though. Instead, I said, "So Walker believes she's a witch."

Sandy nodded. "She broke our vow of secrecy and told him. He didn't believe her at first and made fun of her when she told him she made you fall off the bull. That's why they fought, but when you started winning again, he made up with her and got her to curse you again last week. She freaked out when you had to be taken away in an ambulance. She was afraid she'd killed you, and she'd told Ben she wouldn't do it again. That's why nothing happened last night. But when you beat Ben's score, he bullied her into it, saying he needed the prize money for tuition. Besides, she doesn't like you much."

"Whether she meant to kill me or not, she came damn close. Just what do you plan to do about that?"

"She's been taken care of. You won't have to worry about her again."

"What does that mean?"

"We've blocked her away from her powers. It's a horrible thing to do to a witch. Can you imagine living without magic?"

I looked off into the darkness. I didn't say anything, but the thought terrified me. What would I be without my magic? Whatever I became, it wouldn't be me.

Sandy left, and I stared into the darkness for a long time, trying not to think. When I finally fell asleep, I dreamed of Clenyeth.

He knelt at Fitzrigh's feet. Fitzrigh's eyes were narrowed dangerously. "She's still free?"

Clenyeth had his hands together as if he'd been pleading. "Yes, but she has no idea how to come back, and she hasn't got a Traveler's Stone. Daulphina wouldn't do it anyway. She's not like that."

"I can't count on that. I need her confined where she can cause me no trouble."

"You want me to go back and try again?"

Fitzrigh smiled nastily and put his hand on the side of Clenyeth's face. "I don't tolerate failure."

Clenyeth's screams pierced the air and seemed to go on for hours. Even though he'd betrayed me, it was hard listening to his pain. Suddenly, he jerked and fell to the ground.

Fitzrigh turned to some waiting servants. "Dispose of him."

# CHAPTER 17

I spent most of the next week drunk. I didn't want to think of Clenyeth's betrayal or his face by the candlelight. I was sure I was going to be stuck here forever and Fitzrigh would have my throne. And despite his betrayal, I didn't want to think of Clenyeth dead.

I didn't call in to register for the rodeo. I had no plans for the future, but I wasn't sure I'd ever ride a bull again.

I was stewing in my anguish when someone knocked on the trailer door. "Go away!" I yelled.

"Joshua David Killenyen, you open this door!" Meemaw yelled. Why had Meemaw come to my trailer? Always before, when she wanted to talk to Joshua, she sent Jocelyn over to get me.

I stumbled to the door and unlocked it. "Meemaw, what are you doing here?"

She scowled at me. "Aren't you going to invite an old lady in?"

I glanced over my shoulder. "Er . . . it's a bit of a mess. Maybe it would be better if we talk out here."

"What are you hiding? I've sent Jocelyn over here three times, and she says you refused to open the door." I scratched my head. I had vague memories of Jocelyn pounding on the door and drowning her out with more whiskey.

"I'm not hiding anything, Meemaw. It's just . . ."

Meemaw didn't wait for me to finish, but pushed passed me into the trailer. She stared around in open-mouthed horror. "Jocelyn said you were a bit of a slob, but this place is worse than a toxic waste dump!"

"Er . . . Meemaw, I've just had . . ."

"Don't give me any excuses. I'm not going to let a grandson of mine drink his life away in a place unfit for human habitation! You haven't been yourself since your birthday, and I'm going to find out why. You go get yourself cleaned up. The two of us are going to clean this place while you explain to me what's been happening."

"But Meemaw—"

"No buts!" She pointed toward my small bathroom. "Into the shower now. You smell like you haven't bathed in weeks."

Not knowing what else to do, I stumbled to the bathroom, taking my cleanest clothes with me. My head pounded as I stepped under the warm water, and I wondered how I was going to come up with an answer that would satisfy Meemaw. I washed thoroughly and shampooed my hair twice. I even shaved in the shower. I stayed there until the water turned cold, but I was stalling for time. No answer but the truth made sense. I finally turned off the water, dried off, and dressed.

When I came out of the bathroom, Meemaw was in my small kitchen washing dishes. "Grab a trash bag," she said without turning, "and start gathering up the empty cereal boxes and beer bottles and all the rest of the trash."

I got a trash bag out of the cupboard and started doing as she'd asked. We worked in silence for awhile, me gathering trash and Meemaw washing dishes. After I'd hauled what seemed like the fiftieth bag out to Uncle Gilly's dumpster, Meemaw turned to me. "Explain yourself."

I turned away from her, and tears welled up in my eyes. "There's nothing to explain, Meemaw." Nothing but the loss of everything I held dear.

Meemaw grabbed my shoulder with a wet hand and turned me to face her. I tried to blink away the tears, but I couldn't stop them from running down my cheeks. Meemaw's expression softened. "I'm not the fool you seem to think I am. Something's going on. Now tell me what."

The kindness in her tone overcame me, and I broke down in sobs. "I've lost everything. There's nothing left for me anymore."

Meemaw's forehead wrinkled. "You never had much. What could you possibly have lost?"

I paced the short distance between the kitchen and the bedroom. "Meemaw, I'd love to tell you, but you'd never believe the truth."

Meemaw wiped off her hands on her pants. "Why wouldn't I? It doesn't have anything to do with that parallel realm nonsense, does it?"

"What if it does?"

Meemaw put her hands on her hips. "Joshua David Killenyen, I won't have another of you spouting drunken nonsense to explain your misbehavior."

"What do you mean, 'another of me'?"

"Another one of mine. Where do you think your mother said your father come from? A sixteen-year-old girl gets herself pregnant, and she blames it on some prince named Torvald or Tornor or—"

"Tormaid?" I gasped.

"Yes, that's it. She tell you that story, too? I forbad her telling anyone else."

My head reeling, I collapsed onto the bed. "Holy Cailleach, my father is Joshua's father?"

"What in tarnation do you mean by that?"

I just sat there shaking my head for a few moments. "That must be what Clenyeth meant about the blood bond. Our shared blood must have made the switch possible, and since Fitzrigh did it and also shared our blood, it made his magic much more powerful." I stood and grabbed Meemaw's shoulders. "Meemaw, I know how outrageous it sounds, but you have to believe me. Neither my mother nor I were lying to you, and neither of us is crazy. Her lover was from a parallel realm, and I'm not your grandson. I'm Crown Princess Daulphina of Asteria, daughter of King Tormaid. My bastard brother Fitzrigh used some strange magic to switch me with Joshua. It happened on Joshua's birthday. That's why I've been acting odd. I'm not Joshua."

She stared at me her eyes wide with fear. "I'm calling Lou Ann's husband. You need help." She shrugged off my hands, went to the purse she'd set on the counter, and fished out her phone.

I put my hand on her arm, restraining her gently. "Even your cat Oscar knows I'm not Joshua. He likes me, and you said he wouldn't come within ten feet of Joshua. Animals can sense these things."

"Let go of me, Joshua. I've got to get you help."

"Dear gods, how can I convince you I'm not crazy?" I hesitated. "I know. Stay here and don't do anything." I took her phone to make sure she didn't call Uncle Braeden. I fetched a sock, some string, and a needle and thread. I plucked two of my hairs, and with them and the string, I tied the sock up into the semblance of a person.

Meemaw backed as far away from me as the small kitchen allowed. "Playing with sock animals?" she quavered. "What do you think this will prove?"

"There's no need to be afraid of me. You know I'd never hurt you." Meemaw looked toward the door as if she wanted to run, but I stood between her and it. Ignoring the pain, I breathed on the sock and willed the connection between us. I did it two more times. When the magic coalesced, I pulled my pocket knife and sat the poppet on the counter. "Watch the arm of the poppet while I do this."

"Joshua, let me call Lou Ann's husband. Something's not right with you."

"Just watch the sock," I snapped. I flipped open the knife and made a cut on my left arm. The arm of the poppet ripped open. "Did you see that?" I pointed at the poppet.

"Why are you cutting yourself?" she said, evidently not understanding.

"Now, watch my arm." I threaded the needle and picked up the poppet. I held it in my left hand and angled my arm so that Meemaw could clearly see the cut. I carefully stitched closed the rip in the poppet; as I did so, the cut on my arm started to close. When I was done, I wiped the blood off with a kitchen towel. There was only a thin pink line where the cut had been.

Meemaw looked at the healed cut with her eyes wide and her mouth open.

"It's magic, Meemaw. Nothing to be afraid of, but you know your grandson had no magic. I'm telling you the truth, and so was your daughter. Parallel realms exist. Your daughter's lover came from one, and so do I."

"Good God in heaven," Meemaw whispered. She shuffled around the kitchen, trying to keep her distance from me, until she collapsed on my bed.

I crouched down next to her and held out my left arm with the faint pink line. "You have to believe me."

Meemaw's lips trembled, and she wouldn't meet my eyes. "Perhaps I'd better call my pastor. Perhaps the devil—"

I stood and threw up my hands. "The devil's got nothing to do with it. Why can't you believe me, Meemaw?"

"I can't believe you for the same reason I didn't believe your mother. Parallel realms don't exist. Renee just made up that story about the prince because she didn't want to name the real father of her child. Even showed me something she called a Traveler's Stone that was supposed to take her to him if she changed her mind about being his royal mistress."

I grabbed Meemaw's arm. "My mother had a Traveler's Stone? Meemaw, this is important. Do you have any idea what happened to it?"

She shook her head. "It's probably among her stuff up in my attic. I think I put it there when we cleaned out her house after she died. Nothing but a black rock, but she was so insistent that it was important I couldn't throw it away."

I threw my arms around Meemaw and kissed her on the cheek. "Thank Cernuous you didn't! It may be the solution to your grandson's and my problems. Come on. Let's go find it." I reached out a hand to help her to her feet.

She stared at my hand a moment and then at my pocket where I'd put her phone. "Josh, darling, I don't think a rock is what you need. Let me call Lou Ann's husband and get you some help."

"I'm not crazy." I pointed to the thin pink line of my arm. She just stared at it. "Come on, Meemaw. Help me find this Stone, and your grandson might be back by tomorrow."

She hesitated for a moment more, then stood without taking my hand. I hustled her outside and into my truck. I didn't want to chance her driving somewhere other than her house.

When we entered Meemaw's house, Oscar came and twined himself around my legs, meowing for attention. "See, Meemaw?" I pointed to the cat. "Would Oscar have ever acted this way with Joshua?"

Still looking terrified, Meemaw shook her head. She took me to the base of the attic ladder. "I can't manage the ladder any more, but your momma's things are in the far right corner in boxes with her name written on them. I don't know which one the rock's in."

I scrambled up the ladder, hurried to the far right corner, and looked around for the boxes. It took me quite awhile to find them amid all the junk; all the time my heart thumped loudly. Could I get back? Could I save Joshua and me from what Fitzrigh had done to us?

Finally, I found the four boxes marked "Renee" and ripped into the first one. It was full of mementos. The second contained Joshua's baby things, including a bronze cast of his first shoe. When I opened the third box, I felt a faint tingling, and I was sure I'd found the right one. I started throwing things out. Finally, in the bottom, I found a stone of pure black obsidian about three inches in diameter. It looked like the stone Clenyeth had used to open the void back to Asteria. I touched it reverently, but as soon as I picked it up, I felt sick with disappointment. It buzzed with only the faintest magic. The power must have worn off over the years.

Under the Stone was a piece of paper with handwriting I recognized as my father's. I picked it up and read. It explained the ritual that would open the void and ended with these words, "My darling, I'd hoped you'd understand why I cannot marry you even though I wish to with all my heart. You and the child growing within you mean everything to me, and it's tearing me apart to lose you, but since I am the heir to the throne, I have to do right by my people. If you ever change your mind about coming to me, use this Stone to travel through the void between our worlds, and I will welcome you and our child with open arms."

I put the paper down and stared at the Stone in my hand. Surely there was some way I could bring it back to full power again, a way that didn't involve human sacrifice. This had to be my ticket home.

I gave a whoop of delight and clattered down the attic ladder. I hurried to the kitchen to find Meemaw with Uncle Braeden, Sheriff Wilson, and a deputy.

Meemaw looked at me, then glanced away. "There he is, Sheriff. I hate to do it to him, but he's crazier than a loony bird."

"What's going on here?" I asked, backing away.

"Now, son, come with us quietly," the sheriff said. "No need to make this hard on yourself."

"I haven't done anything wrong," I protested. "You can't arrest me."

"I'm afraid they can commit you, Joshua," Uncle Braeden said. "If what Meemaw says here is correct, you're a danger to yourself."

"Well, that will be for a judge to decide," the deputy piped in. "After a seventy-two hour observation."

I rounded on Meemaw. "How can you do this to me? Meemaw, I'm not crazy. You know I'm not."

Meemaw looked away and didn't answer. Sheriff Wilson hit me from behind and slammed me into the counter. He wrestled my arm behind my back and slapped a cuff on. I wanted to fight him, but I knew I couldn't win, and fighting would only make the situation worse. So I shoved the Stone and piece of paper in my pocket and let him take the other hand. Then he and the deputy took me out to the patrol car and drove me to the county hospital.

At the hospital, they took everything from me, made me strip, and put on one of those short gowns, then locked me in a padded cell with nothing but a cot and a toilet. I collapsed on the bed, shaking with anger. I couldn't believe Meemaw had done this to me. I felt almost as betrayed by her, as I had by Clenyeth.

I laid there and tried to think of a plan for bringing the Stone back to life. I fell asleep and dreamed of Joshua. He lay on the bed in the tower room. Sylvia burst in. "Come quickly, Your Highness." She hurried to the bed and grabbed Joshua's hand. "Duke Tearlach has cleared the way for you and has a coach waiting below."

"He has?" Joshua jumped to his feet and followed Sylvia out the door.

If you enjoyed this novel, please leave a review on Amazon or Goodreads.

Then subscribe to my mailing list to

get monthly updates on my writing, specials,

and advanced news on upcoming releases.

You will also received a free ecopy of my short story collection,

*Blood Cursed and Other Tales of the Fantastic.*

http://jamie-marchant.com/newsletter/

Following is an excerpt from the first book of my *Kronicles of Korthlundia* series, *The Goddess's Choice*. If you enjoy it, the novel can be purchased on Amazon.

# The Goddess's Choice

## The Kronicles of Korthlundia

## Book 1

### Expanded Edition

# By: Jamie Marchant

# THE GODDESS'S CHOICE

# CHAPTER 1

"Please, no!" Robbie Angusstamm screamed as his father's heavy strap came whistling down on his bare back. He tried to yank his hands free, but his brother Boyden held his wrists tightly against the dining room table. *Sulis curse it! Why do I have to be such a worthless weakling?* He promised himself he wouldn't scream again, but he screamed just as loudly the next time the strap hit.

"Sleeping by the river in the middle of the goddess-cursed afternoon! How many times must I beat you before you learn responsibility, boy?" His father brought the strap down even harder.

"I didn't mean to!" But Robbie's explanation turned into screams of pain as the strap landed again and again.

Robbie let out a humiliating whimper when his father finally stepped away and Boyden let go of his wrists. Clutching a chair for support, Robbie struggled to hold back his tears. *By the goddess, don't let them see me cry.*

His father towered over him. "Learned your lesson, boy?" Angus Camlinstamm was the largest man in the Valley, even bigger than the village blacksmith. Although Angus had become a bit round about the middle, he was still strong as a team of plow horses. His blonde hair, flowing past his shoulders, was only just starting to show some gray. His broad face was red, both from anger and exertion. "Well? Have you?" he demanded when Robbie didn't answer at once.

"Yes, sir," Robbie said, ashamed of how pathetic he sounded.

"I'm not going to have to send your brother looking for you again, am I, boy?"

"No, sir."

"All right, then. Stop lazing around like a fool and get your chores done." Angus hung the strap on its peg by the door. "If you finish before dinner's over, I may consider letting you join us."

*Like that will ever happen!* Robbie clutched at his empty stomach, knowing he'd get nothing to eat before breakfast. Careful of the welts on his back, he pulled on his shirt, which was made from crude homespun. Although Angus could afford better, he didn't believe in wasting coin on workday clothing. His father and brother had better quality clothes for holy days and other special occasions, but Robbie didn't.

As he passed through the kitchen, one of the servants quickly drew the star of Sulis in the air to ward off his evil. He hated it when people did that, but how could he blame them? His reflection in the shiny pots that hung from the kitchen wall showed dark black hair-- the color of night and demons. Green eyes, unlike those of the children of the goddess. Skin, darker than natural. He was also so short his brother called him a worm.

Outside, Robbie drew two large buckets of water from the well. He staggered toward the barn, the weight of the buckets bending him forward and pressing his shirt against his back. Praying none of the servants or farmhands would see him, he set the buckets down and emptied some of the water. His father would beat him again if he knew, and Boyden would laugh at his weakness. Boyden could carry hundred-pound sacks of grain as if they contained feathers. Boyden was everything their father wanted in a son.

Boyden hadn't killed their mother.

When he reached the barn door, he shouted for Allyn or Darien to open it, but no one came. The two farmhands were supposed to help him with the animals, but this wouldn't be the first time they'd used Robbie getting in trouble as an excuse for taking the night off. They knew he wouldn't risk another beating by telling on them.

Robbie sat the buckets down to open the door. The barn was large, with plenty of room for the dozen cows, ten horses, and four mules as well as for the large pig and her half-dozen piglets. When he entered, the cows mooed happily. The horses and mules neighed and stomped their feet in greeting. A bird whose wing he'd mended flew down from the rafters, landed on his shoulder, and nibbled his ear affectionately. The animals' joy seeped into his body like a warm, living current, strengthening him against both exhaustion and pain. Animals couldn't sense the evilness in his soul. Only here was he loved.

The animals' welcome quickly turned to cries of thirst. Cursing himself for making them wait so long for water, he began filling up the water troughs. He hadn't meant to fall asleep by the river, but he'd been up most of the night helping a neighbor's goat with a difficult birth. "It will be alright. Robbie's here now. Just be patient, and I'll get water for all of you." Knowing they could depend on him, the animals all quieted.

It took several more trips to the well to get enough water, and by the time he'd finished, he saw spots in front of his eyes. But he was far from finished.

When he started the milking, the large, gray-striped barn cat twined around his legs, mewing for attention. "Hello, Ronan. Taking care of the mice and rats for me?"

*:Of course.:* Ronan licked his paws as if getting the last taste of a recent kill. *:Good hunting.:* Robbie didn't exactly hear Ronan's words; it was more that he got an image or feeling from the cat's mind. He didn't know why he could understand animals; he'd always been able to. Perhaps it was another sign of his demon blood.

Robbie placed the milk in the icehouse. He then turned to cleaning the stalls and feeding the animals. When he entered Wild Thing's stall, the mare neighed. *:Wild Thing stomp father bully to mash.:* Robbie hugged his horse around the neck.

With Wild Thing, communication had always been particularly strong, and her mind seemed much more complex than other animals' because Wild Thing wasn't a normal horse. Four years ago he'd found the days-old foal out on the plains, near the body of her dead mother. She'd been half-mad with hunger and fear. Her brilliant coloring, somewhere between chestnut and auburn, and the stars on her chest and forehead made it obvious she was a Horsetad. The herd of wild horses roamed free on the plains of Lundia, and people said they could never be tamed. The origin of the Horsetads was highly debated. Ages ago, some said Sulis herself had ridden her chariot in the land, and her horses had mixed with those of earthly origin. Others said the Horsetads had escaped from the seven hells and their demon masters and were forever unwilling to allow anyone to master them again.

Rubbing his face against her, Robbie choked back a sob. "Wild Thing, girl, why can't I do anything right? Why did I have to be born evil?"

Wild Thing stomped her hoof. *:Not evil. Robbie good.:*

Robbie knew she was wrong, but he didn't argue. Many in the Valley thought Wild Thing was a demon herself.

Very late, he finally stumbled up to bed. Despite his hunger and the pain in his back, he was so tired he fell almost immediately asleep.

\* \* \*

Early in the morning, Robbie stirred. He winced as he sat up. But he knew the pain in his back wouldn't last too long. His demon blood made him heal more quickly than normal people. Struggling to his feet, he carefully got dressed, brushed the tangles from his long, curly hair, and tied it back with a strip of leather. Wondering if he'd ever grow a beard, he felt the smoothness of his face. At sixteen, a lot of boys had at least some hair on their faces. Then again, who ever heard of a demon with a beard?

As he left his room, he was nearly brought to his knees and just avoided crying out. It took him a moment to realize that this time the pain wasn't his own. He blocked it away and hurried outside to find the injured animal. A faint mewing came from the other side of the barn. He followed it and found Ronan covered in blood. Trembling, Robbie knelt beside the cat and stroked his head. *No, not Ronan!* "What happened to you, boy? Don't worry, Robbie's here." Robbie cradled the cat in his arms and carried him inside the barn where he kept his medicines.

As Robbie examined the injury, he sighed in relief. "It's not as bad as I thought, my boy. Some of this blood isn't yours. Got a few licks in yourself, did you?" Ronan mewed feebly, and Robbie saw an image of Ronan fighting several overgrown rats. Robbie cleaned the wound carefully and treated it with one of his salves. Robbie couldn't explain how he knew how to make his remedies. No one had taught him. Certain plants just seemed to make good medicines, and certain medicines felt as if they'd help a particular problem.

As he rubbed in the salve, a trickle of energy moved through his fingers into Ronan. The sensation resembled other men's descriptions of the pleasure to be found with a woman. Ronan's wound began to heal. *Holy Sulis, what is this I do? If being a demon feels this good, maybe I shouldn't mind being one!*

By the time Robbie finished bandaging the wound, Ronan had drifted into a peaceful sleep. He carried the cat to a spot where it could sleep without being disturbed. "You'll be fine, Ronan, my boy. I'm not so sure about me, though." His father wouldn't be happy he'd spent all this time healing a cat, especially after the beating he'd given him yesterday for neglecting his chores. Angus didn't consider cats important animals.

Realizing he'd have to forego breakfast to get the chores done on time, he put his hand over his empty stomach.

* * *

After completing the morning chores, Robbie found his father outside the barn talking to Cullen Bevinstamm, a neighboring farmer. "You think I have no use for the boy myself?"

"Angus, you know I wouldn't ask if I wasn't desperate. This is my only plow horse. If she dies, I won't be able to feed my family."

"Is your horse sick, sir?" Robbie asked.

The farmer glanced nervously at Robbie, and his father snapped, "Stay out of this, boy." Angus turned back toward the farmer. "Just what do I get out of letting him go with you?"

"Angus, you know all my money's gone into seed, but I'll pay you a tetra at harvest."

Angus scowled. "How do you know you'll even have a harvest?"

Robbie clenched his fists. *Why can't he ever think of anything but money? If the horse is sick, I have to help.* "What's wrong with your horse, sir?"

"Boy, I told you to stay out of it!" His father rounded on him. "Do you need another lesson?"

Robbie clenched his fists even tighter, but he didn't dare say anything more.

"Do you have any of your wife's preserves left?" Angus asked the farmer. Cullen's wife was rumored to make the best preserves in the Valley, not that Robbie had ever tasted any.

The man nodded, glancing nervously at Robbie. "Yes, I think there are four or five jars."

"Send all you have back with the boy, and I'll wait for the money." Angus stomped back to the farmhouse without even looking at him.

Cullen licked his lips nervously, and Robbie looked down at his feet. "Your horse?" he asked, still not meeting the man's eyes.

Cullen backed farther away as he explained what was wrong with his plow horse. It sounded like the lung sickness. He fetched his supplies and saddled Wild Thing.

On the ride to his farm, Cullen stayed far away and said nothing. Robbie tried not to mind. Farmers came to him because he was far better at treating animals than anyone else in the Valley, but Robbie knew they wished they had another choice.

When they neared the farm, Cullen rode a little closer. "Just so you know, I've sent my wife and children to her sister's for the day."

*Just what do you think I'd do to them? I'd never hurt a woman or a child. I'd never hurt anybody.* But even as he thought it, he knew it was a lie. Couldn't his demon blood cause harm even if he didn't mean it to? It had killed his own mother.

They dismounted in front of Cullen's small stable. Cullen had far fewer animals than Angus: a single cow, a few chickens, the sick plow horse, and the old mule he'd ridden to fetch Robbie. The farmer led him inside, still careful to keep his distance. As soon as Robbie entered, his lungs tightened, making it difficult to breathe. A bay gelding coughed and wheezed. Talking in his usual soothing tones, he approached. "Hello, old boy, not feeling so well, are you? It'll be okay.

Robbie touched the horse to be sure of the extent of the illness. "He has the lung sickness, like I thought."

He had the man light a brazier, and he set about brewing a remedy for the horse. "I'll give this to him now, but he'll need the dose repeated three times a day for a week. Come fetch me again if he's not acting better in a day or so." As he put herbs of differing amounts into the mixture, he explained the process to the farmer.

"Sounds a bit complicated," Cullen said. "I'll fetch you some paper and ink, and you can write it down."

"I have better things to do than writing down remedies," Robbie snapped. He wasn't about to admit he was too stupid to either read or write. Father Gildas hadn't allowed him to attend the temple school, claiming the knowledge of the goddess shouldn't be shared with the seed of demons.

* * *

Just after noon, Robbie started back to his father's farm with three jars of strawberry and two jars of peach preserves in his saddlebags. His stomach ached with hunger, and his head swam so badly he feared he might fall off Wild Thing. Cullen hadn't offered him so much as a piece of bread, and healing left him ravenously hungry, especially for sweets. By the time he reached home, the noon meal would be over, and there'd be nothing to eat until supper.

As he took a shortcut through the woods, he got out one of the jars of preserves. "My girl, do you think my father would ever know there were five jars instead of four?"

Wild Thing's ears flicked in answer. :*Robbie hungry. Wild Thing hungry. Nice grass there. Nice jar thing here.*:

Wild Thing was suggesting they stop at the abandoned stable up ahead. He'd found this stable when he was twelve, during one of his wanderings through the woods looking for plants for his remedies. The stable consisted of a small barn with four stalls and a fenced-in paddock with grass for grazing. A small stream ran alongside it, and it had been in surprisingly good condition for an abandoned structure. He'd fixed it up to use as a private retreat. Stopping beside the stream, he opened the jar and reveled in the sticky sweetness of the fruit; it was the best preserves he'd ever tasted. Before heading home, he made sure to wash any sign of the preserves from his hands and face.

\* \* \*

In Robbie's dreams that night, the demon lady came to him. He'd dreamed of her for as long as he could remember. She always dressed in clothing more brightly colored than any he'd ever seen; tonight she wore scarlet, trimmed with bright silver braiding. Like him, the lady had black hair, green eyes, and dark skin. As a child he'd longed for sleep, where he could curl up in her arms and listen to her stories and songs. But as he'd gotten older, the dreams had begun to trouble him. If demons loved him, didn't it mean he was as evil as people said he was?

*Tonight she approached through a fog of mist, sunlight forming a halo around her. She hugged him to her chest. "I love you. You won't always be alone."*

# CHAPTER 2

The Princess Samantha sat at her dressing table and glowered at her reflection as her maids dressed her hair. She detested balls and loathed the hundreds of suitors who flocked around her: "I have never seen a lovelier flower, Your Highness!" or "Your eyes rival the brilliance of the stars, Your Highness!" *If I hear that one again, I'll vomit. It wouldn't be quite so bad if even one of them meant it.* Sometimes she wished . . . She pushed the thought away. As the heir to the throne, she couldn't expect romance.

"Let us be painting your face tonight, Your Highness!" Ardra begged. Samantha's maid was as small and slight as the princess herself and had hair so blonde it was almost white. The princess smiled at the quaintness of her speech. Although both Ardra and Malvina had been in Murtaghan for over ten years, they still hadn't lost the peculiarities of their western Lundian accents.

"Yes, Your Highness," Malvina chimed in. "Lady Shela's maids said just yesterday we couldn't possibly be knowing our business 'cause you never be wearing paint." Malvina, more of a typical Korthlundian woman, was tall and broad and not nearly as pretty as Ardra.

"Lady Shela," Samantha snorted in disgust. Shela wore so much paint she resembled some ghastly sea creature. Samantha knew she wasn't pretty, but she was fond of the freckles that speckled her nose and thought the emerald green brilliance of her gown set off her white skin and auburn hair beautifully. Besides being appallingly uncomfortable, paint would absolutely spoil the effect. The princess gestured toward the huge portrait that covered one wall of her bedchamber. "Do you think Danu wore paint?"

Malvina shrugged. "The Princess Danu was said to be a powerful sorceress, Your Highness. She probably didn't need to wear paint to attract men."

Samantha laughed bitterly, as she thought of the army of men waiting below. "I wish not wearing paint was all it took to scare them off. They say Danu never married, and see how happy she is."

Samantha yearned for Danu's freedom. The long-dead princess was laughing as she galloped across the fields with her auburn hair flying out behind her in the wind. The stars on the forehead and chest of her horse shone against its gorgeous coat. Samantha loved this painting, which was just as well because it was bolted to the wall and couldn't be removed without tearing her chambers apart. She'd decorated the rest of her bedroom to match. Tapestries of horses covered the walls. Her dressing table, armoire, and large four-poster bed had horses carved into the woodwork. A quilt, embroidered with horses and stars, was spread over the bed. The mantle over her fireplace sported figurines of horses in gold, silver, jade, crystal, and precious stones. Every new ambassador added to her collection.

"Your Highness, you'll be having to marry one of them eventually," Ardra persisted. "The king won't be letting you hold out forever. You are seventeen, after all. Your mother was only thirteen when she married the king."

"You needn't remind me, Ardra." Samantha picked up her silver-backed brush from the dressing table, a gift from the Neasarian ambassador that was inlaid with an amber Horsetad; diamonds marked the stars at its forehead and chest. She fingered it lovingly. "Do you think it's true Danu rode a Horsetad?"

"So the bards sing of her," Ardra said.

Malvina made an impatient noise in her throat. "And they also be singing she turned suitors into toads with her kiss! You don't really believe such nonsense, do you, Your Highness? Nobody can tame a Horsetad."

"No, I suppose not," the princess sighed wistfully, then smiled at the toads that hopped around the feet of Danu's horse. *How I wish my kiss could do that!*

Finally, her maids were finished weaving the jewels through her hair and had attached the simple gold circlet of the heir. Samantha tried to take a deep breath, but was prevented by the tightness of her corset. "That's it. This is the last time I wear a corset. Have my dresses altered to fit without one. And don't lecture me about fashion. I'd rather be able to breathe."

Before her maids could protest that without a corset she was almost as flat as a boy, she left the room. She passed through her reception room, which was decorated in a similar style to her bedroom and contained more ambassadorial gifts. Pausing in front of her favorite tapestry—a white mare at the edge of the forest, helping her newborn foal stand, she wished she were heading for the stables instead of the ballroom. She forced her face into a court smile and left her chambers.

Her two bodyguards bowed and fell in behind her. The princess couldn't remember a time when she hadn't been followed by two heavily armed men. She'd grown so used to them she often forgot they were there.

\* \* \*

*A full crowd tonight, of course. While the possibility of wearing a crown still exists, not even a deadly plague would keep the hordes away.*

Behind the dais at the top of the ballroom was the king's standard—a brilliant yellow sun on a field of red. Next to it was a smaller standard in her own colors—the head of a white horse on a field of emerald green. The walls were lined with the standards of all the noble houses of Korthlundia; most sported images of ferocious beasts or weapons of war. *If I'm supposed to be maintaining the peace, why do I have to dance in a room that celebrates war?* Her father claimed they couldn't redecorate the ballroom without the risk of offending one or more of the Korthlundian noble houses. But Samantha doubted she'd like balls any better no matter how the room was decorated.

As she moved through the crowd, the courtiers parted and bowed. All the men attempted to catch her eye, and the smiles of the women failed to mask their jealousy.

As she mounted the dais where her father and members of the royal council awaited, King Solar beamed at her. His long white hair and beard flowed around his head, giving him the appearance of the wise old man from the bards' tales. She bowed to him, and he quickly extended his hand, raised her, and gave her a kiss on the cheek. Despite his insistence that she marry, her father did love her. The princess knew she should consider herself lucky. Most royal children had no choice in a spouse, but her father had left her free to choose among the men of appropriate rank. But as she looked over the sea of hungry male eyes, the thought of marrying any of them nauseated her. *If only marrying them didn't mean I had to bed them.*

Beside the king, Uncle Caedmon smiled at her. Caedmon, Duke of Tuath and Boirche, was her mother's uncle and had been her father's chancellor since she was two years old. He had very bushy eyebrows that gave the impression he was always looking down on people. But he was one of the few members of her father's council she liked, and he was the only one who exhibited no designs on the throne. His only son had married before she was born.

Immediately after the king announced the opening of the ball, Argblutal, the Duke of Handgriff, stepped forward to claim the first dance. No one else ever dared ask her until the duke had had his turn. Like every Korthlundian man, Argblutal was tall, broad-shouldered, and blue-eyed. Many of the girls found him handsome, but she wasn't sure why. He was nearly twice her age. He was dressed in a surcoat of black leather with long black velvet sleeves, trimmed in gold and crimson braiding. He had several thick gold chains around his neck. From the largest of these hung a pendant of a panther, the symbol of his house. In defiance of court fashion, he wore his blond beard and hair cropped short. He and Duke Sheen were her closest living relatives on her father's side, not that they were very close—third cousins or something. Both had thought to inherit the throne until her birth gave Solar a direct heir.

Argblutal bowed. "May I have the first dance, Your Highness?"

"I'd be honored, Your Grace." *Father would throw a fit if I refused.* She smiled her fakest smile and accepted his hand.

As the dance began, the duke bowed low over her hand, sliming it with a kiss. "Your Highness, you are the brightest star in a shining crowd tonight." *It's only the first dance, and I get the star thing already. Is there some book they all read? Fifty-two Compliments for Ladies.* The duke danced stiffly, as if he disapproved of frivolity. "Your dress, it's Saloynan silk, is it not, Your Highness?"

"No, it's Neasarian. I find the weave so much finer. Don't you?" The silk did feel delightful against her skin, but she found talk of fashion and fabric tedious. She'd never understood the other girls' obsession with it, just as she never understood why they giggled so much.

"So I have heard, Your Highness, but it's very difficult to come by. The Neasarians are more interested in trading spices than silk."

This was true, but equally boring, so she smiled and made some inane comment. When the dance finally ended, Argblutal slimed her hand again. "Perhaps we can share another dance before the evening's end, Your Highness." Surreptitiously wiping her hand on her gown, Samantha merely smiled. *Only if all seven of the hells freeze over.*

The next suitor in line was Lord Devyn, Duke Sheen's oldest son. Devyn was only a couple of years older than the princess, but he looked younger. His chin was covered with only the lightest and most delicate of fuzz. The princess thought he'd look better if he shaved. But, of course, he couldn't do that; only the clergy shaved. "May I . . . may I have this dance, Y-y-your Highness?"

As the dance began, Lord Devyn turned a dozen shades of red. "Y-y-your Highness looks just like a-a-a flower tonight." It was obvious he didn't want to dance any more than she did, but Duke Sheen was bent on controlling Korthlundia through his son. She'd heard the duke had threatened Devyn with the lash to force him to court her. Devyn was only comfortable among his paints and canvases. Besides, he was in love with Count Morfran's daughter, Lady Aislinn. She wished just once some man would look at her the way she'd seen Devyn look at Aislinn.

Samantha noticed blue under his fingernails. "And how is your latest creation coming? Working in blues, I see."

Devyn gaped. "I'm doing a seascape, Your Highness, but how could you know?" When she glanced at his fingers, he curled his fingernails into his fists. "Your Highness, how could I have been so neglectful? My father will kill me." Devyn was a nice boy, but she wished his father would leave him to his art and his lover.

After Devyn, the princess worked her way through her father's council—Count Kayne, Duke Torin, Count Weylin, Baron Arawn's son, Baron Teague, and a host of other nobles of varying degrees of importance. Nola, Count of Meillid, looked on wistfully. The count was nearly as round as he was tall, and it was rumored he'd do away with his wife if he thought he stood a chance of capturing the princess's hand. He had a five-year-old son, and Samantha thought it a wonder Nola didn't send the toddler to court her.

After the majority of the king's council had had their turn, ambassadors and foreign envoys began to present themselves. She knew each one was eager to negotiate the most important treaty between their two countries—one that would give them power over the Korthlundian throne. The princess enjoyed the variety of their appearance, but at heart, they seemed little different than the Korthlundian nobles. The vast majority were nearly twice her age, and the talk of stars and flowers sounded little different in a Mintarian accent than in a Korthlundian one. However, the princess smiled when Phomello, the son of the Neasarian ambassador, took her hand. As with all Neasarians, everything from his hair to his skin to his eyes was a deep rich ebony. It was he who'd given her the silver brush and the silk for her gown, and she'd seen him several times in the stables. He seemed to share her love of horses, but the best thing about him was that he could barely speak Korthlundian, so he couldn't bombard her with mindless chatter.

\* \* \*

The king went to bed at midnight, but Samantha was forced to stay and dance with suitor after suitor.

"Might I dance with the stars of heaven tonight?" Count Pandaran, the only member of her father's council with whom she hadn't yet danced, asked. He always danced with her late in the balls; maybe he felt he was saving the best for last. He wore a surcoat of bright turquoise, edged with yards and yards of delicate lace. His hair and beard hung in long, blond ringlets. When the princess took his hand, she cringed at the smoothness of his palms. *The damned fool doesn't even know how to wield a sword.* The hands of most of the men at court were like hers—rough and calloused from weapons training. Knowing she would rule after him, her father had always treated her more like a son than a daughter. Despite what other members of the court might think of it, he had insisted she receive weapons training since she was strong enough to hold a sword.

As they whirled around the ballroom floor, a soft glow of rotten orange erupted around Pandaran. A steaming heat seeped from the orange and poured over her, coating her body with a slime so thick a dozen baths wouldn't cleanse her. The princess nearly cried out in despair. *Not the colors again! I thought I'd gotten rid of them!* It had been several months since she'd spent all night kneeling at the altar in the palace chapel, praying for the goddess's help. She'd felt the goddess's peace and thought the terrifying colors gone forever. But again she'd been wrong. When she'd first seen the colors, she'd gone in disguise to the Temple of the Mother's Love. It was the only time she'd ever given her bodyguards the slip. She'd told a priest about the colors. He'd insisted she was under the influences of the denizens of darkness and that her soul was in great peril and performed an exorcism. It hadn't worked. Nothing had. *Maybe it's not demons; maybe I'm insane.*

The princess was so upset after her dance that she fled the room without giving an explanation. She ignored the questions from her bodyguards and her maids, but she was shaking by the time Ardra and Malvina had finished undressing her and taking down her hair. When she was finally alone, she curled up into a ball on her bed. The colors had to mean something, but after the exorcism had failed, she'd never dared tell anyone else about them. Tonight she again prayed to the goddess for help. At last, she fell into a troubled sleep, her dreams full of people who glowed as brightly as the jeweled horses on her mantelpiece.

# ABOUT THE AUTHOR

Jamie began writing stories about the man from Mars when she was six, and she never remembers wanting to be anything other than a writer. Everyone told her she needed a back up plan, so she pursued a Ph.D. in American literature, which she received in 1998. She started teaching writing and literature at Auburn University. One day in the midst of writing a piece of literary criticism, she realized she'd put her true passion on the backburner and neglected her muse. The literary article went into the trash, and she began the book that was to become *The Goddess's Choice*, which was published in April 2012. Her other novels include *The Soul Stone* and *The Ghost in Exile*. In addition, she has published a novella, *Demons in the Big Easy*, and a collection of short stories, *Blood Cursed and Other Tales of the Fantastic*. Her short fiction has also appeared in the anthologies--*Urban Fantasy* and *Of Dragons & Magic: Tales of the Lost Worlds*—and in *Bards & Sages, The World of Myth, A Writer's Haven*, and *Short-story.me*. She claims she writes about the fantastic . . . and the tortured soul. Her poor characters have hard lives. She lives in Auburn, Alabama, with her husband and four cats, which (or so she's been told) officially makes her a cat lady. She still teaches writing and literature at Auburn University. She is the mother of a grown son, who is a fantastic young man.

# CONNECT WITH JAMIE ONLINE

Email:

jamie-marchant@jamie-marchant.com

Website:

http://jamie-marchant.com/

Blog:

http://jamie-marchant.com/blog/

Facebook:

https://www.facebook.com/jamieofkorthlundia/

Twitter:

https://twitter.com/JamieMarchantSF

Goodreads:

http://www.goodreads.com/author/show/5258855.Jamie_Marchant

Amazon:

https://www.amazon.com/Jamie-Marchant/e/B009L7ZGH0/

# OTHER BOOKS BY JAMIE MARCHANT

*The Kronicles of Korthlundia*

> *The Goddess's Choice*--original edition (2012)
>     Expanded edition (2017)
> *The Soul Stone* (2015)
> *The Ghost in Exile* (2016)

*Blood Cursed and Other Tales of the Fantastic* (2016)--short story collection

*Demons in the Big Easy: A Novella* (2013)

Story Collections including her work

> *Waiting for a Kiss: A Princess Fairy Tale Anthology* (2017)
> *Of Dragons & Magic: Tales of Lost Worlds* (2014)
> *Urban Fantasy* (2013)
> *Best Genre Short Stories Anthology #2: Short-Story.Me! (Volume 2)* (2010)

All works are available on Amazon.com and other online retailers.